BE BAD NOW

HOCK HOCHHEIM

WOLFPACK PUBLISHING
— EST 2013 —

WOLFPACK
PUBLISHING
— EST 2013 —

Paperback Edition
Copyright © 2020 (As Revised) Hock Hochheim

Published in the United States by Wolfpack Publishing, Las Vegas

Wolfpack Publishing
6032 Wheat Penny Avenue
Las Vegas, NV 89122

wolfpackpublishing.com

Paperback ISBN 978-1-64734-938-7
eBook ISBN 978-1-64734-937-0

BE BAD NOW

FOREWORD

My name is Archie Lennox. It was Archibald Lennox. I once insisted that all my contacts, even my family and friends call me Archibald. As a graduate of Yale University in Journalism, I once considered myself an intellectual of sorts, a dogmatic historian, and a published authority in international history and world affairs. Indeed, I have collected a cache of awards from news associations and think tanks so elite that you've probably never heard of them.

Then in the '90s while preparing an expose on the world trade deficit for the United Nations, I was introduced to a man I will call here, simply "Denny." He was, as you will later surmise, in the Mafia. La Costa Nostra. The Mob. Organized Crime. Denny helped control the docks of New Jersey and knew insider trade information - he called it the "skinny", or the "dope" - on certain imports and exports. That included heroin.

I first met Denny one night in a Newark, New Jersey restaurant, and then and there I suddenly became "Archie"

Lennox. Transformed. He wouldn't call me Archibald. He refused. Goombas never use the proper, full name. They use a nickname or a street version of the name. Hence, Archibald became Archie. Through the years Denny transformed me into a different human being and because of him, my career and starched, self-image took a sharp turn. And because of him and the shocking things he told me; I began writing non-fiction, crime books.

I wrote several books you probably have heard of, all based on a spiderweb of contacts, interviews and research--thanks to Denny. Books like The *Guys Who Are Wise*, which was made into a movie starring Ray Lewaldin and Robert Dennichi. I served as a consultant for eight years for the HBO hit crime show "The *Sontenellis* and co-wrote the screenplay "The Italian Brotherhood". I was paid to connect writers and producers with mob insiders for the academy award winning project *The Big H Gangland.*

Thanks to these books, films and projects I have made a lot of money. I own a brownstone in New York City and a house in the Hamptons near former President Bill Clinton. Archibald couldn't accomplish this. Archie did. You see, Archie knows the Mob.

I have laughed, cried and commiserated with all these criminals. It's a sick, yet addictive lifestyle. I have amassed thousands of hours of audiotapes from mobsters in exchange for Hollywood and book publisher money. Ol' Archie here is still invited to the house parties that are surveilled by the FBI in vans up and down the street. We all know. We all know we know. We all wink at each other. And yes, I know about killing and torture directly from the minds and hands that pluck eyeballs out and twist fingers off.

Vendettas and revenge. Respect and street justice. Through the years I learned how criminals take territory by a ruthlessness that even the modern militaries won't dare do, least of all the poor hamstrung, street cops and detectives who are supposed to protect us. I learned that with threats, seduction, corruption and murder, "coppers" almost always lose in the end.

Almost always. In the midst of writing these crime projects, in hanging out in bars and restaurants and meetings halls, in state pen interview rooms, I began to hear some casual gossip about an attempted mob invasion of Texas back in the 1980s. It was an era when the first real oil industry crunch hit the marketplace, and Texas tycoons fell from grace. Some did more than lose grace. They jumped out of skyscrapers to commit suicide. Some were pushed. Support industries followed suit. Lifestyles tanked. New York mobsters saw a weakness, an opening in Texas. The threats, the seductions, the corruptions, and the murders that work everywhere else, soon attempted a migration into the Lone Star State. A sea of button men and lower level crime bosses infected Houston, and Harris County. I found out that some of these immigrants intertwined with the local thugs and drug runners called the "Cowboy Mafia." It was an uneasy alliance, full of prejudices, conspiracies, and Shakespearian drama.

The older Yankee wise guys would occasionally laugh and tell stories about the '80s and "da hicks" and "da cowboys" and what happened in Texas. What happened was - it didn't happen. The mob actually returned to New York. I asked once what went wrong in Texas, and a few of them told me about a certain Houston area, police detective.

"Jack Kellog." Denny blurted out. "Jumpin' Jack Kellog. Ha. Like fuckin' Matt Dillon. Or, or, like da "Man with No Name" in all da spaghetti westerns."

Denny put down his cigar and positioned the fingers on his hand like pistols and snapshot them in the air. "Hey-heeey. Bang. Bang. Bang. Dis motherfucker was untouchable."

I watched his strange glee mixed with respect as his cigar smoke almost blended with the barrel shaped ends of his pistol fingers.

Jack Kellog? Who was this guy? One night while taking a break on "The Italian Brotherhood" project, I mindlessly typed this name in on the Internet and Lexus-Nexis. He was a detective in West Forge, a suburb attached to Houston. I found some newspaper photos of Kellog. Photos at crime scenes, or courthouse appearances. I can't explain why, but I found the photos haunting. Captivating. He looked at bit like the movie actor Burt Reynolds when Burt was in his late 40s or early 50s, only stockier. Long, gray hair brushed back. Thick, gray moustache. Western cut jacket and pants. In each photo it looked to me like he was always captured in the beginnings of a dodge, like he was trying to dodge the photographer. Impatient. In one photo he looked agitated and sneered at the camera.

I searched further. I found the '80s batch of Houston Chronicle stories containing his name. Crimes waves and gunfights and shootouts. There was even a bloodbath at a Houston bus station that would rival a military battle in Iraq or Afghanistan, least of all the OK Corral. I saw where Kellog even testified before an organized crime committee in Washington DC. His name also came up for killing two hit men in Las Vegas in a casino shopping mall. Another story covered an attack in his home by three, armed ex-cons. He killed two of them. Who IS this guy? This Matt Dillon?

One news story reported he suffered a nervous breakdown in 1990 and he was fired. Within a year they pressed him back into service as a Texas Ranger to assist on a state-wide manhunt. He was the first Ranger in years to be appointed by the Governor without being a trooper in the Texas Department of Safety.

I printed all this out and stuck it in a file I labeled the

"Kellog Chronicles," and then dove back into the "Italian Brotherhood". Archie knew how his bread got buttered, but I was still distracted by this Jack Kellog. Was there a story here too, to butter more bread?

After the 2002 Academy Awards, my wife and I were sitting on a hotel balcony in Malibu, watching the waves break on the Pacific coastline. I was as restless as the tides. Everyone involved in *The Big H Gangland* went home with Oscars. Everyone but me and the other writers involved. Of course! I had several book pitches and a screenplay to sell, but no solid offers. I told Linda I was going to do a little background work on this Kellog storyline. Go to Houston. Find him. Find others. That week, I told my agent and book publisher of my plan. They told me, no. I had to write more crime stories about mobsters, not cops.

"No formula changes, Archibald," they told me. "Too risky. Stick to the mobster stories. That's what you do best."

Archibald would have obeyed, but the "Archie" in me told me otherwise. Linda and I flew home to the Big Apple. I asked Denny more and more about this Jumping Jack and the Mafia invasion of Texas. I showed him the news clippings. He nodded and smiled and told me they were all true. Then he filled in the blanks with what he knew. Not even a fictional story could match the action and intrigue in this one. Book company or not, I was hooked.

Linda and I rented a condo in Houston for 6 months. We wound up staying there a year. After much preliminary work, I girded my loins one muggy afternoon, under a warm, drizzling rain off the Gulf of Mexico, and walked right up to the front door of Jumpin' Jack Kellog's house - the very same place where he killed those intruders decades before. It was a fine, two-story house in an exclusive neighborhood. I rang the doorbell.

A man in his 70s answered. Same black and grey hair, receded, thin, yet wrestled into the same pompadour style. Same moustache. White Astros t-shirt. Jeans, and barefoot. But Jesus, he looked like he would shoot me dead if I moved the wrong way, and I couldn't see his right hand behind the door.

"Yeah?" he asked.

"My name is Archibald...Archie Lennox. I write books, movies and screenplays. You've heard of the *Sontenellis* on HBO?" I smiled my charming smile that even worked getting serial killers to talk to me.

He grimaced back and stared at me. A bushy eyebrow went up. The door moved an inch toward close. In my hand was a thin, paper bag. From it, I pulled out a bottle of El Conde Azul Blanco Tequila.

"This is yours if you talk with me a bit. Just a few minutes. I have some questions about the '80s."

"I have some questions about the '80s, too," he said.

I smiled big again. Maybe a bit sheepish?

He looked down at the bottle, shook his head twice and half smiled at me.

"El Conde. My brand," he noted. His voice sounded like gravel.

"I know."

He almost smiled back. He squinted his left eye, tipped his head with a nod inward and opened the door all the way. From behind the door, I saw he held a big, semi-auto pistol in his right hand. After all these years with mobsters and killers, I can smell a dangerous man up close. And a gun close to going off. And this guy stunk of quick, crazy trouble. But, a vigilante kind of trouble. I followed him into his plush living room. Despite his age, he still moved like a damn cat.

We talked that first afternoon for about two hours, over margaritas. I told him my story mostly, in my most charming way, much as I have written it here for you. He seemed reluctant to say anything, but I am a professional, investigative reporter at heart. Sell me. Sell him. And, I told him up front I was going to write the story of this New York and Cowboy Mafia Crime Confederation with or without his help.

The next promised bottle of El Conde Azul Blanco meant another trip to his house and that time I brought a tape recorder. On that visit, he mostly talked. I'd interviewed a lot of cops. City, County, State and Feds. But all of them from the northeast. I knew some very dedicated, sacrificing NYPD investigators much like Kellog, but Kellog was different. He was old school, Texas. And unlike the mobsters I knew whose lives were full of flashy cars, wine, wives, children, women and song, I began to realize that Jack Kellog lived alone and quietly. Simply. He enjoyed tending his roses outside.

Over the next few months, I collected pieces of this man's story and of his soul, as well as the stories from the surviving friends, enemies and strangers around him, to compose the most fantastic story of crime, action, law and order adventure I'd ever heard of. How the New York Mafia joined the Cowboy Mafia and how a lone Texas detective had stopped them both, cold. Dead cold. If you want to know about the subsequent nervous breakdown? The Ranger appointment? The manhunt for vicious killers? You'll just have to read the next Kellog book. That is, of course, if this first one sells, because Archie knows how Archie's bread is buttered.

The story you are about to read, though based on research and interviews, is told in what we call in the business *third person format*, and as New York Times book reviewer Mel Dellava said once about me, my books *read like fiction*. All my books are done this way. Writing junkies call this *God's view*, but it's the only way I can cover all the crazy events happening all at once, and anyway—who doesn't want to play God—once in a while. It's not like I killed somebody.

It's Kellog that killed all the people. Not me.

CHAPTER 1
DEATH COMES IN THREES

"Yeah, Kellog. He's a bad mo fo. He threw me off a balcony once and killed my two homies. Put me away here for life."
- Walter Wayne Hill, Huntsville, TX Penitentiary

Archie Lennox interview tape 8

WEST FORGE, TX, FALL, 1984

Two a.m. A good hour. All the rich folks on the block asleep, even Jack Kellog. The trio of men, a macabre sight, ducked and weaved through the suburban shadows cast by ornate streetlamps, and from the night lights of expensive homes and lawns full of lush shrubbery and thick, ancient trees. The three sinister shadows moved amongst buildings and around fences. A car turned the corner.

"Shit."

"Shut up."

The men evaporated into the dark expanse of a front lawn and waited, tense and silent, until the car taillights disappeared. The man slinging a sawed-off, Remington shotgun around, slowly stood, his K-Mart, disco shirt flapping in the night wind. This Remington served as his pet tool of violence and, because of it, his friends on the street knew him as "Shotgun." This Remington, its muzzle ready to bark death with another pull of its fang-like trigger, had already knocked down five unsolved Harris County murders and one in San Antonio. Shotgun clutched the rusty, monstrous weapon to his thigh, motioned to the others to come on, and all three dashed ahead to Kellog's house.

Jack Kellog had destroyed Shotgun's life with the threat of life-long imprisonment. Killing the detective now would not stop this punishment, but at least the bastard would pay for messing with him.

Close behind Shotgun, the second man sported a crowbar "port-arms," the same way he'd carried his M-16 in Nam. His knit stocking cap covered an Afro that hadn't seen air or daylight in a week or soap for a month. His breath came in short gasps, his heart pounded. Jack Kellog's time to die had come. This cop had meddled in too many lives for too long. Crowbar and Shotgun were tight, and no man messed with Crowbar or his brothers. Not even his brothers from a different mother. Victims of Crowbar's wrath were ambulance and emergency room challenges. Some even tested the talents of experienced undertakers. Crowbar fell in line on the street behind Shotgun.

The third man followed periodically tapping the .32 semi-auto pistol tucked in his belt, concerned that it might bounce loose. He'd always "tote me a piece" a .32, and had never lost one from his beltline yet, unless you counted two police confiscations that resulted in two trips to the Texas State Penitentiary in Huntsville.

"Gonna kill me a muthafucka," he thought as he panted, loping down the street behind the other two, shoring up his confidence with rough self-talk. This would be his first kill. He felt tight and ready. He'd always hated Jack Kellog. The man stuck his nose into everybody's damn business all over the hoods in Harris County. Kellog had messed with .32 since Kellog worked the streets of Houston as a patrolman, and even though he was now a detective in West Forge, he still messed with brothers. "Yeah. Gonna kill me a muthafucka tonight."

Shotgun and Crowbar knew their way around this type of excursion. As a team or apart, they had crept up on many victims. Just three weeks earlier they'd stalked a black man from Ft. Worth who owed some Houston people gambling money. Off a busy, late night, Houston street they stepped into a slum club called *The Funky Whiskey* and shotgunned the gambler into mincemeat as he was losing even more money shooting pool. Amid the drunken and drugged screamers, the club owner grabbed the gambler's shirt and beltline and hauled the carcass across the floor, out the front doors, and dropped the body in the gutter across the street. Then he ran out the crowd, already well in gear to leave, locked up, and split.

People walking by couldn't miss the 260-pound bleeding gambler's carcass lying in the street, but for 22 minutes no one called the police. Shotgun and Crowbar split too with this welcome head start, and with two hundred dollars each for the job. They had gotten away with murders like this for years. Hey. Why not Jack Kellog's murder?

Shotgun led tonight's assault. They trotted across the detective's well-manicured lawn, crushed the freshly planted pansies bordering the brick sidewalk. Mister .32 crept past an antique porch swing, and slowly twisted the front doorknob. Locked.

"Should I bust a winda?" he whispered.

Shotgun shook his head, cursed and said, "if you can bust it quiet."

The panes in the door, like those of the front windows, contained thick stained glass, way too noisy to break. The three moved in stealthy silence around the house. The brick driveway forked to a garage and to a patio in the rear. Jack's 1982 Cadillac Seville was parked by the patio. Shotgun's grim smile showed even in the dark.

"Wha?" Crowbar asked.

"He home. That's his ride."

Crowbar scanned the second-story balcony overhead. The house looked pitch dark, but he heard music, some honky, big band shit. It sounded muted making it impossible to pinpoint the source. He swung around to the muffled tinkling of breaking glass.

Shotgun had broken a small kitchen window and reached his arm inside, flipping a latch.

"We in," Shotgun grunted.

.32 grinned. "Gonna kill me a muthafucka."

******

The old familiar tightness, like a sore muscle, gripped Jack's throat as Old Blue Eyes crooned from the record player inside the house. Jack steadied the cool, wet tumbler of Tequila resting on his bare stomach, felt its weight rise and fall with each breath. The song ended. Clad only in jockey shorts and stretched out on the lounge chair of his second-story, bedroom balcony, he studied the thick treetop branches beside the balcony as they swayed, hypnotized by his thoughts and by the October night sky - its racing clouds, its one-eighth moon.

A cool, fast Gulf wind cleansed the air of summer humidity. The Sinatra album finally fell completely silent, but for a last crackle, as the arm of record player lifted the needle off the last groove and settled into its cradle. He should get up, go inside and hit the sack.

"Hell," he whispered and drained the Tequila glass, setting it on the deck beside him. Beds. Up and down these tree-lined streets people slept peacefully in beds with lovers, wives, with children down the hall, with dogs and cats by their bedsides. Normal families living normal lives. Not Jack. The lounge chair provided as good a place as any to collapse his 51-year-old, exhausted bones. Why go back into an empty bed? He sank deeper into the cushions, but he didn't drift into that, "who am I, why am I here?" feeling that so many stargazers catch. Other ghosts grayed his hair and leeched onto his very soul.

Who abducted that 70-year-old woman, shot her in the head, left her in the field off Interstate 45? Who was the "Steak Knife" rapist? What higher power from within those stars allowed Barbara Corawick's father to rape and kill that cute, four-year-old, blondy-haired girl?

Jack searched the stars and the dark spaces in between them for these kinds of answers. It wasn't easy living in a world of twisted, greedy minds and time-bomb personalities that ripped around the world like meteors. Jack read once that meteors killed off all the dinosaurs and would one day strike the planet again killing all the people. But for now the small minds were killing folks off one at a time like shrapnel from space.

Meteors bounced around his brain and detective cases crowded his thoughts like a rowdy bar - his cases, his friends' cases, past cases, 28 years of cases and crimes, solved and unsolved. Sometimes he felt like he would suffocate. Cases starting from his rookie days at Houston PD right up to that very morning's caseload at West Forge PD. While he might forget his car keys or misplace his checkbook, he never forgot an angle on a case or a crook's name. Monsters trekked across the sky in his mind and went bump into the stars of his night.

Bump…?

A bump brought Jack back to earth with a flash from his bedroom ceiling light. Illumination suddenly flowed across the balcony and railing. What the hell?

Jack had his back to the sliding glass door of his bedroom. He froze. Long shadows fell onto the balcony deck around him. Someone was in his room?

Jack slowly turned his feet downward so they wouldn't protrude from the lounge's shape. Ever so slowly, he peered around the chair back. One? No, two. Two men stood in his bedroom. One stood with his back to the glass door holding a shotgun. The other raised a pistol and snapped on the light in the room's bathroom.

Jack's breathing came fast and shallow. His Colt Combat Commander lay on the nightstand beside his bed, his magnum revolver rested inside the locked Caddy glove box on the driveway below. But, hey, that may as well be on a shooting star or the moon to him right now. Silently, he rolled off the lounge, then inched tightly into the corner beside the door and stood still. The searching shadows cast onto the balcony. Grunting. Whispers.

"He ain't here."

"He's here somewhere. Look in dem otha' rooms."

One shadow disappeared. The second, brandishing the shotgun, crossed in front of the light. Jack strained to hear more. Something thumped on the carpet. Silence. Could he make the jump from the balcony and run to the neighbors? Then he heard a click. It was the handle to the balcony door. The sliding glass door inched open. Jack pressed tighter against the wall. The barrel of the shotgun appeared. Next a huge, left wrist, then a forearm on the gun. A snarling profile glared at the lounge chair.

Jack clamped his right hand on the muzzle of the shotgun and yanked it forward and away from the intruder as hard as he could. Only the man's arms moved, not his body. The gun didn't budge from his hands. Jack reared back with his right fist and backhanded the man square in the face, on the nose. He felt his knuckles strike bone and his skin break across teeth. The massive man's head snapped back, but no TKO here. Jack seized the stock of the shotgun with both hands, and the two men began a desperate dance for possession of the weapon.

The man, whether dazed or body smart, surrendered some space to Jack, feeding him the shotgun by extending his arms. Jack won the space unexpectedly, and lost his balance, He fell backward. The intruder charged him then, using the weapon like a battering ram, sideways across Jack's chest.

They crashed into the balcony railing. Pieces of the redwood gave way with a cracking sound and ripped partially loose from the decking. The big man now towered over Jack, his shotgun gouging into Jack's chest, pushing him down, down, with steady, angry momentum. A searing pain pulsated in the small of Jack's back as he arched over the loose, creaking railing. Another post splintered away, and Jack's bare feet - his only anchor - began to slip. Soon he would either topple over the railing ledge in a rain of lumber or just break in two.

Their faces were now inches apart. The other man's bloodied nose drained onto Jack's face. It was then Jack recognized his assailant, Walter Wayne Hill. Hill had an upcoming court date, his fourth armed robbery. Out on bond - Hill wanted to kill Jack, the detective who'd arrested him three of the four times. Hill smiled - a serious mistake.

Hill's smile enraged Jack. He lurched forward and buried his teeth deeply into Hill's broken nose. Hill shook his head, causing even more pain, and twisted to escape. Jack held on, and bit down harder. Hill's concentration broke. His grip loosened on the stock of the gun. Jack ripped the stock from Hill's left hand, let go of Hill's nose, and swung the stock up hard into Hill's face, crushing and collapsing bone and teeth. Hill stumbled back and released the gun barrel. Finally in full control of the weapon, Jack bashed it full force across Hill's forehead, over and over. Like a savage machine, Jack battered Hill across the balcony and up against the far railing. With a last vicious swing, Jack catapulted Hill over the top. He watched the giant man silently fall, almost in slow motion, into the darkness below.

Jack collapsed to the deck gasping for breath. He spat out skin and blood. The struggle had lasted less than half a minute, maybe 20 seconds? But Hill's accomplice had to have heard it. Scrambling to upright the weapon, he pointed the shotgun at the door. Jack waited. Would the shotgun still work? No one appeared in the bedroom doorway.

Fighting dizziness, Jack rose and moved inside. He kept the shotgun leveled on the door into the hall. With one hand he reached for his Colt Combat Commander pistol beside the bed. He snapped off the light. Steps creaked on the stairs. Moving fast, Jack clicked off the Colt's safety, lay the shotgun on the floor by the bed, and flattened himself against the wall next to the door.

"Yo, Shotgun?"

He heard from the hallway. Jack peeked around the doorway, spying the man with the pistol. Offering nothing as a target but his .45 and a fraction of his right eye, Jack settled his sights on the figure on the stairs.

"Drop it, fella," Jack barked.

The man froze. Jack heard his hissing curse, saw his gaze dart from the Colt, down the stairs, and back at the

.45. Jack read the look like a book.

"Drop your gun. Drop it." Jack's eyes narrowed on the face. Lusk. Herbert Lusk, a parolee. And Hill's cousin.

"I'll shoot you dead, Lusk."

Hearing his name, was like a message of pending doom. Lusk banged off two shots and dove for the stairs.

Jack's instant, explosive response, braced and accurate, caught Lusk in mid-air, punched through his chest, and bounced him off the stairway wall. Jack saw the man's face register utter shock before he crashed upside down onto the stairs, tumbling in a lifeless heap down the stairs and onto the floor below. The dumb bastard died before he hit the ground.

Jack slid down the doorframe until he sat on the floor and stared at the splattered remains of Herbert Lusk left on the wall. Painfully, he rose and walked to the top of the stairs and leaned on the banister. It didn't take a mental giant to piece together the motivations of his attackers. Revenge. He straightened up and winced. Tomorrow he'd have the burglar alarm installed that he'd promised himself for years.

But for now, he still had tonight to clean up, after his comrades at the PD raked through his house. And outside too, as Walter Wayne Hill was still outside on his driveway for starters. Call 911. If the fall hadn't killed Hill, the son-of-a-bitch would need an ambulance and a new face. Jack started down the stairs and looked around. The kitchen window curtains billowed out softly, drawing his attention. Their entry point. He had done Harris County a favor with regard to Herbert Lusk. No more prison space, no more trials, no more victims. Hill, on the other hand, would...

WHAM.

A crowbar welted across Jack's mid-section. It doubled him in half. His Colt ejected from his hand and clattered into the darkness below.

"You muthafuckin'...." screamed a voice.

A third madman appeared from nowhere swinging into Jack's vision, his eyes wild, arms reared back for a killing blow. Jack rolled, and the crowbar crashed into the banister beside him, splintering wood as the man's screaming obscenities exploded in Jack's ears. Jack somersaulted over Lusk's corpse on floor beside the stairs into a clumsy roll.

The intruder charged him, stumbling over Lusk. He rose to his feet. He lunged and stunned the back of Jack's right leg with the crowbar as Jack bolted into the living room. Jack twisted a living room chair over into the man's path, then fell atop the coffee table. Jack slipped off the table just as another blast cracked into the table's middle, splitting it in two, shattering the glass top like a small bombshell. Crowbar took another swing in this relentless offensive, striking just above Jack as the detective half-fell, half-ran. The iron bar plowed into a winged chair, tipping it over spinning it on one leg. It toppled into Crowbar's path giving Jack a few precious seconds to escape.

Skidding across the entryway, Jack ran into the dining room, swooped up a dining room chair, and raised it like a shield against the next blows. The antique chair shattered under Crowbars madman bashing. Jack picked up another chair and threw it, then threw another - like throwing glass against a brick wall as Crowbar swung his tool like a buzz saw, batting and destroying each seat into wood shrapnel. Then, Crowbar charged, and Jack had nowhere to go except over the huge dining room table. His weight and momentum tipped the table over on its side, and Jack landed on his back in a heap amid the centerpiece crystal, candles and busted chairs. His hand closed around a thick but narrow crystal vase. He fired it like a missile at Crowbar's head. The vase struck the man's face, his left eye and forehead, with such force it glanced upwards into the ceiling fan, and the attacker almost dropped to his knees.

Now the overturned table stood sideways between

them. Jack scrambled to his feet, grabbed the last chair and bashed it into Crowbar's side. He dove over the upturned table and tackled Crowbar chest high. They fell into a wall of shelves, and dropped within the avalanche of books and statues, Jack swinging his fists at the man's head and throat every inch of the fall.

Driving full force into each other, they both got knee-high. Crowbar reached out with his free hand, caught Jack's neck and squeezed. Blood gushed from his vase-cut forehead, staining his face. He roared like an escaped lunatic from hell, his eyes wild and wet, his fingers puncturing into Jack's throat, ready for the kill.

Entangled, they somehow both stood. Jack clamped down on the giant hand choking him. He stuck a thumb deep into Crowbar's eye, and the criminal let out a pathetic whine, like a wounded wild pig. He released Jack's throat and Jack seized the opportunity. He began pile-driving punches, carrying the punk across the wall. He didn't let up until Crowbar collapsed unconscious against the serving bar between the dining room and the kitchen. He hung, half on the bar, half tangled in the bar stools.

Then Jack fell back, tripped on debris, and landed, gasping, on the floor. His lungs burned with and intense agony, and his heart raced out of control.

Unable to move, Jack studied the bloodied face of the man splayed over his bar and could not identify this petty hood who had almost beaten him to death with a metal bar. Cheap, amateur prison tattoos plastered his sweat, slick arms. Jack gazed at the largest tat - "We Aim to Pleaz " in an uneven scrawl over the artwork of a barrel of a gun. Scowling, Jack turned his head away. The room looked like a missile had exploded within.

"Christ," he mumbled.

His heart, which had begun to slow, sped up with new

thoughts. What if Jack's brother Robert and Robert's wife and their two kids had been here tonight, on their yearly visit from California? What would have happened? He stumbled to his feet in rekindled rage, tossing wreckage aside, searching for his .45. Jack's hand wrapped around his gun handle and he kicked back through the broken furniture and grabbed Crowbar by his shirtfront.

"Wake up." He yelled and yanked the man's torso away from bar, forced him onto his feet. Crowbar's eyelids fluttered, then flew open as he registered he was at the business end of Jack's Colt, inches from his nose. Faces flashed in Jack's mind - his brother and sister-in-law, their innocent, grinning kids, then to his surprise, the visage of the curled-up lifeless form of the 19-year-old grocery clerk killed in Hill's last supermarket robbery. Jack even pictured the clerk's family at the funeral. The sounds. The tears.

A blast of air, saliva and blood exploded from Jack's mouth, in an undistinguishable bark of a growl. And he squeezed the trigger. The gun erupted. The hot shell flipped to the wall as Crowbar's body jerked violently from Jack's grip. It slammed in a red blur back onto the bar stools.

Jack wrestled his gasping lungs under some control and reached for the wall phone. He forced his shaking fingers to zero in on the numbers.

"West Forge Police Department. This conversation is being recorded so we may better serve you," Dotty Gonzalez, the midnight shift dispatcher answered.

"Dotty. This is Jack. I've been attacked in my home. Three guys..."

"Are you all right?"

"I had to shoot two of them. The third is stretched out in the backyard. Call the cavalry. Get everybody out here." A "cavalry call" at West Forge PD was a nickname for major call-out, starting from alerting the mayor and then the Chief on down.

"Jack. Are you okay?" she asked.

"Yeah, yeah. Beat up. But - yeah. Okay."

He hung up, and realized he was still in his underwear. He went to the utility room off the kitchen and slipped on the mechanic's overalls hanging there, then flipped on the front porch lights for the responding units. He still needed to check on Hill in the backyard.

Jack limped past the dead man sprawled on the dining room floor and stopped. Whoever this "We Aim to Pleaz" tattooed, freak, wanna-be punk, was, Jack was certain he had done Harris County, and Texas, yet another big favor.

"I did all the aiming tonight, fuck-head," he growled over the corpse.

******

"A Harris County Grand Jury yesterday cleared Sgt. "Jumping Jack" Kellog, West Forge PD, of any criminal charges in the shooting of two of three late-night intruders who broke into his fashionable West Forge home. Indicted for attempted capital murder in relation to this investigation is Walter Wayne Hill, the surviving third of the trio who attacked the detective with a shotgun. Hill is currently in custody of deputies in the Blair wing of Duchess Memorial Hospital as a result of injuries sustained in the attack. Hill had been indicted for aggravated robbery of a West Forge supermarket, a case investigated by his quarry, Sgt. Kellog. Leading the investigation was Texas Ranger Weaver Wisdom who had these comments, 'It was more than apparent, that Detective Kellog acted in self-defense.' Revenge is believed to be the motive for the attack on the police detective." - HOUSTON CHRONICLE

CHAPTER TWO
THE LESSON OF DILLER BAILEY

"Jack Kellog was a hound dog. Day and night. He got more things done in our county, more crimes solved than anyone else. He was a gangbuster of a soma-bitch." - Rye Edleson, former Harris County assistant district attorney

Archie Lennox, Interview Tape 22

Jack heaved the Houston Chronicle across his old wooden desk with a bruised arm and sore hand. The desk was a virtual museum piece of humor, horror and fascination. It contained photos and objects from years and years of crimes. Equipment like bugs, recorders, cameras, and binoculars lay tucked away beside envelopes containing hair from murder victims, old suspects' guns, and forged checks. Things that should have been locked in the evidence department safes, but for one reason or another, not excluding distraction, never quite made it that far. It was like any other veteran investigator's desk, much like his partner that of Jack Breasley's desk just inches away in the small room. A brass sign on their door read "Robbery Squad." If you could call two men a whole squad?

Jack's partner looked up from his steaming morning coffee, studied Kellog's healing but still bruised and swollen face, and shook his head.

"You ugly," Breasley said.

Nicknamed "The Two Jacks," Jack Kellog and Jack Breasley did not resemble each other at all. Breasley stood tall, lean, and handsome with jet-black hair and a jutting hero's jaw, while Kellog barely topped six feet, barrel-chested and getting heavy-set. His graying hair rubbed his shirt collar and a full western moustache drooped just beyond the corners of city PD grooming regulations. Breasley owned the clean-shaven good guy's face, a leading man's demeanor, while Kellog could look like his impatient, grumbling villain.

Breasley, the born and bred, Houston city boy, appeared each day in a business suit with the required tie that managed a disappearing act after lunch. Kellog looked like the cowboy from Yoakum, Texas that he was, inclined toward western leather blazers, Levi jeans, and a rotating collection of boots to rival that of the Governor's. Kellog's tie vanished years ago and emerged only when Chief "Shrewdy" Collins demanded it, and then only for a little while. He preferred the bolo tie, which wasn't "city policy."

Breasley wouldn't be caught dead in a cowboy hat while Jack wore his white Stetson with regularity, especially off-duty. Breasley carried a S & W Model 66 in a Cordura shoulder holster. Jack tucked his Colt Commander in his western beltline. Fact was, there wasn't much twin-like about them except their first names and their never-ending, robbery division caseload.

Both in their early 50s, they'd survived police business

for a long time. Both received each robbery report as an old familiar challenge, deep down hoping the next case they caught might be of "Super Bowl" caliber, a pending case that kept them still playing on the field. Most weren't. Ordinarily there weren't many homicides in West Forge, the suburb of Houston, so any veteran detective might be assigned those cases. So, realistically expecting little, Jack reached slowly for his Houston Oilers coffee cup and asked Breasley, "What's new this morning?"

"First, gotta go home and get my gun," Breasley muttered. "Lisa took it again."

Jack let out a short growl. He wanted to know about the crime reports not about Lisa and his empty holster. "Where's Lisa's gun?" he asked.

About every six months or so, Lisa Breasley somehow wound up with Breasley's pistol. Most of the time it happened due to Breasley's shoulder holster. It felt extremely uncomfortable to carry a weapon full time in such a rig, and Breasley often pulled it and parked it for relief here and there. He got used to the holster being empty. Then, when he would leave the office of the house, he'd holster up, then grab the gun from it's last location, unless he forgot to look and left the house. The gun wound up in his wife's car a lot.

"That Starsky and Hutch Hollywood holster gonna get you killed yet," Kellog complained.

Breasley thumbed through the six new robbery offense reports. "Oh, Lisa gave her shiny pistola to her friend for the weekend, and she got in my car and took my gun out to go shopping." Mrs. Breasley was not supposed to be taking a city detective car shopping, least of all toting the police handgun in her purse.

"A sure-fire recipe for a disaster," Kellog muttered shaking his head.

"Over the weekend, let's see," he scanned the top report. "One strong-armed robbery. A guy, Diller Bailey, got the shit and his teeth kicked out of him on the Blass Shopping Mall parking lot by two white males, all for a whoppin' 11 dollars. Next one, an ol'-timey gal, 80-year-old Erma Faye Frederick, had her purse and a…a small pine tree plant she was carrying taken…ever in your pea-pickin' life had a case with a pine tree stolen? Snatched from her on Twitty St. by a white male. The poor ol' gal was shoved down and broke her hip. Admitted into East Duchess Hospital. This one here is a truck driver from Moore, Oklahoma, robbed at gunpoint by a hitchhiker at the Meredith truck stop."

Breasley paused, frowning. "…and the Steak Knife rapist struck again. Broke into another apartment early Sunday morning, robbed and raped a woman."

"Cut her?"

"A bit."

Jack finger-motioned for the Steak Knife report, and Breasley pinched the papers in the middle and sailed them over. They landed square in the middle of Kellog's desk, as Breasley had perfected the skill having used it well over a thousand times.

Kellog followed the violent crimes of the Steak Knife Rapist, a black male who had selectively chosen eight victims in as many months throughout the Harris County area, two of those women on their turf in West Forge. The M.O. was always the same - he'd break into the home of a single or divorced woman with a common kitchen knife. Then he'd rape and sometimes cut, and always rob. The first victim told television news reporters that a knife man had 'come a callin' with a sharp steak knife, thus the quick, media nickname. Since this uncluded a robbery, and there was no official rape division, these cases found their way to the Two Jacks.

Breasley rattled off a few comments while Kellog half-listened, reading every word of the rape report in his hand. This time, as the body of the report disclosed, West Forge PD's Crime Scene Search Team lead by Leon "Right-away" Attaway had actually located some apparent workable fingerprints, a rarity in the real world of policing despite what the public usually believed from watching TV. Seemed like every other week Efrem Zimbalist Jr. solved a crime on the FBI show with a fingerprint. But now, just like a Quinn Martin Production, all they needed was a suspect with which to compare the prints.

Kellog finally looked up to the top of the sheet to read the name of the victim-Ida Bell. "Hell, I know this gal. Ida Bell. Somebody robbed her about six years ago. Her cousin, a real scumbag, stole her entire life savings from inside her mattress. Now she's been robbed again. And raped too. Damn shame. She's a good, hard working woman."

"Your turn to pick 'em," Breasley said."

"We'll, I'll damn sure take this steak knife rape. Give me the "shit and teeth kicker" and the pine tree plant deal too, I guess," Jack chose. They were always fair, trying to spread a "major," a "minor" and a "damn silly" between them.

"Fine with me. Anybody want the rest?" Breasley shouted to no one. Jack sighed at that tired joke.

"Okay," said Breasley as he slapped the reports on his desk, "In that case, let me run by the house and get my damn gun. See ya at Birch's for java." He downed his station brew as did Jack.

Kellog painfully rose from his chair, and the two Jacks left the station bound for their cars. The daily routine, barring emergency, was a morning breakfast at Birch's café. This might sound like slacking off to a novice or an ignorant taxpayer. But both Jacks averaged a 60 or 70-hour work week, 20 or 30 of those hours unpaid. But that's just the life of a detective. The department forgave them for their breakfast ritual. Plus, the breakfast was an unofficial meeting place, one might say a daily intelligence gathering of sorts, where several DPS Highway patrolman, local ATF, DEA, Ranger Weaver Wisdom, and some deputies might be found. Sure, they talked about deer hunting, fishing, the Oilers and the Astros, but they also talked cop shop and crime.

"Detective Sgt. Jack Kellog. Please report to Captain Melton's office." The tinny voice sounded over the back-parking lot loudspeaker just as Jack's boots touched the asphalt of the lot. The smokers congregating by the back door all chuckled. West Forge's City Council, mostly yuppies from Houston, outlawed smoking inside all city buildings. The parking lot door was a designated area where smokers angrily fed their addiction and spent a good 20 minutes on the hour wasting time.

"OOOHHHHH, whatcha do this time, Jumpin' Jack? Leave the water fountain on too long? Flush twice?" a records clerk said. Captain Danny Melton was in charge of budget.

"Snip-snip." another wisenheimer added.

"Je-SUS," Jack mumbled, turned and headed back inside.

"Snip-snip" was often whispered around Danny Melton. A few years back, Melton suffered from severe hemorrhoids. But to save money, one night he decided to climb into a bathtub of hot water with a pair of scissors and a handheld mirror. The hot water - it was presumed - to dull the pain. The mirror, after much rehearsal, was positioned just right in the corner between the tub and the wall. In a circus act of contortion, Danny maneuvered his body in the tub so as to pull out and access the anal growth. With a deep breath, he squeezed the scissors into action. Snip-snip. Off went the exposed part of the hemorrhoids.

Blood spurted out into the water. A lot of blood. Danny expected some blood but not this much. He pinched it off but still the warm water become a transparent red. He began to fell faint. He lost his pinch. He called out to wife Reba for help. She burst into the bathroom to see Danny reeling into unconsciousness in a tub of red water. Ordinarily, one might suspect suicide, but Reba was wise to Danny's penny-pinching ways.

"DANNY. You've done cut yer roid off and bleeding like a stuck pig."

She shoved a towel into the crack of his ass and called for an ambulance.

The tape of the call was collected and distributed by department pranksters. It went like this:

"West Forge Police Emergency."

"This is Reba Melton. My husband Danny has cut off his hemorrhoid. He's bleeding to death in the bathtub."

"Reba? You mean Lt. Melton is bleeding to death?"

"Yes. The Lieutenant is bleeding to death. He snipped off his own god-damn roid with my best pair of goddamn sewing scissors and he is bleeding all over the goddamn bathroom...DANNY, Danny you get back in the bathtub, you'll ruin the carpet..."

Needless to say, the nickname Danny "Snip-Snip" Melton stuck.

Jack walked into the Captain Snip-Snip's office.

"Jack, have a seat. How ya feelin'?" Melton asked.

"Still sore as hell, Danny."

"Jack...you bought gas in Amarillo about three months ago? On the PD credit card?" Melton showed him a form.

Kellog looked it over, "Yeah, went out there to their county jail. Inmate there said he knew something about one of our robbery cases. Antonio authorized the trip and gave me the card for gas."

"What's this part?" He pointed to a second line with the charged price of 87 cents.

"Ahhh, I got a coke? I think." Jack said. "Oh, I know. That was a popsicle. I got gas and an ice pop."

Melton stared at Kellog for about 10 seconds, then said, "Jack, you can't buy a coke or an ice popsicle." Melton sounded mildly astonished at Jack's fumbling of protocol.

"Well Danny…. I didn't eat a meal. It was an eight-hour drive each way. I believe I would have been authorized to eat an entire sit-down, $10 meal. One going. One coming back. $20. Any other nimrod in this building would have stayed one night and cost a hotel room. I didn't spend that dinner allotment or that hotel money. I just had the ice popsicle. I was in the middle of a case and had to get back. I believe I saved the city nineteen bucks and whatever a hotel costs." Jack stood and took out his wallet. "But looky here Danny, here's a buck."

"Okay Jack." Danny said, now fumbling for words.

"I had an orange popsicle for dinner." But Jack could tell Melton's spreadsheet universe was still out of joint. There was to be no buying of ice popsicles with city money. And handing him a dollar bill was a puzzle he couldn't solve easily either. Now he would have to deposit a dollar bill under some kind of title or category. And sweat out what to do about the 13 cents profit. What account would that go into?

"Popsicle for dinner," Danny mumbled.

"Orange."

"Orange."

Kellog stood and left the room. Deep down Jack liked Danny. They'd spent five years on the same patrol shift together back in the 70s. But Danny sure made himself hard to like sometimes - the anal-retentive bastard.

"Lighter in wallet, Jack?" The gauntlet of smokers cajoled as he walked hastily by them back in route to his car.

"One buck for an orange popsicle," Jack grumbled. And the smokers howled in absolute delight. And coughed.

This type of crap always annoyed Jack. The admin seemed to quickly forget all the free hours Jack worked as well as the fact he used his own car for work. And paid for his own gas at 50 cents to the gallon. Jack slid behind the wheel of his 1982 Caddy. He even parked it on the back police lot. There was no way he and Breasley could function with the one sedan assigned to the robbery unit. What would Mrs. Breasley run to the store in on weekends? Besides Jack liked his eight-track player, FM stereo and the smooth, cloud-like, Caddy ride.

Kellog and Breasley met some 40 minutes later at Birch's Cafe to inhale omelets with two highway patrolmen on their breakfast break. Eventually, all four wandered back outside, each with a toothpick clenched between his teeth, to begin their days.

******

"Police are on the hunt again for the infamous Steak Knife Rapist, a serial criminal who has struck repeatedly in Harris County, and may now be responsible for another assault last night, this time in the Houston suburb of West Forge."

Jack listened to the radio newsman's report as his Caddy floated over a set of country railroad tracks and down a winding, two-lane road bordered by the hilly, open farm-land of northern Harris County. It had been a 30-minute drive from the West Forge city limits in pursuit of the complainant: one Diller Bailey.

Box 242, Rt. 2 - a policeman's dilemma. The first mystery was to locate the right house amongst a maze of unnamed back roads. Fortunately, most postmasters did forego usual federal formalities and reveal box locations over the phone, as this lady had done for Jack. But things were starting to get real funny. Privacy-funny. Some post office people wouldn't tell police such information anymore. Apartment complex managers were not always helpful with info on their residents like they used to and just last week the East Duchess Hospital's new office manager wouldn't turn loose of a victim's medical record without a signed release or a court order. How would investigators investigate?

Searching the horizon, Jack flipped open his tooled, brown-leather notebook to its yellow, legal pad, ready to decipher the directions that involved a series of turns at this or that natural landmark and included a number count of old wood frame houses. "Fourth white house past Bob Day's Quarter Horse Ranch on Farm to Market Road 1222. East side." After that, Jack was on his own.

Four down and there it sat, an old, barren, one-story place beside a weather-beaten barn that would have put the Leaning Tower of Pisa to shame, for one good mountain-cedar, allergy sneeze would knock it right over. Jack turned in, rocked over the cattle guard, and crunched up the gravel driveway to the house. He parked beside a brand new, black Ford pickup and stepped slowly out into the chilly Andrew Wyeth landscape.

He knocked on the door, then turned to survey the flat landscape in front of the house from the porch. A semi-truck maneuvering poorly on the road blew by in a roar. Jack noticed that the Ford pickup had been in its share of accidents, both major and minor.

"Who is it?" shouted a muffled voice.

"The police."

"The police?"

"The police."

A bed sheet-turned-drape opened in the front window.

"Show me some badge," ordered the figure.

"Sgt. Jack Kellog, West Forge PD. I'm here about your robbery," Jack said, displaying a gold shield from his wallet. Through the years he had been greeted by all kinds of identity questions. One time he was even locked in a hallway by a resourceful old woman while she called the PD to confirm his pedigree before letting him in - or out.

The drape closed and Jack heard several latch chains hit the wooden door. The knob turned, allowing the door to creak ajar.

"Come in."

Jack pushed the door open to see his complainant limping backward away from him until he collapsed on a worn, ragged couch. Small and slightly built, the man wore a blue T-shirt filled with holes, almost white blue jeans, and a black cap with "Jack Daniels" on the crunched front. Jack had seen the likes of this type of guy many, many times. He looked like an unhealthy version of Sonny Bono, which was unhealthy to begin with.

A beat-up black and white TV drew through its wire-hanger-and tin-foil antenna the fuzzy images of cartoon superheroes doing galactic battle. The smell of marijuana permeated the air. Pill bottles, half empty and full, lay scattered everywhere. But it was a long-barreled, 12-gauge shotgun cradled in the man's arms that drew Jack's attention. On the sofa cushion beside him rested a blue steel revolver. The complainant sat back with a low groan, threw his hurt leg up on a wobbly coffee table adorned with empty beer cans and cigarette ash.

"You Diller Bailey?"

"Yupster."

"Goddamn, man. Just who are you expecting?" Jack stared at the handy arsenal.

"Shit, man. That robbery bidness yesterday gots me

scared," he replied, his eyes wide and words garbled by the swollen black and blue damage around his mouth. The cotton gauze stuffed between Diller's gum and cheek looked blood stained. "Have ya a seat. Ya wanna beer?" He asked.

"No thanks." Jack unbuttoned his tan blazer jacket and sat down carefully. The rickety chair's bowed leg brushed his calf muscle that had been smashed by the crowbar only a week ago.

"Well," said Diller, "I'm a hurtin' for certain. My damn teeth is knocked out. I'm ace-bandaged up. My leg is killing me. That som-a-bitch got me good." Diller grabbed an ice pack from the couch and pressed it to his swollen face. He chucked off his cap revealing a burr crewcut. Jack easily envisioned a once proud ponytail growing from his round fuzzy head. It belonged with that Fu Manchu moustache dangling an inch below Diller's chin, along with a small silver star in his left ear.

"That's a whole lotta hurt for 11 bucks," Jack said. He noticed a large diamond ring on Diller Bailey's finger. Something these robbers missed? He pointed at the ring.

"Ain't that the truth." Diller's head moved side-to-side like an Egyptian dancer.

"Since you have no phone and there was no place of employment listed on your report, I took the chance you'd be here."

"Yeah. Say man, you look like you been through some hell or yer own, too."

Jack partly smiled, though it hurt a little. His tongue and jaw were still sore. "I've been beaten up myself here lately. You wearing that ring when this happened?"

"Uh - yeah," Diller said hesitantly.

"Listen," Jack said, "I won't take a lot of your time." He flipped open his notebook and reviewed the facts given in the crime report. Diller chimed in to support the report that he had left the mall and a white male attacked him while another white male stood by a customized van watching. Tan, gold maybe. Fancy van. Tricked out. These boys ordered Diller to surrender his wallet, then punches flew. Diller fell, then his attacker kicked his face and stomach. Diller couldn't supply a decent description of the men and his account to Jack was a little different from the reports. Throughout his dramatic, head-weaving narration, he kept peeking at the Super Friends cartoons on TV. Jack was not impressed.

"Says here, Diller, you didn't want to report this. The hospital called it in."

"Yeah, well, you know," he said, "nuthin' much can be done. I knows that, so why bother you guys, ya know?"

"Diller," Jack said while standing and adjusting his gun-laden beltline, "Do you really think they'll come up here to get you?" He looked down at the wepaons.

"Well, man, they gots my wallet, gots my ID, gots my driver's license with my address printed on it." he replied.

"Yeah," Jack drawled. "Diller Bailey, Route Two." He pulled out his business card and tossed it on the coffee table.

"I sure thank ya fer coming, Sergeant. I don't expect much, ya know, these robbers, these boys could be anywhere - anybody. I sure appreciate your time. Don' cha be worryin' about it. Don't work too hard on this. I don't expect much," Diller said.

"Yeah, well. Hope you get better," Jack said and walked out. The sounds of locks being re-sunk followed him as he left the sagging porch. Back in his Caddy, Jack inconspicuously jotted down the Ford's license plate and injected a Merle Haggard tape into his stereo. He backed out of the drive and turned south. Over the hill, he ran the pickup's license and requested the criminal history of Diller Bailey from the West Forge dispatcher.

"I'm just an ol' lump of coal. But I'm gonna be a diamond someday…"

Jack's and Merle's singing was interrupted by the dispatcher, "West Forge 101. Registration check - 1985 Ford pickup to a Diller Bailey, 2113 Chelsea, Apt. 4-B, Houston. Texas. No lienholder. Arrested seven times. Four drug-related offenses, two convictions, currently on Harris County probation."

"Save that for me, dispatcher."

"1152 hours."

A dope deal, thought Jack. All the signs of a dope deal gone bad, plus, Diller, the hippy, skinny Bailey, owner of a brand new but dented pickup that was completely paid for. Use to live in Houston, but now lives on "Route Nowhere" with a garbage can TV. Big diamond ring. Four drug-related arrests. He was in the hospital beaten to a pulp but doesn't want to call the police. It was the emergency room who reported the incident as was their standard procedure on assaults. Usually, such victims scream for the police. Not ol' Bailey. When confronted by the questions of patrolmen, his best fantasy was, "I was robbed." Diller had obviously fallen into debt or trouble with some druggists. He said not to worry or work on his case, yet he hid at home fondling a shotgun and waiting for a robbery team he just couldn't seem to describe to the police. It was a collection team he was afraid of.

This was going to be another case that would die a graceful death in Jack's filing cabinet. Jack wasn't going to work for a lying, drug dealer complainant who should have known exactly what happens to folks who play around "in the business," especially when there were people like Ida Bell who really need to see some justice.

What a strange, thin man with the Egyptian twitch,

the star-shaped earring, and the Fu Manchu. Damn hippy freaks. Justice comes in many forms, Jack thought as his Caddy took the railroad tracks gracefully. By the time he turned onto the highway, he was already plotting out the next steps in his other pending cases.

"101," called the dispatcher.

"Go ahead," answered Jack.

"Have a public service for you. Can you copy?"

"Go ahead."

"10-4," finished Jack after, blindly scratching the dictated phone number on his note pad while driving into West Forge's city limits. He pulled in at a Mobil station, got out, bought a bottle of Dr. Pepper, and walked to the outdoor pay phone, dialing the number from memory. The cold bottle felt good on his swollen fingers.

"Hello," answered a male voice.

"This is Sgt. Jack Kellog of..."

"Yeah," interrupted the voice. "This is Carl Fredericks. My grandmother was robbed yesterday. She's been in the hospital ever since. Why haven't you spoken with her yet?"

"I just received the case this morning," said Jack calmly, sipping his Dr. Pepper.

"We want something done about this, damnit. Where the hell have you been?"

"Well sir, I have been working on robbery cases. I was assigned three this morning of which your grandmother's case was one. The other two were a vicious robbery/rape, and a robbery beating. I also have nine robbery cases open from last week and since the first of the month, another 11. Fact of business is, your grandmother's case is the 67th robbery I've had since the first of January," Jack sipped again. This was a patented speech he used about 50 times a year.

"My grandmother is in the hospital, Sgt. Kellog. She was attacked and robbed. She's upset. She's in pain. The police need to deal with this, that's all."

"I deal in very tragic offenses, Mr. Fredrick, with many upset and hurt victims. We do the best we can."

"I know. I know you do," the voice mellowed, a little.

"I plan to get over to St. Duchess to see your grandmother as soon as I can."

With an uncomfortable goodbye, Jack hung up, drained the soda and tossed the bottle into an overflowing trash barrel on his way back to his car. Mr. Fredrick and his grandmother would have to wait until after Jack had interviewed Ida Bell. The Steak Knife Rapist had priority over a purse and plant snatcher.

******

Jack drove to Swillum Products, a small Houston factory listed on the report as Ida Bell's place of employment. It was in the sweatbox beyond the air-conditioned front offices where the real work was done. Every machine in the place generated heat like an oven. With the floor manager's cooperation, Jack commandeered a small office and some time for Ida away from her 10-pound, metal press. No one there knew Ida had been raped over the weekend, and Jack was careful to reveal only that she was a witness in a police investigation.

"Sgt. Kellog," the woman murmured quietly, her eyes widening with recognition when she entered the room. She walked stiffly and concisely, as though she didn't want to disturb or offend the very air in the room. Jack smiled. She patted the perspiration on her face and slipped into an office chair. She was wearing a faded print housedress and worn, black work shoes. She folded her hands in her lap.

"Hello, Ida. How are you?"

"I don't know," she admitted, and a great sadness fell over Jack. He studied this thin black woman in her early

40s. She was an absolutely hard-working woman, the kind of woman who would probably work three different shifts to support her fatherless family if she didn't need sleep. Mister Bell disappeared the day after their youngest son, Bobby, was born. All this he learned from working that prior robbery case years back.

"How's Bobby?"

"Well as expected."

Jack leaned back in the swivel chair and released a long sigh. "Ida, I really am sorry to see you again under these circumstances. Can we go over what happened the other night?"

"Sgt. Kellog...I can...I have..." Ida stopped, swallowed. She began again. "Do you remember that time before, when you arrested my cousin Rasp? For stealing my mattress money? You were the one who arrested him."

"I remember. Raspus Wilson. They call him Trampus on the street now."

Ida's eyes filled. "I swore to the Lord above, Sergeant, that I wouldn't tell. To the Lord." Her fingers curled in her lap. "Until I saw your face when I walked in here. You are a good man, Sgt. Kellog." She took a shaky breath and stared at Jack with wide, watery eyes.

"What, Ida?"

"He did this to me," she whispered. She looked to the floor.

"Rasp? The rape? He raped you?"

"Yes. He raped me."

Jack leaned forward. He could barely hear her words as she spoke them with a mix of shame and disgust.

"He came back to steal my money again, and he raped me this time, Sergeant."

Adrenaline surged through Jack's body like the seven or so legal decisions that simultaneously pumped through his head.

"Ida, you are positive it was him?"

She looked up. "Of course I am."

"How positive?" he repeated slowly.

"What do you mean? I know him, have known him his whole life."

"Ida," Jack interrupted, "did Rasp Wilson say all the things and do all the things to you that were in the police report?"

"Yes, sir," she said solemnly. "I told the patrolman every detail. I need the police report to show my landlord because I have no money for the rent. I told him evetything except who it was because," her hand shot up in warning, like a shield. "He's crazy. Crazy mean. I am so scared of him." She closed her eyes. "He...he hurt us after you arrested him last time, Sgt. Kellog, after he got out of jail." She lowered her head and whispered, "He hurt us."

"How?" Jack asked. "Tell me, Ida."

But the woman would not look at him, would only shake her head. Her palm opened again before him was like an emotional barrier, but it slowly faded down to her side.

"I wasn't going to tell anyone Rasp did this to me, not till I saw your face," was all she said.

"Ida, there are fingerprints from the bedroom. Prints from your attacker. If they are Trampus's...Rasp's...is there any other possible reason for his prints to be there?"

"No sir. I have not seen him in six years."

Jack picked up the phone on the desk and pounded away on the buttons.

"Attaway," he requested of the Crime Scene Search Team secretary.

"Attaway here."

"This is Kellog, Att. Do you know which team went out Saturday night to the Ida Bell robbery/rape?"

"Yeah, me. I was there," Att said.

"Pull the arrest records on a Raspus "Trampus" Wilson. I can't remember his birthday, but he's about 32 years old, black male."

"Raspus was born in February, 19 hundred and 57." Ida interjected. Jack nodded but didn't need to tell Attaway. Attaway being Attaway remembered Jack's old case.

"Check the prints against anything you all picked up Saturday. And, Att, check the Wilson prints against any other Steak Knife latents any agency might have."

"Gotcha," said Attaway, obviously charged with the prospect. "I'm on it." The receiver went dead. The man wasn't nicknamed "Right-away" Attaway for no reason.

Ida watched Jack pound out another number. This time he called the Houston PD Rape Division number and reached a Detective Ignacio Lupus, quickly tipping him on Trampus Wilson and the prints.

"Jack, I am almost certain all we ever lifted were smudges in our five cases, but," Detective Lupus said, "with a definite suspect in mind maybe we can do something. I'll get back to you."

Jack got up and sat on the edge of the desk right in front of Ida.

"Ida," Jack said, "have you heard about the Steak Knife Rapist?"

She nodded her head.

"We have purposely held back many details of the rapist's actions - I mean the exact things he's said, some of the exact things he's done. Your cousin did these same things to you. There's been other women who have been assaulted like you were assaulted, but you are the only victim that knows him - can identify him." Jack took a deep breath, reading the fear in Ida's eyes. "We need a statement from you so very desperately about every detail. And about your very solid identification of him."

The woman closed her eyes. "He is a very, very angry man," she said.

"We...all...need your help," Jack said simply, "or this

meanness will go on and on."

"I know. Will he get out on bond?"

"Not if I can help it."

She looked into Jack's eyes with a calm resolve. "I know you will. The Lord knows it too."

******

Back at the station, Jack sat Ida down in the CID waiting room and jogged over to his ringing telephone.

"Kellog, this is Right-away," said the voice on the phone. Jack sat down in his office chair when he heard Attaway's voice.

"Go."

"On the Ida Bell case, we got some workable ones off the metal headboard of the Bell bed. The report said during the rape, the suspect held onto the bed railing. Also, we lifted some from the bathroom medicine chest mirror. Both areas matched with Wilson's right index finger and a thumb."

"YOU are one of the world's great people. Can you get me all this in a statement?" Jack felt ecstatic.

"Right away."

They hung up. Jack peered at Ida through his office door as she sat with a female officer giving a statement. He walked up to them.

"Ida, did Rasp ever go into the bathroom?" he asked quietly.

"Yes. Yes, he did. He looked through my medicine chest for drugs."

"Get that in," Kellog told the officer, then returned to his office. The statement would now also support the fingerprint evidence found on the mirror.

He sat at his desk waiting impatiently for the statements to come in. He mindlessly toyed with a switchblade knife he had wrestled from a Spanish gang member 22 years ago when he worked as a street cop in Houston. It now served as his letter opener and fingernail cleaner. It never ceased to amaze him what strange occurrence might break a case, or this time, a series of cases. You work and work with no leads on what appears to be unsolvable assignments. Then, suddenly, a break comes from nowhere. Well, it wasn't really from nowhere, Jack thought, snapping open the switchblade. It usually came from a chain reaction caused by the police investigation. If they worked hard enough, if they questioned the right people, if they scoured the crime scene for evidence, if you threw your best punch each time, many cases were ready for a break. Jack had a wall of filing cabinets full of unsolved cases, many "gracefully dying" like Diller Bailey's, many others waiting for a break. Jack also considered sending the Diller Bailey report down to Narcotics for their intel when the phone rang.

"Kellog, Robbery."

"This is Fredericks." A long silence. The grandson again. "Where the hell have you been?" The man sounded angry.

"Mr. Fredericks, I am about to go to the Harris County D.A.'s office and file a case against a serial rapist, someone who has beaten and raped eight women."

"Well, damn, can't it wait till tomorrow?" he demanded.

"No, sir, it can't wait. I will be by the hospital to see your grandmother as soon as I can."

"I want something done."

"I know you do, so do..."

"There is a criminal loose in this town attacking old women." the voice complained.

Jack heard a dial tone and, sighing, slowly hung up.

Right-away's enormous frame filled the doorway. "Jumpin' Jack. Here ya go, proof positive Wilson's yer man." Attaway tossed a stapled packet on the desk. Stocky and bald, forever clad in polyester Levi dress pants and short-sleeved western shirts, Leon Attaway looked more

like a retired pro-football player than the forensic policeman he'd been all of his adult life. "There's a statement
from our scene man that actually lifted the prints. We
have a 10-pointer from the bed rail and a seven-pointer
from the medicine chest." He referred to specific matchups
between Wilson's fingerprints and the prints lifted from
Bell's apartment. Jack explained the fast-breaking case,
and Leon hung on every word.

"Lupus from Houston PD called me. They just can't
discern anything in the smudge prints they lifted on his
cases," Right-away added.

The female officer stuck her head into the office. "She's
through."

Jack brought Ida back into his office. He collected all
the paperwork, made many copies for all the records chan-
nels. When he was ready, he drove Ida back to the factory.

On the ride, Kellog explained, "Ida, if anything happens, you must call me. I'll do whatever I can to help you,
protect you, whatever."

She remained quiet, staring ahead.

"Id-AAHH." Jack repeated with a loud, long final accent to her profile.

"Yes, Sergeant, I'll call you," she mumbled.

Jack did not like the tension between them as he dropped
her off, but it was something he had to worry about later.

She stepped out of his car and looked in and told him,
"you have a blessed day." It was almost robotic. Jack decided he had to insist on some fast counseling for her. There
was a victim's rights representative right at his next stop.

He also hoped his old amigo, Rye Edleson, an assistant
criminal prosecutor with the Harris County D.A.'s office would
be in and available to author a probable cause arrest warrant.

******

"Jumpin' of the Jack of the Kellog," roared Rye Edleson across the open bay area of legal secretaries, sounding and even looking like Teddy Roosevelt right down to the suspenders. Jack smiled and wove his way through the computer terminals toward the lawyer.

"Congratulations on your recent murders of Herbert Lusk and Jay Bishop, your aggravated assault on Walter Wayne Hill, and your subsequent no-bill by the grand jury." Edleson broadcast to the enjoyment of those who could hear. Jack chuckled and shook his head. It was good-natured fun to all, though Edleson would never be convinced that both Lusk and Bishop were killed in self-defense *quite* the way Jack testified to.

"What can we do for you today?" Rye asked, but Jack barreled non-stop right past him toward Rye's office before he answered.

"Let's arrest the Steak Knife Rapist," he declared behind Rye's back.

"Let's." Rye curiously raised an eyebrow and he followed after the detective.

******

"101," said the dispatcher.

"Go ahead," said Jack.

"101. You have a visitor."

"10-4, dispatcher. ETA in 10 minutes," Jack responded as he crossed the west city limits of Houston into West Forge. He was planning on a run to St. Duchess to see Erma Fredericks, but again another delay. The grandson would probably assassinate him if he showed up this late anyway. The distant downtown Houston skyline was a silhouette against a red-setting sun, mammoth and modern compared to the approaching old western-style buildings that still made up more than half of West Forge's downtown streets.

Once upon a time there was a break of countryside, a flat no-man's-land between Houston and West Forge where a soul could ease into a transition from modern metropolis to a rural-flavored, West Forge, a place where downtown sidewalks were still some two feet high from street level and a rancher could still find a feed store and red pole barber shop on Main Street. But West Forge had quickly emerged from a town with one Sears catalog store to a place with two complete Sears chains merged into wings of two huge shopping malls. West Forge transformed into a super suburb in a metroplex.

Houston annexed all the county no-man's-land and built on it until it had to re-invent Laredo Boulevard in 1978 from a bumpy two-laner to a four-lane thoroughfare. One side of Laredo Blvd. was West Forge's, the other, Houston's. Like so much of West Forge's style, decor, and personality, Jack had difficulty identifying with the melting pot Houston of today and how closely it touched and forever changed what used to be a quieter place away from the big city. Though West Forge steadfastly held to its cowboy charm, Houston sprawled down all around and amongst it like an octopus.

But the octopus was slowly being poisoned. The whole bottom of the oil industry, the lifeblood of Houston and much of Texas itself, had fallen out from a series of international oil cartels, price fixing, gouging and bad luck. Discretionary oil monies that once bankrolled all kinds of capital projects and fattened countless wallets had dried up. The governor had called a special legislative session to battle the eminent budget crisis.

Banks failed every week; some of them were one-hundred-year-old institutions. But it was the subtle signs around Houston, as well as other Texas "oil cities," that spoke most of the financial tragedy. You could find a surplus of expensive homes on the auction block or for sale at extremely low prices. You could find any kind of exotic or foreign car sitting on the used car lots, or in the "For Sale" newspaper columns, all available at desperation must-sell prices right beside jewelry, guns, computers, golf clubs - deals, deals, deals. Heavy equipment was going for a fraction of its true value. "Oil wasn't worth spit," an executive said.

People who'd been related to someone in the oil industry in a million different ways suddenly weren't anymore. Unemployed, perhaps for the first time ever, were 10s of thousands, most were use to living at a certain stature with the jewelry and clothing, cars, furs and leathers, and golden bathroom fixtures that went with it.

The oil businesses vacating the county left and right only added to the glut of un-leased and empty new office space in the Houston area. Construction died as hundreds of companies each month filed for bankruptcy, leaving in their wake more unemployment. While Houston was one of the largest cities in the country, a diverse place of many different businesses and people, a goodly portion of it just wasn't paying bills or spending money like it had, and that hurt.

Jack was back at the station, pulling his Caddy onto the lot. After exchanging some brief words with a passing patrolman, he bounded up the stairs to the detective division carrying an arrest warrant for Trampus Wilson inside his notebook. He didn't need to ask who was there to see him. He spotted a sullen Diller Bailey sitting on a bench outside his office, studded earlobe and all. Jack stopped and stared at the man's anxious face, noticed a new cast on Diller's left hand. Kellog sighed, a sound often mistaken by many as a growl - sometimes it was - and he sauntered into his office. Diller hobbled in, and Jack shut the door.

"Never been in a police station before," Diller began, looking around.

"Cut the shit, Diller. You've been in one at least seven times as far as I know."

"Well, yeah," said Diller.

"Well, yeah," repeated Jack gruffly.

"They got me again," he said, painfully lifting his arm to show Jack.

"They did?" he returned sarcastically.

"At a phone booth. They must have follered me, Detective. They follered me, then they jumped on me. I stopped there just one minute to call my girl, man. They's on me."

Jack noticed Diller's eyes water as he re-lived a bad flashback.

"Two of 'em. One grabbed me from behind, the other, the other one slowly broke all of my fingers on my hand. Bent 'em back- back till they snapped."

"Diller, you must owe someone one helluva lot of money."

"I do. I do, man. I need me some help. These motherfuckers gonna kill me. They're not just gonna kill me, they're gonna torture my bald ass - my goddamn hand, man!" He started to choke up and cry. "They just snapped my fingers like pretzel sticks." He stared at Kellog and tears rolled down the cheek still fat with the gauze.

"Diller, I am not going to help you until I hear the whole story," Jack said, leaning back in his chair.

Diller's gaze dropped to the floor. He wiped his nose on the sleeve of his filthy thermal shirt and mumbled, "I've been working, selling drugs. All kinds of drugs - coke, PCP, heroin, grass, crystal meth -" his head jerked up. "Look, if this comes out of my mouth, man, I'm dead meat."

"Okay," said Jack, pitching forward to stand and leave.

"No. Shit. Wait, man," sobbed Diller. "I'll tell you. After those motherfuckers broke my fingers, man, I decided I was going to kill them, but I can't, so I came to you to hurt 'em. I want you to put Ray Pontecorvo and Baker Tanseed away. And the dudes that snapped my fingers. Them, too. All away."

With one arm folded across his chest, the other up where his hand covered his jaw, Jack stared at the dust strings hanging from the ceiling. Visions of Baker Tanseed danced in his head. Tanseed. He knew of Tanseed, owner of the big, new Western World, a store on Laredo Blvd. where a fellow could stroll in and buy any kind of western wear, horse tack, cattle trailers, shotguns, pistols, camping gear, everything from a gold and diamond hat pin, hundred dollar shirt to a snake bite kit. Hell, he could even ride out on a quarter horse or a thoroughbred they sold in the attached stable and show arena out back.

Tanseed had started in the quarter horse business years ago and almost finished in it, too. He found himself bridled to an over-extended ranch, deep in debt, artificially inseminating horses left and right without real buyers. Used to the high-dollar life, he had only foreclosure to look forward to. Then suddenly, a sign appeared on some prime real estate on Laredo, *Future home of Tanseed's Western World."*

A massive store was built and to its rear, a huge country mansion surrounded by the last undeveloped acreage of south West Forge. There were airstrips, showplace stables, a fleet of trucks - magic money. It was as suspicious as hell.

"Who is Pontecorvo?" Jack asked.

"New York City mob, a nephew from some mafia family up there." Diller squirmed with every word.

"Is he investing in the future of Texas?"

"Yeah, yeah. He's investin'. He started investin' in Baker Tanseed. Baker was donkey dick broke before they met. Broke. His old lady spent more in one afternoon what he was making in a month. I knew them then. Desperate for money, Baker took the Amtrak train to New York. He was gone three weeks. But, that motherfucker flew back first class. Pontecorvo came down the next week with some of his crew a week later. It's been first class ever since. Now,

Pontecorvo lives with Tanseed in that big house on the hill behind the store."

"What exactly do they do together?"

"They read the Wall Street Journal every goddamn day." Diller's tears were gone and the head started its Egyptian, bobbing motion. "Hey, this part of the country is a hot place for their kinda' business. They know oil's down, construction's down. It's a loan sharkin' paradise. Then they get their grip on all kinds of business - and people."

"Loan sharkin'," Kellog repeated.

"Portecorvo's people, about 20 of 'em, just read the papers, hang out in titty bars, go to parties and to businesses. Country clubs. They offer up easy money, man. As much as anybody wants er needs. They got it." Diller snapped the fingers on his good hand. "People who, you know, want to keep their house for their family, want to keep up an image with a new car, whatever. Ray's boys give it to 'em, whatever they want. Then comes the interest rates. You can't be late for their date. Broken bones," he raised his cast, "Finger-breakin. Fires. Even murder. Loan sharkin', Sgt. Kellog. That's what they do. Now theys training Tanseed's men in the business. Loan sharkin'. You see "The Godfather" movie? Yeah. But theys fer real godfathers. There's more."

"More?" repeated Kellog quietly.

"Yessir," Diller continued. "The dudes run a lot of dope. Regular. They grow grass on whole plantations in Louisiana and East Texas. They run dope through the Bahamas. Pontecorvo has even met fucking Castro once. They get cash from back East all the time. I used to drive a van every two weeks to Nashville and meet two Yankees from NYC. I would pick up cardboard boxes and boxes of hundred-dollar bills, man. They brew methamphetamine. They pimp. They even kill a little. Anything for a buck."

"Why you?"

"Baker Tanseed and I go way back. I met him when he was still in the quarter horse business, in a bar in Houston, a country dance hall. I used to deal some then, he liked to snort, to smoke. I'd set him up with some pussy. We was runnin' buddies. When he needed the money, I got him some dope to sell. I knew a pilot that flew some coke in and out of Florida. I had connections. I got this pilot together with Tanseed - next thing Tanseed takes the pilot's advice and off he goes to New York to meet people." Diller's head bobbed. "You might say I set Baker up to what he is today." He seemed strangely proud of that.

"Really." Jack watched as Diller lit a Camel cigarette with an inexpensive gold lighter.

"No smokin' in here, bubba."

"No smokin'? That shit's crazy." Diller put out the cigarette, but he still stuck it back in the corner of his dry mouth.

"Just last month I boogied up to New York State in a semi-trailer disguised as a ketchup truck. The fucker was full of guns. All bought on Western World's books. The boys up north needed 'em. Shit. You got 10 years, I'll tell you some shit, man." Diller's flag waved, but the wrong colors for Jack to salute.

"Did you steal some of this mob money?"

"No, no," Diller's head zipped back and forth. "Last month I drove a shipment of cocaine to Denver for Tanseed, some kind of deal I didn't know much about. This dude Johnny Handline - or Handell, Handlip, some kinda' last name like that, he was the mule on the trip. He rode shotgun with me. I was the driver. Well, it was a lot of coke, and we snorted just a little on the way. A pinch. So on the ride, I gets alone with the shit for a minute and, you know, I skims me some for me and my girl - just a little. I know this Johnny got him some too. Just didn't know how much. The deal went down in Denver and them Colorado boys called Tanseed and Pontecorvo complaining the shipment was off weight, big time off-weight. Now I know that fucker Johnny blamed me, said I took it all. I took the rap. Next thing I knows, him and this other dude, they're kickin' my teeth out and breakin' my fingers.

The other one, one of the New York City guys, he's telling me I owe them the coke or the money. Shit, I don't have it. That fuckin' Johnny Handline dude is who's really got it. I'm his fall guy. He fuckin' knows well I don't have it, and he'd love to beat my ass to death and let me die with his rap." Diller became physically pale. This time, his rendition came minus the theatrics, just a straight steady tale. "I know Johnny took a bunch of that coke before Denver. If I didn't take it, he did. And I didn't take it."

"How much, Diller?"

"Fifty grand."

"Fifty grand?"

"Yeah. A fucking fifty grand. Do you think I took 50 grand of coke? Me? Do you think I'd still be livin' in Pricksville, USA if I had 50 grand worth of blow? Do you think I can pay $50,000 back with interest?"

Jack took off his blazer and hung it on the rack. He sat back at his desk, opened a drawer, and threw some switches. His Radio Shack telephone tape recorder engaged.

"Diller, I want you to call Baker or Pontecorvo. Get them to talk about anything - the 50 grand, coke, guns, anything. Ask 'em, plead with them to quit beating you up."

Jack handed him the phone. "Say your name, the date, the time, say my number and the number you're calling at the beginning of my tape, then dial the number, and try to get whoever answers to identify themselves." He had to repeat the instructions twice.

"Is this legal?" Diller mumbled while dialing.

"Just get 'em talking."

"Western World," came a female voice.

"Is Baker Tanseed there?" asked Diller.

"Whom may I say is calling?"

"Diller Bailey."

Waylon Jennings music came on for several minutes.

"Bailey." barked a voice. "This is Ray. You got something for us?"

"Please, Ray, please," said Diller, his tough-guy, big-shot demeanor completely gone, "don't beat my ass anymore, please," he pleaded. "I'll...I'll pay up."

"What pay? What beatings?" asked Pontecorvo in a calm voice.

"The fifty thousand. They broke my fingers."

"Where are you?"

"At...at the mall."

"What's the number?"

Diller read off Jack's office number. Jack grimaced and shook his head "no."

"Ray. Ray?" He looked over at Jack.

"He hung up."

"Shit." Jack grabbed the receiver from Diller's hand and replaced it. "If they trace my..."

The phone rang, startling them both. Jack motioned for Diller to answer it.

"Hello?" said Diller.

"Diller, this is Tony Tetro. Listen ta me, weasel boy, I'm gonna say this once. Ya know what's on da line. Baker is not gonna help you." His New York accent sounded heavy; his threat undisguised. "Ya understand that lessons fa the future are made by the dispositions of circumstances like yours. Ya take care of ya business, Diller, or be remembered as a lesson."

Dial tone again. White-faced, Diller sat frozen, his good hand clenched around the phone.

"Tony Tetro, he's the other dude. The one with With

Johnny, both times, when they beat me up, Sergeant," he finally whispered. "Tetro's a New York City cop."

"He's a...cop?"

"He was, I mean. He's an ex-cop. He's like, I don't know, like a mafia specialist, a pro. He grabbed me so fast, and calm, man, like he was thinkin' 'Oh, here we go again, just the old finger-breakin' hold again, you know?" Diller inhaled deeply on his extinguished Camel cigarette.

Jack rewound the tape. Tetro's little speech convinced him that at least part of Diller's story was true. He punched play and listened to the tape again.

"Fuck." Diller lit up the cigarette.

Jack let him this time.

"A lesson," Diller muttered. He looked over at Jack. "What the fuck am I supposed to do?"

Jack rewound the tape. "You're damned if you do and damned if you don't, Diller. On the street, here, anywhere... you're a dead man."

Diller swallowed, went from pale white to ash grey. "This Johnny' Handline's got you one way. Baker and Pontecorvo the other. With us, you got a chance."

"Us?" asked Diller.

"Us. Me. I'm gonna call my captain right now, then the chief. We can protect you - if and only if you tell us... everything, Diller."

"Snitch city." Diller whispered to himself and pulled the cigarette out of his mouth. "Shit."

"Everything, Diller, you got that?"

"Yeah." The man closed his eyes. "I think I'm gonna be sick."

He wasn't kidding. Diller's grimaced and his gray face faded to another level of off-white. His upper body visibly shook.

Jack dialed the division captain's home phone, then leaned back in his chair and considered this slumping, broken-down, husk of a man in front of him while the phone rang. Perhaps, he thought, perhaps Diller Bailey could teach a few lessons of his own.

CHAPTER THREE:
SHIT FIRE, YANK!

"Yeee-who. Ye who, West Forge 101," called a sweet, overly feminine voice from a parked van.

Jack had just finished his chicken fried steak dinner at the Crossroads Truck Stop and was on his way to his car, toothpick clinched between his teeth. He turned and smiled.

"Hello, Clara," he said and walked toward the woman waving at him from the van window.

"Hi, Sugar 101. How are you?"

"Hi yourself, Honey Pot," he replied, glancing down at the CB radio and police scanner on her dash. They both had radio names. She knew his from her scanner. He knew hers because she was a traveling prostitute, beckoning truckers off the Interstate via CB radio, to make her van payment and whatever else she owed.

"You back in town?" he asked.

"For a little while, till ya'll run me off again." She laughed. Clara Netler was 47 years old, possibly attractive depending on the lighting. She was undeniably well built and did a fairly successful business broadcasting free commercials on the CB airwaves for relatively inexpensive rates. Jack ran a CB radio in his Caddy and knew the advertising usually went something like this:

"Hey, ya'll, this is Honey Pot, just melting down and smelling sweet for you at the Crossroads Truck Stop. Forty dollars for a lay, 15 dollars for a blow job. Will do custom work for custom prices," was the usual traffic, seducing folks off the road to various Harris County truck stops.

They talked and laughed briefly, and she offered Jack some free public relations, but the lighting just wasn't right, and Jack declined.

"Remember, Clara," Jack said as he walked away, "a watched pot,"

"Never boils, darlin'. Don'cha be watchin' me now. Boiling over is my main business."

Jack shook his head and crossed toward his car.

"Jack." A man's voice shouted from the parking lot.

Jack turned again to see a large, curly brown-haired man leaning on a new bronze colored, *Good Times* van. The man's baby face seemed familiar, but the hard-eyed features of the bearded man inside the van's window watching him didn't.

"Jumpin' Jack, do you remember me?" asked the man who hailed him. He walked toward Jack with a cocky strut. "I beat the holy hell outta you, in 1965. Palawa Sportatorium."

The man's face, younger, much younger, came back to Jack in a disturbing vision, bouncing around him in a smoky black and white atmosphere. He recalled the face above two arms pelting him and pelting him some more. The memory clicked into full color. It was Jack's fifth, no sixth boxing match. Johnny Handell. Was this Diller's Johnny Handline? John the Killer Handell, former Marine turned boxer?

"Long time, Jumpin' Jack-off," Handell declared with a sinister grin. He and Handell had met only during promos and their one fight. That was it. 1965.

In 1965, Handell was on his way to minor league, boxing stardom with Jack serving only as a bloody stepping-stone along the way. Jack didn't last four rounds. At the time, Jack had made the career mistake of quitting his patrolman's job with the Houston PD to fulfill his lifelong dream of being a professional boxer. After 11 fights, no victories, he returned to policing but at West Forge, having been turned down for rehiring in Houston because the recruiting officer decreed Jack had quit Houston under the "frivolous circumstances" of becoming a boxer. He'd left the ring and returned to police work but had inadvertently carried the "Jumpin' Jack" boxing moniker ever since. Jack stared a moment longer at Handell, then turned back for his Caddy.

"Hey. Jack-off." Handell used his long reach that Jack couldn't outbox two decades ago to hook Jack's bicep and twist him around.

Jack sighed/growled, "What do you want?"

"You wanna go at it? I'm ready." Handell looked more than ready. He appeared raring to go. "We can go somewhere, or we can have us a re-match right here."

Jack sighed again, stood with his thumbs in the pockets of his jeans and one hip thrown out. He stared at the gravel below, then raised his head and met Handell's belligerent glare.

"The Marquee of Queensberry rules knows no home here on this parking lot," Jack said.

Handell only grinned. "We're gonna take yer' ass somewhere," he whispered.

Both men turned to see a bearded man approaching, his look as cool as his partner's was hot. Jack frowned. Handell. A bronze van. These were the men Diller told him about.

"Like to talk wid ya," the bearded man said as he stopped in front of Jack. "Like to introduce ya to our friend, a Mr. Raymond Pontecorvo, tawk some business wit ya. He'd like a word wit ya, dat's all." The man spoke calmly, all in a heavy New York City accent. Thick. He offered his hand. "I'm Tony. Tony Tetro."

Jack ignored the man's hand. Not so much to be unsociable, but rather to avoid being grabbed and sucker punched.

"Talk about what?" asked Jack, now fully aware of whom he was dealing with.

"Business, ya know," he shrugged his shoulders. "Police business. Life business." Tetro smiled, but there was menace in it. "Diller Bailey kinda business. Something funny happened da other day. Diller called me. Diller said he was at da mall. He gave me his phone numba, see. But when I call it back? I get da police department. I get…your phone…funny. Funny, huh?"

Clara's van pulled up beside them, spitting gravel with her hard stop.

"You all right, Jack?" she asked, staring at Handell and Tetro.

Handell moved toward the prostitute's van door. Clara yanked the mike up from her CB. "I'll have 20 truckers here in 10 seconds, Jerk."

"Then, you gotta live through the next 10 seconds."

"No, you gotta, fuck your nuts." She pulled up a big silver revolver in her other hand and pointed it at Handell's balls.

Handell made a move for his waistline.

Jack made a move for his .45 on his belt.

"HOOOOO." Tetro interrupted with both of his hands up. "Hoooo. Everybody relax. Okay?"

"I'm fine, Clara," Jack cut in. Handell stepped back from her van. "Just go on. I'm fine here." He winked at her, hoped he looked unconcerned. She nodded, then slowly drove off while watching the trio in her rear-view mirror.

"I'll go see your man," Jack said to Tetro while the New Yorker continued to stare at Clara's van.

"Good," he grunted.

"You're coming with us, Jack-off," ordered Handell. He looked at Jack's hip. "The gun." He held out his hand, palm up.

Jack let out a short laugh. "I'm not going anywhere in your van," his voice and face cooled down to look of death, "and I'm not giving you - or anybody else - my gun."

Handell curled his lip, but Tetro tapped the ex-prize fighter's arm, and they both turned toward their van.

Tetro adjusted his coat and shoulders as they walked to their bronze van. "Just follow us," Tetro said over his shoulder. He spoke easily, like they were buddies and all they were doing was going for a beer.

Tetro was by far the more dangerous of the two, Jack decided as he climbed into his Caddy and turned the key in the ignition. He alerted the dispatcher of his situation that he was off to a meet some suspects for "questioning," and he requested a "28" on the van plate. It came back to a leasing company in Corpus Christi. The Good Times van turned out of the parking lot onto to the access road picking up speed. Jack drove by Clara and waved. He followed the van, his mind tripping back to the Palawa decades ago, to the bloody beating he'd received from the big fists of "The Crucible." He made a note to study Handell's career during and especially after boxing, but his notes turned to scribbles as he relived that bout, recalled his powerless legs in the third round. He couldn't even remember the fourth.

******

Headfirst, the pit bulls bashed into each other, snarling savagely while their teeth snapped at each other's muscular necks and chests. With this fresh attack the small, fashionable crowd circling the dogfight roared in excitement.

Jack, walking directly behind Handell and Tetro, glanced through the howling crowd of men and women. He caught glimpses of the two battling pit bulls in the arena. A tall, shapely blonde eyed Handell as she reached for a Coors from one of the six strategically placed iced-down barrels. The place looked like a set for a nightmare on Twilight Zone. It was dark and smoky and loud, and everyone was enjoying themselves drunkenly in a place built for dizzy good times. A dogfight in full swing unfolded before him in this closed roller-skating arena.

Overhead in a long balcony, Jack could see a series of windows without glass and seated figures watching from rooms that had once housed a DJ spinning rock records, maybe, or a manager's offices. The three men filed through the edge of the raucous crowd and up a narrow wooden stairway to these suspended rooms.

At the top of the stairs, Handell stopped, turned and said, "the gun," his hand palm up, his fingers waved inward.

"Fuck off." Kellog walked past him.

"Mr. Kellog," said a tall, middle-aged man with an unusually protruding belly that hung over an expensive belt. Gold seemed to hang everywhere possible from him: cufflinks, buckle, multiple rings, thick neck chain, lapel pin. His features were distinctly European. His clothing looked distinctly western, a walking contradiction, like a bad actor dressing up to play a rich cowboy. The wrong actor. Bad part.

The noise crescendo behind him caused him to turn and glimpse the fight below. Jack took in the room. It appeared huge with plush chairs and a portable bar complete with a blonde bartender, 6'2"- eyes of blue, in a flaunting, body-yielding gown. These were the only additions to the otherwise dingy rink surroundings. The elite, about 12 people, watched from up here where gambling monies rested in piles on the counter tops of the long balcony.

At the far end of the counter sat a couple. The man, wearing an expensive dark hat, casually glanced at Jack, then looked back at the fight below. His female companion, overdone in thick makeup, swayed drunkenly on her stool. Her head tottered, sweeping off to a shoulder, nodding down to her nape. Startled awake, she jerked upright and sipped her cocktail. They were Mr. and Mrs. Baker Tanseed. Jack hadn't realized until yesterday when he studied Tanseed's arrest records that he had arrested Baker for DWI way back in 1964. Twenty plus years had changed him a bit - he'd lost weight, groomed up, shaved off a beard, but the quality of his shirt and hat couldn't hide what he was - a shallow, selfish redneck jerk who wouldn't think twice about peeing off of his front porch even if he lived in a high rise in downtown Houston. He apparently didn't recognize Jack.

A big expressionless Indian, American style, with harsh, almost demonic features stood solemnly by the bar dressed in a black suit, his hands huge slabs at the ends of his jacket sleeves. Looked like an explosion waiting for the right place to happen.

"Like a boot at Texas Stadium, hey Mr. Kellog?"

"You mean a booth," Jack said, eyeing up the man of gold.

"We put a couple fights together like dis' about one a week. Main events now." He motioned for Jack to follow him as he walked toward an office door. "I'm Raymond Pontecorvo. Let's tawk just a little business. Ira."

Ira the Indian followed them, shutting the door once all three men were inside the office. This smaller room also had a view overlooking the rink, but this room had a glass wall, baffling the sounds and smoke below. Jack leaned against this window and crossed his arms, his elbow inadvertently rubbed the butt of the .45 under his blazer, giving him a passing reassurance. The Indian glared at him, probably reassured by his own means. Means unknown to Jack, but he could guess.

"Sgt. Kellog," Pontecorvo began, "we have come to discover that an ex-associate of my partner, Baker Tanseed, one Diller Bailey called for me, to tawk to me," he paused, "right from your office phone." He stared at Jack. "He gave us your numba to call him back." He walked around the desk. "This makes us wonder if maybe our conversation... well, ya know," he met Jack's impassive gaze, "were ever recorded and like dat?"

Jack refused to show any reaction.

"Now, Mr. Diller has disappeared. We can only guess that you got him somewhere. I thought that...I don't know why...I should explain a few things about Diller, about what's going on around here. Now I am da new business manager of Mr. Baker Tanseed. Comptroller. Money comptroller. Baker here is a local boy. Hometown boy. You know him. I handle many things for him."

Kellog remined silent.

"My corporation plans to set up a nationwide chain of Western World stores. Now, Mr. Tanseed...he's had some poor business associates in the past, very poor. Dis Diller Bailey for one. I don't know how much you know about dis' Bailey, but he is just a little hick scumbag. We have broken off associations like dis and business like dis. No more. No more. That is all in the past." He smiled. "Part of my job here is to clean up Mr. Tanseed's past."

"Next thing to clean up is dog fighting. It's illegal in Texas," Jack said, engrossed at the man's pockmarked face. He thought of Diller. In a pinch they rattled off his desk phone number to this man one day ago. Of course they checked the number, but how? Did they call again later, and a secretary gave Jack's name and position? Did they have a contact at the phone company? Did they only think calls were routinely taped or did they know? It had really been such a legally harmless and ambiguous conversation. Perhaps Tetro forgot exactly what he said on the phone and thought it worse?

"Ahhhh, dawgs. Dawg fighting is a sport. Nobody gets hurt. Except maybe, you know, da dawgs. But, Diller deserves anything he gets. Police officers don't care about people like him. He is hardly worth a police investigation," Pontecorvo concluded with a half-smile.

Jack remained expressionless.

"Sgt. Kellog, we would like for you to lose Diller and his paperwork. Let him deal with his own problems. They're his, not yours. If you have him somewhere," Pontecorvo raised his shoulders, "lose him. You know, West Forge is going to be the national headquarters of our chain. We will need all kinds of help and all kinds of dings like...security. Whatever. We would like to work with you. This could mark our first association, our commitment to da world peace, you know what I mean?" He stopped, waited. Jack remained silent.

"A national headquarters here means big warehouses, lots of jobs, lots of local business, lots of taxes for your city here. We need plenty of help. Very well-paid security managers and like dat. We don't want to handle any bad publicity like Diller Bailey and all the vicious lies from da past I am sure he's telling you about Mr. Tansee. Or myself even."

The dogs below thundered against the partitions in a ferocious brawl below.

The three men turned as the door opened.

"Tony Tetro." Pontecorvo barked as Tony walked in. The older man gestured to Tetro and smiled back at Jack. "Look at my friend, Sergeant. Tony Tetro here? Twenty-seven years with the NYPD. You know what he had to do for most of them years? He was a steel worker on weekends, a construction worker part time - just to make ends meet, to send his kids to school for Chrissake. Sgt. Kellog, in one year with me - one year." ...he held up his index finger, rings flashing from the lights... "I swear to God he makes more money than he did in 27 years police working and steel working. Put together."

Jack's silence appeared to either be getting to Pontecorvo or making him mad, maybe both. He leaned forward suddenly on the desk, his weight on his hands. "Tony did the smart thing. You do the smart thing, Sergeant. This unfortunate business really could turn out to be your lucky break, you know? Our introduction. This could be the beginning of something big for you - for us. Think. Think about a price that would make you busy on all your other cases and not Diller Bailey's case. We will eventually take care of Diller Bailey, anyway." He straightened, waved his hand. "Ah. This is all a lot at one time, I know. Get a message back to me, think things over. No answer now."

The two men stared at each other. Pontecorvo took a deep breath.

"Tony." Tetro straightened from where he'd been leaning on the wall beside the door.

"Pat him down," Pontecorvo ordered.

Tetro smiled at Jack as he approached him.

"Business, Jack" he said, and his veteran police hands began a professional pat down, obviously aware of the gun, but searching for a recorder or body mike of any kind.

"I am the one that checked your phone number yesterday, Jack," Tetro said to him. "Seemed fishy to me Diller would call like that. I mean we would never make such a call when I was in Organized Crime."

Jack looked away to the crowd below. The pit bulls sprawled in a pitiful pile, barely able to move yet still tearing, growling. Tetro stepped back. Tetro's message was clear. Using Jack's office phone was a dumb strategy in a war against organized crime. Especially when the criminals were staffed by ex-OC cops.

"He's clean. I mean, ya know he's got a fuckin' gun. Dats all."

"Let me tell you a story, Sergeant," Pontecorvo said, "about the dying hick cowboy of the '80s. It took years for organized crime of any kind to get settled into other states like Texas. Our people from the east came down here in the '50s and '60s and we got run off. Run outta here. Know why? People down here just wouldn't lie down. They fought us, beat us, hell even shot us.

In the '50s we had a button man - muscle - a soldier walk into a Houston pawnshop to set up a protection racket. He walks in, looks around, sez to Billy Bob Hick, the owner, he sez, 'Hey, I like dis place. I'll like owning dis place.' Ol' Billy Bob Hick, he sez, 'Golly, Mister, what?' The button man sez, 'I'm your new partner.' Hick sez, 'Golly, don't need a partner.' Button man sez, 'Yes, you do. Either that or I'll burn up your store and your home with your wife and kids in it.' The hick...he's fucking bewildered, right? Hick sezs, 'Shit fire, Yank. You'd do this to me?' With that, he pulls up a fucking shotgun by the cash register and - BAM. - the button man dies right there. The fucking button is like, is like, exploded all over the fucking place. Shoulder here. Brains there. Holy shit, right?

Houston PD shows up, runs a check on the button man, the guy's got racketeering criminal history. From New Yawk, no less. They listen to the Hick's story. Da' Hick's a fucking hero. It's in all the papers. Hometown boy kills Yankee mobster. Yeah, true story. Cross my heart."

Tony Tetro chuckled. The Indian didn't. Pontecorvo came around the desk and got in Jack's face. His breath stank. "That was 19 and fucking 54, Marshal Dillon. Things are different now. The laws are different. The laws are pussy laws now. We are in and we are here, baby. We are now."

His index finger shot up close to Jack's nose. Jack didn't flinch. Pontecorvo growled, "You listen to me. Don't you tape my calls, baby. Don't you come after me or my friends." His voice dropped low. "You might find out that you are da very last hick in the OK Corral."

He straightened and stalked away, throwing his shoulder forward like it was out of socket and needed an adjustment.

"You don't have much choice, Sgt. Kellog," Pontecorvo said calmly, all Mr. Businessman again. "So tink about all this. Get a message to me, here, Friday." He glared across the desk at Jack, apparently finished.

Jack looked over at Tetro who smiled at him. Ira, the Indian with gorilla hands, stared blankly into space. There wasn't much else to do but leave. Ira opened the door, and Jack left the office, walked through the outer room past the Tanseeds, Handell and the statuesque bar maid, and the other "sports" fans. He walked down the narrow staircase and onto the rink floor.

Above him Ira, Tetro, and Pontecorvo watched as Kellog made his way across the floor below.

"I thought this rink scene, all this, would impress him. Do you think he was impressed?" Pontecorvo asked.

"Nope," said Tetro.

They continued to watch Kellog below as he snatched up a Coors from one of the barrels. He slung ice off the top, stalked past the dogs lined up against the wall in cages. They lunged at him and snarled at his passing.

"You went at him in at least three different ways, boss" Tetro commented. "He didn't hit the ball back once. Not a lie. Not a stall. Not a scam."

"Did he even say a fuckin' word?" Pontecorvo said,

half-asking, half perplexed.

"PPPPHHHTT. Not that I hurd," Tetro shrugged.

"He said dog fighting is illegal in Texas," Ira the Indian said.

"Yeah, well. I tried. I mean, if he's talked with that fucker Diller at all, he knows the score. We ain't hiding anything from him." Pontecorvo scowled. "That fucking little hick scumbag."

Jack disappeared out the front doors.

"And dis guy. A fucking Matt Dillon or what?" Pontecorvo looked over at Tetro and asked, "Any kids? Wife? Ex? Family? Grandkids?"

"Nope," said Tetro.

"None?" Pontecorvo looked surprised. "Nobody to with with?"

"None. Unmarried, never married, parents dead, no ladies."

"Men friends?"

"He's not a queer. A female hooker almost shot us tonight to save him. He's got a married brother in Los Angeles. That's it." Tetro answered.

"What the fuck does this guy do with himself." Pontecorvo shouted.

"He...detects." Tetro shrugged. "He's a detective. As our man in the station puts it, boss, Jack Kellog...'fights crime.' Dats all he does...fight crime."

"Shit." Pontecorvo shook his head. "A fucking Matt Dillon." He turned, leaned against the glass. "Well, he is a big fucking wart on my ass as of today."

******

The next morning at the PD, Jack reached for his desk phone and placed a call to the patrol squad room.

"Officer Timmes," said Jack, "This is Jack Kellog."

"Yeah, Jack, how are ya?" Timmes strained to hear over the clamor of the patrol room shift change. "What d'ya need?"

"Do you remember that report you took about two weekends ago, a Mrs. Fredericks? Mugged on the street, an older gal, had her purse and a plant taken from her? She broke her hip when she fell."

"Yeah, sure do."

"Could you look into that for me when you get a free minute? Try to turn something up on it. Her grandson is driving me crazy, and I just can't get to it now. Things are - well, you know what I'm doing. I saw your name on the Diller's bodyguard detail for a few nights this week."

Timmes and a rotating protection team of officers were watching Diller in an apartment in West Forge until the Feds had enough evidence to take him over. The overtime costs were driving Captain Melton crazy.

"Yeah, I'm watching your boy, but I'll see what I can do," said Timmes.

"Thanks. Make a point to let the son know we're working on it, okay?" Jack hung up.

******

Sunday afternoon. Barefoot and clad in baggy old Levis and a huge robe, Jack stepped out of his front door during the Oiler football game halftime. Having missed Saturday, he checked the mailbox, then bounded down the porch steps and brick walkway to retrieve another poorly thrown Chronicle. As he approached the Sunday Edition way down by the curb, he heard an ignition roar and, while bending down, turned toward the sound.

A dark blue Lincoln Continental with four male figures inside, two wearing cowboy hats, slowly pulled from its parking place two houses down and across the street from Jack. It was not a familiar car.

Suddenly, it bolted forward, barreling down the street on Jack as though it meant to jump the curb after him. Jack turned so fast parts of the newspaper flew from his hand. With his robe flapping, bare feet slapping bricks, he raced for the house. The car approached Jack's curb, cut back to the street, tires screeching. Jack lunged for his door and heard hearty male laughter as the Lincoln straightened and then slowly continued on down the street. Jack rushed inside, closed the door and leaned against it, adrenaline shooting through him.

From the surprise and his mad dash he was way out of breath, already, quickly perspiring. He had let his guard down so low he didn't have any. He slammed his fist against the door behind him. He could have been maimed or killed, just walking outside.

He'd had meetings with Diller Bailey for several hours, collected great amounts of criminal information. The mobsters now knew that Diller Bailey was cooperating with the police and Jack might or might not cooperate with this bastard child - this new crime confederation of New York mobsters and Texas outlaw cowboys. Jack straightened, looked carefully out his window. At least now his house and garage were wired against intrusion. But what of car bombs, what of ambush? Their terror tactics were only just beginning.

After the game, Jack stared at his naked body in the bathroom mirror. It was white and almost flabby, could very easily get real flabby. His once big, boxer's arms had lost their definition, those sinews were gone from his chest, and his once ripped stomach had given way to a soft bulge. There would now be a network of men following him, after him, men trained in terror, in pain. Strong men. Fast men. He decided he needed to get back in shape. Get mean. Recover some kind of edge. Or, was it too late?

CHAPTER FOUR:
RANGER WEAVER WISDOM

"Looky here, I've worked with Jack Kellog hundreds of times through the years in some of the biggest manhunts and investigations I've been involved with. If my family was ever in danger? The first man I would call is Jack Kellog to protect them. I know he'd give his life for them, and me."- Texas Ranger Weaver Wisdom, Ret. Round Rock, Texas, 2003

Archie Lennox interview tape 16

Weaver Wisdom swung his large feet off the bed to the wooden floor, his huge black body startled awake by his children and their game of backyard chase past his window. He rubbed his sleepy eyes and scratched his short Afro and listened to the high-pitched laughter. Weaver had four children from Luella - his one and only wife of 23 years - and two children from an "armed robbery." That was an unexpected "birthing" that had occurred seven years earlier, well before his promotion into the elite state police group, the Texas Rangers, back when he was still a Department of Public Safety uniformed highway patrolman stationed in Lubbock. On duty one Sunday afternoon, he responded to a Lubbock PD dispatch of a "Signal 36," an armed robbery at a 7-11 convenience store. Weaver arrived at the store beside a City of Lubbock unit and an ambulance.

The clerk lay dead, draped over the counter from multiple gunshot wounds. Outside in the parking lot, two customers quivered near death in the bullet-ridden front seat of their 1974 Pontiac. They had the misfortune of pulling up just as the crazed robber fled the store, and the killer opened up on their car. Miraculously, two toddlers huddled unhurt in the back seat.

As the E.M.T. crew fought back the couple's imminent death in a fury of hoses, tubes, equipment, and care, Weaver reached into the back seat and pulled the traumatized three-year-old boy and two-year-old girl into his big arms. Both became orphans in the following moments. Weaver put them in his squad car and took them home to Luella. He called in and got temporary approval from a child welfare worker he knew.

The children stayed with Weaver and Luella during the search for their relatives. Through collected identification from San Antonio police and child welfare workers, Weaver traced the children's family back to Bexar County. But, a few weeks after the robbery, having discovered uncaring uncles and apathetic aunts, the children remained virtually unclaimed. No one would even make the drive to Houston to see the kids, lest of all take them to raise. Soon they stopped answering their phones.

Weaver sat in his cluttered kitchen and stared at these two scared, lost kids in borrowed clothing while they nibbled on a lunch of soup and sandwiches right beside his own four.

Weaver buried his head in his hands and began to cry. The children, all six of them, froze, wide-eyed. Weaver raised his head and met Luella's gaze across the table. They'd begun the adoption proceedings the next morning.

They all remained as a family tightly together through Weaver's different duty stations - trooper in Odessa; Narcotics in Houston, Brownsville, and Dallas; Auto Theft in Tyler; then finally back to Houston as a Texas Ranger - the first black Ranger ever appointed.

Weaver sat on the bed and watched the two kids "born to him by armed robbery," Bobby and Della, dash past his window.

"Weaver." shouted Luella down the hall. Weaver stood and walked into the kitchen and looked at the clock. It was late afternoon. He'd been up all night on a case and slept in. The kids must have just gotten home from school.

"Jack called," she said, "around one, but he didn't want to wake you."

"Thanks." Weaver reached for his notebook on the counter and punched a number on the phone. He carried the receiver with its extra-long cord back to the bed.

"Jack Kellog, please. This is Wisdom." A moment passed.

"Wea-vah," Jack drawled as he came on the line. "Whatcha know?"

"I'm sleepy." He flipped his notebook to a different page and scowled at the notes. "Jack, Jack, Jack, Jack, Jack, who are you running with? Some bad folks?"

"Running after, not with. Did you get anything back for me?" Jack asked.

"Hell, yeah. These people," he took the mug of coffee Luella offered him, "they don't have simple records - they've got libraries."

"Thought so."

"Their records have records. On this Raymond 'Ponty'

Pontecorvo. I got ahold of the NYPD Organized Crime Task Force. He's a native New Yorker, born in the Bronx, an important nephew in the Ervine Gallanti family. They call him a lieutenant. No formal criminal history, only some tax evasion problems. They say he's into anything and everything: gambling, small - and big-time heists - and listen to this. A Lt. Rozonko said that the closest they came to making a case on him was in 1978. A local New York Laborer's International Union president brought 'Ponty' in to establish a dental plan for about 20,000 members. Your man Ponty hired one dentist in a single office and siphoned off 68 cents from every dollar of the $5.1 Mil deducted from workers' checks. Almost all of that nest egg went back into the Gallanti network, labeled as 'legitimate' business investments. Then they say Ponty's been behind some hits - some labor related, some of it drugs. But Rozonko says in the last few years Ponty has fallen from grace."

"He has? How?"

"The Gallanti family, old man Ervine in particular who's 86 years old now, doesn't like dealing with Hispanics and Mexicans, a racial thing. They bought their drugs in Asia, shipped in from France, never dealt with South Americans. Ponty thought this was an expensive mistake. He eased on down to Columbia and set some deals. Rozonko even heard Ponty met with Fidel Castro."

"Yeah. I heard that from my end too."

"When old man Ervine finally caught up with him and what he was up to, Ponty lost some of his face - you know, power. Ervine banished Pontecorvo out of the immediate family, exiled him to Texas looks like to me."

"Lucky us," mumbled Jack. Weaver could hear him scribbling notes through the receiver.

Weaver took a sip from his coffee mug. "Leaving New York for Texas. Some exile."

"Is he on his own down here then?" Jack asked.

"No way. Family is family." Two of Weaver's six crashed into the kitchen in an uproar about something outside. This was Luella's beat to handle.

"Hold on Jack..." Weaver waited until she'd shooed them both back outdoors. "Pontecorvo will forever have their support, and they still are heavily involved in this Texas connection as a matter of family and business. Rozonko was glad to hear from us. They did't have much on this satellite project down here."

"What did you find out on Wishing Well Industries, the company that bought the property off of Loop 9 for Western World and the mansion behind it?"

"Wishing Well is owned by Brigade Growth which is a holding company for..." Weaver flipped through his notes, "well, when you knock all the cards down, it comes back to the Gallanti group. NYPD has a chart on all this corporate structure shit, and about halfway down I met Rozonko halfway up with company names down here."

"We need to see what Wishing Well buys up around here, don't we," said Jack.

"You bet."

"And Mr. Tetro?" Jack asked.

"Anthony A. Tetro." Weaver rubbed the bridge of his nose. "Lt. Rozonko knows him personally. Both of 'em worked together on the Crime Task Force six years ago. Rozonko said Tetro was one of the most talented cops New York has ever had. Highly decorated. Service in Harlem, Manhattan, the Bronx, a half-dozen task forces. Rozonko said Tetro was, and I quote, 'allergic to desks.' He was a street cop's cop."

"There was trouble on their OC task force in '82, and "T", as they called Tetro, resigned and retired after 27 years on the force. Turned rich overnight. They later discovered some of

Tetro's informant connections had recruited "T" into the mob. They say Tetro's behind some big heists, is a consultant to the mob on police procedures and security. And it gets worse." Lou refilled Weaver's mug. He took a deep drink.

"In 1983, a non-criminal, corruption-fighting candidate announced a run on the presidency of Local 332 of the LIU in Philadelphia. Five armed men in Halloween masks broke into the candidate's home, bound and gagged the wife, and beat the guy to death while she watched. The same thing happened in Baltimore to someone else two days later. Rozonko is pretty sure that Tetro was one of the five killers. Just informant talk. No arrests in either case. He said Tetro is now a family troubleshooter. He can smell a wiretap and an undercover cop in a heartbeat. Watch out for him first, Jack, and don't forget about him...ever."

In his West Forge office, Jack had given up on taking notes and was kicked back, glued to the phone, memorizing each of Wisdom's words.

"Rozonko wants in on anything we do," Weaver continued.

"Yeah," Jack said, deep in thought.

"Next is John David Handell, carries the nickname Killer."

"From his boxing days," Jack said.

"He's strictly a Texas boy, born in Ellis. Has quite a misdemeanor record for disorderly, did a short stint in 1981 for involuntary manslaughter in Greenville. I called the Ranger up there and he took a look at Killer's records. Handell had a traffic problem with a 55-year-old corporate type. They both pulled over, got out of their trucks, and Handell wound up beating the man to death and got 10 years' probation - which he promptly violated in Marshall, Texas where he went berserk at a Sonic Drive-In. Took six cops to arrest him. Must have been fired up on drugs because, says here, they hit him with flashlights and nightsticks and nothing stopped him. His parole was revoked and he did three years. Our State

Intelligence Unit said Handell is a suspect in the murder of a Colorado businessman in 1986. He was questioned, but no charges were ever filed."

"Organized crime deal?"

"Yeah," sighed Wisdom. "And then we have this Ira Tenpenny. Where did you meet these dudes, anyway?"

"Over a Coors at a dog fight," Jack laughed.

"Remember A.I.M? The American Indian Movement?"

"From back in the '70s."

"Yeah. Some FBI agents got shot up tangling with them. Color your Mr. Tenpenny - A.I.M. Very militant, very radical. This guy's got a black belt in several forms of karate and chop-suey. Been arrested twice in Wyoming for assault on a police officer. Did his time, finished parole. His current whereabouts were unknown by the Feds until now."

"Trust me. He looks as bad as he sounds."

"You've seen this soma bitch?"

"Eyebrow to eyebrow."

"What's up, Jack?"

There was a long pause on the other end of the line.

"How would you like to bust 'em all?" asked Jack in his offbeat, methodical way.

"Say what now?"

"I've got someone who can take them all down. At seven tonight I've got a meeting set up with the Assistant U.S. Attorney Bob Pellen, Rye Edleson from our DA's office, my mystery guest - and you. Can you bring all those files?"

"The boys in New York begged me to let them know if we were gonna make a move on any these people. Said they'd fly a team down in a New York minute."

"No," Jack said quickly. "No. We don't want any of those people in on this. Maybe at the end. No can do, no can trust.

You know I never liked any chili sauce from New York City. Okay. I'll be there, seven sharp."

"Government building. And afterward, we need to arrest a rapist, the Steak Knife guy."

"Ohhhh, no shit?" Weaver was delighted. "Sounds like a good night."

The two friends hung up. Weaver and Jack worked together many times before. They completely trusted each other. Weaver Wisdom thought Jack was a relentless, talented cop with bottomless grit. Jack Kellog thought Weaver was the smartest, meanest, most impressive Texas Ranger to ever pin on a badge. When push turned into shove, Jack was push and Weaver was shove. Or, was it the other way around?

Jack often told the story about the night he and Weaver were part of a manhunt for a murderer and the county dispatcher said over the radio,

"Ranger 210, be aware, the suspect is armed and dangerous."

Weaver's gravel voice returned over the county airwaves,

"Be aware, dispatcher, so am I." So he was.

When Weaver Wisdom, all 6'5", 250 pounds, strapped on his tooled leather western belt carrying two engraved pistols and tapped on his white Stetson, he brought a whole new definition to the term "lawman." In short, he was a criminal's worst nightmare come true.

Jack also liked calling on Weaver because Weaver had all kinds of power and statewide jurisdiction. Red tape disappeared before the Texas Rangers. They could usually cut through it like a hot Bowie through butter. The governor's office stood right behind the Rangers. Weaver had a handle on all kinds of information, bank records, work records, snitch money, photos, evidence processing, helicopters, planes, and high-tech surveillance, and could get it all in one-tenth the time it took Jack. Anytime Jack came upon something larger than his department could handle or a significantly dangerous situation, he called on Weaver Wisdom.

CHAPTER FIVE:
ATTITUDE ADJUSTMENTS

Jack and Weaver both thought a few six packs of Coors might loosen up the intensity of the federal crowd and certainly that of the tongue of their honored guest, Diller Bailey. Jack left the Coors and cooler in his trunk to check out the Holy Roller level of the questioners. It was always a good idea to get informants a little drunk. Jack and Weaver would often sign out prisoners from the jail, drive them around Harris County and give them a bottle of booze or beer. Soon, loose lips would sink ships. Then, a variety of the pure, high and mighty, even teetotalers came into administrative power and the once successful practice came to an abrupt end.

Once inside the front door of the county building several well-known, soul-saving Baptist prosecutors greeted them and the six-packs never left the cooler in the trunk. Instead, the State Attorney General's conference room offered only coffee and a tangy twist of limelight for Diller. The meeting began and the limelight alone was proving to have its own considerable loosening effects on Diller. Jack sat back and watched Diller's mini-mental wheels whiz under questioning through the tale of Baker Tanseed's horse business, drug deals, his near bankruptcy, then his trip to New York, and his eventual love/hate affiliation with Pontecorvo family and all that was Western World.

"Money controller, well, comptroller or controller is what they call Pontecorvo. He holds the purse strings of the whole sordid bidness," Diller reported.

Rye Edleson, there to represent the county DA, leaned on the conference table and studied Diller over his bifocals. His eyes darted about like a spectator at a tennis match to keep up with the bobs and weaves of Diller's quixotic head movements.

A clean-cut, shorthaired supervisor from the FBI named Merryweather was also present. He sat beside Bob Pellen, the young Texas, Assistant Attorney General who possessed that magical trait of communicating maturity and competence through humble mannerisms and brief conversations. A stenographer worked diligently in the corner. Investigators for Pellen stood by the double doors. Another one stood outside. Both looked like tasseled- shoe Wall Street boys, except if one did a quick pants cuff-high inspection one would spot expensive cowboy boots instead.

"I met Tanseed when he was nothing but a dirt-poor redneck, a fucking cowboy. I mean, he ropes and rides and all that cowboy shit, walks around with his Levis like a piece of cardboard. His jeans and shirts be starched like cardboard. Hey - he cracks when he moves, ya know? We used to hang out in the Houston clubs and bars chasing that afternoon pussy. Ha. You know - Crockpot Pussy? Know what that is?" he looked over at Pellen. "It's a woman in a club drinking all afternoon with a good ol' reliable crockpot cooking dinner at home. When her old man gets home after a long day's work, it looks like momma been home a cookin' his dinner all day. She wasn't. She sometimes was a running with me. Beehives. Hairspray. These ladies? They had hair so big it hurt.

"Just like Tanseed's wife thought Tanseed was out on the range hisself, workin'. We was chasin' that crockpot pussy and doin' a little drug dealin' too with these ladies. They think it will make 'em skinny. A little pot, some speed - them women, they love that speed, love it. - and some coke too. Tanseed realized quick enough that it was easier to sell this stuff than it was to work those quarter horses of his. He asked me if he could meet some people I knew." Diller's head was a rocking to and fro. "I set him up, see? He started playin' the game, played mean too. He's gotta whole lotta mean in him. Became one helluva drug dealer."

Jack looked like he was studying the wood grain in the table, but he was listening.

"Don't ever owe Baker Tanseed money," Diller went on, "Oh boy." He raised the cast on his hand. "Rednecks will be after yer ass. One time a horse doctor, Doc 'Blue' Boone they called him, messed up. He did things for us like phony up horse death certificates so Tanseed could collect on insurance. But he also inserted packs of drugs in horses that Tanseed would ship all over the country for sale or fer horse shows. A bag broke once inside a Palomino and Tanseed was madder than a Jap. The horse got poisoned. OD'd right there, sure enough. And the heroin was gone too. Well, the doc drove home to his place out in the country right after that. He was real fond of some dogs of his. Ya know? Irish Setters, real beauties. He drove up, and on the front porch found all four of them dogs with their throats slit. Johnny Handell. He and some other punk did it for Tanseed. Killed them dogs like butchers. The doc didn't get any more jobs under the table, and his fancy equestrian clinic shut down without the extra drug money coming in." Diller's head bobbed. "Guess ol' Blue is in the red now, bankrupt." He laughed.

Weaver scribbled something on his note pad and showed it to Jack. A Houston veterinarian named William Boone had been questioned along with Johnny Handell regarding the murder of the Colorado businessman back in 1986, a case for which no arrests had ever been made.

"An' Tanseed's wife Sharlene? She's MONEY mad. She likes the high life. She likes to boogey. She could spend more on one shopping trip to that Neiman Marcus store than Tanseed could make in a week of horse dealin' an' drug dealin' together. Hell, she's crazy. But the shit, it caught up with 'em. Sharlene will fuck anybody. Everybody was pumping her. They say Pontecorvo is fuckin' her an' Tanseed doesn't seem..."

"Spare the cock stories," growled Weaver quietly.

Diller was startled still by the gruff interruption and stared at the Ranger nervously. He looked at Jack, then cleared his throat and continued. "Yeah, well...ah...the way I set Tanseed up is this. On one drinking session back then, Tanseed and I got to talkin' an' I tells him I knows this pilot, a border runnin' boy. Nick Tips is his name. Tips is doin' deals with the boys in Chicago, LA, New York. I gets Tanseed and Tips together and they set somethin' up for Tanseed to see some people back East. New York." Diller sat back finally in his chair. "Like they say, the rest is history, boys."

He lit another cigarette. The room was bar room gray with the Camel smoke he'd already exhaled. Diller took in a deep drag, blew it out. "Raymond Pontecorvo. The New York man. Tanseed's store is just a big starched front for Western World, that's all. Them New York boys, they operate the business. Their big painted horse trailers get them all over the country to rodeos and horse shows, smuggling guns and drugs everywhere. No pig stops a fancy horse trailer on the road, right? Johnny Laws just lets the cow-boys go on down the road. They are even carrying coke inside the horses - inside 'em. Pig gonna check that out? No way. An' they ship these horses all over, to Canada even. They got vets on the payroll loading horses with containers of drugs, like Doc Blue. An' that ain't a half of it."

Encouraged by his captive audience, Diller's head began weaving, and he warmed again to his topic. "They brew amphetamine and PCP, fence stolen property, an' keep 'em a small stable of hookers. Top dollar hookers to fuck local politicians and businessmen. They loan shark big time, are into video game hall protection rackets, gam-bling. An' they love the unions. The more unions in Texas, the happier they'll be. They lease muscle. But loan sharkin' and drug dealin', that's their main draw."

"Who hurt your hand, Diller?" asked FBI Merryweather.

"Johnny Handell. The fucker who framed me, set me up." A shudder rippled through Diller. He crushed the cig-arette in the overflowing ashtray on the table and reached for another one. "Johnny and that Tony Tetro." He puffed on his new Camel nervously. "When Pontecorvo came, muscle came. Handell is a Texas boy, but Tetro is from New York. Tetro is a psycho. Joe Cool, Joe Sharp. He's a hit man, the kind you see in the movies. I'm not shittin' ya. When Johnny broke my fingers, Tetro held me from behind, held my head forward and me so's I had to watch what was happenin'. Not just feel it - watch it. I'm tellin' ya, Tetro knew what he was doin'. That Indian, Tenpenny? RAD-E-CAL. Radical. He's Tanseed's man. Tanseed got him and Handell to sorta offset Tetro. Handell is big but he's just a fuckin' red neck bully. On that trip to Denver, he bossed me around like I was his slave. Tetro's the real muscle, the professional. But I do believe Tenpenny could whip both their asses."

Weaver began his recitation of the official police biographies of the men Diller had talked about. All the men in the room paid intense attention, especially Diller who must have felt like a privileged spy learning police secrets. Jack played the tape of Diller speaking on the phone with Pontecorvo and Tetro, then related his encounter with the group at the skating rink, dog fight. For the next two hours Diller was deluged with more questions that led to more criminal knowledge of this Tanseed/Pontecorvo confederation.

"Mr. Bailey," said FBI Pellen, "we need to make you a credible," he paused, re-phrased his words. "We need to substantiate you and your information. The bigger the substantiation, the better. Once this is accomplished, I will personally insure a position for you on the Federal Witness Protection Program. Tell us something we can use, right now, something we can prove."

Diller glanced over at Jack. "The Sergeant, he told me you might need that." His head bobbed once, twice. "Okay. How about a marijuana farm - a garden, man - just acres and acres of grass growing tall in East Texas, near the Louisiana line? That make ya happy?" He sat forward. "I understand that they're cookin' serious batches of crack out there, too. I been there, okay? I've seen it, know the cultivator, the ol' boy who tends the crop. Donny Mecher. He's just an ol' hippy, graduated from UTA." His voice dropped. "Mecher, he's a peaceable fella, ya know?" Diller pulled on his cigarette. "But they's some mean boys guard it, though, a bunch of 'em from Cuba. Refugees. They all live out there and guard the place day and night. Them Cubans an' the others, they're raised on shotguns. Mean fuckers. Bad news, every one of 'em."

"Mr. Bailey, we have a form, a contract, if you will, that will detail our relationship with you if you are eligible for the protection program. Read it and sign it, so that if and when the time comes, we can put you straight into the program," said FBI Pellen. He handed Diller a large manila envelope.

Diller took it reluctantly, shot a look at Jack, then shook the typewritten pages from the envelope with his good hand. Silently, he read them as the others watched.

This document will serve to confirm the agreement reached between Diller Bailey and the Organized Crime Strike Force for the Eastern District of Texas.

"You could have a lawyer..."

"No, no I got it."

It read:

This office is conducting an investigation of possible illegal activities on the part of Baker Tanseed, Raymond Pontecorvo, and others in connection with illegal trafficking of narcotics, controlled substances, weapons, prostitution, gambling, loan sharking, assaults, and murder.

You have agreed to inform officials at the Department of Justice of everything you know concerning the above-mentioned crimes and any other criminal activity in which Tanseed and Pontecorvo have participated. In addition, you have agreed to testify, if called, before all federal grand and petit juries hearing these matters. It is understood that no information or testimony given by you (both before and after the making of this agreement), or evidence derived from information or testimony given by you will be used against you in any criminal proceeding other than as indicated below. It is understood that this office will forego any prosecution of you, which could arise out of this matter in light of your cooperation in this investigation. In the event that any other law enforcement authorities contemplate prosecuting you in connection with your involvement, we will recommend they not do so.

It is understood that in the event that any other law enforcement authorities in connection with any violation of the law prosecute you, this office will bring to the attention of the prosecuting authorities the cooperation, which you furnished in connection with this agreement.

It is further understood that this office will seek to place you in the Federal Witness Protection Program along with any wife and children and any other associates who become in need of protection as a result of your cooperation with this office. This understanding is predicated upon your complete cooperation with the Government including the immediate, full, and truthful disclosure of all information in your possession, which is relevant to these matters. This agreement will not prevent the Government from prosecuting you for perjury should it be discovered that you have given false testimony in connection with these matters. In addition, in the event that you do not fully comply with all the other terms of this understanding (immediate, full, and truthful disclosure, testimony, etc.), this agreement will be nullified. Should this occur, the Government will be free to prosecute you with regard to any and all violations of the federal criminal law in which you may have participated, and to use against you any and all statements made by you and testimony you have given prior and subsequent to the date of this agreement.

Diller Bailey signed. Rye Edleson signed, Jack Kellog signed, FBI Pellen signed. The stenographer notarized. Two West Forge officers in plain clothes took Diller away to his motel room where he was under 24-hour protection. Pellen stood and began collecting his notes. The stenographer gathered her belongings as well.

"If," Pellen said, "you can successfully raid this marijuana plantation, a bust of that size is the sort of thing that will convince my superiors to put Diller Bailey on the program and assign some special Federal investigators to him. I know protecting Bailey is a drain on your department, but our budget is such that we can't protect him until I can justify doing so. After the raid he will become our security problem."

Jack nodded his understanding.

"I also believe we are obligated to notify a few other law enforcement agencies," Pellen continued. "The Alcohol, Tobacco, and Firearms people from Treasury, of course, as well as the state narcotics, and the NYPD."

Jack held up his hand. "One thing at a time, sir. Let's not bother them until we substantiate Diller." When FBI Pellen looked unconvinced, Jack spoke bluntly. "I don't want to involve any more agencies just yet, for security reasons."

FBI Pellen nodded. He snapped the lock on his bulging briefcase and stood up. "Good work and good luck, Sgt. Kellog. We will send an local FBI tactical officer with you, even though this is all contained within Texas right now. There are some good allegations of interstate crime." He shook hands with Jack, then extended his hand to Weaver. "Ranger Wisdom." He paused and let the stenographer exit ahead of him. "Get back to me," he said and followed his people out of the room, their arms burdened with multiple briefcases.

Jack and Weaver stood at the table. Rye Edleson paused at the door.

"Your boy's a character, but I believe him," Rye said. "We'll take any good cases you can deliver in Harris County."

"His attitude sure changed - from reluctant snitch to superstar," said Jack.

"He likes the spotlight all right," Weaver agreed, working on the fresh pinch Copenhagen in his lower lip.

"East Texas, huh?"

"Let's just raid that sumbitch," said Weaver.

"Local bidness tonight comes first," Kellog said.

******

South Houston projects. Lower east West Forge. These two neighborhoods bordered each other for miles. Third world, old rotten shacks and decaying apartments spilled across the city limits, backdrops for crowds of unemployed drinkers and drug abusers, young and old. Nightlife lasted well into the late morning. The young mingled in crowded knots inside and outside dingy clubs and pool halls with names like The Jungle, Soul Key, and The Cook Spot. They engaged in traffic-stopping conversations while hitting on bottles of cheap bootleg whiskey and grocery store wine. They shot up "H" or speed in parked cars or in lots beside dice games, their ghetto blasters screaming songs like "Don't Push Me Cause I'm on the Edge."

The old rested on porches and cars, their faces wearing the burn of every drink they'd ever had. They festered in endless domino games, collapsed on endless curbs. Ex-convicts, too old now to commit crimes, sat on porches smoking dope and drinking. Cars cruised the streets steered by men with blurry, bloodshot eyes and liquor bottles balanced in their urine-stained crotches.

Tonight there would be car wrecks and fights, beatings and thefts, heavy gambling, often a knifing or two, maybe a rape. Maybe the police would be called, maybe not. Tonight, Jack and Weaver trolled these streets in Jack's Cadillac dodging the slow-motion pedestrians and drivers.

Tonight, Rasp Wilson needed an attitude adjustment by way of an arrest warrant.

"Hey, what yo doin'?" snarled a voice from the sidewalk. Jack braked. A short, stocky teenager stepped off the curb and stood in front of him, defiant. Jack recognized the teen, a neighborhood regular. Jack could remember a much younger boy playing on this same Houston street corner with plastic cars and tanks back when Jack was in patrol. Now that child was an unemployed, blossoming tough guy.

"Yo think yo gonna get somethin' down here?" The teen challenged them.

Jack kept his response to, "Yeah."

"You ain't gonna get nothin' heah," the boy shot back.

"No people down heah, be tellin' off on their own color."

Weaver Wisdom leaned forward from the passenger seat and, with his deep and resonant voice said, "People be rapin' and rippin' off on their own color down here. People be killin' their own color, too."

The teen mumbled and shuffled off down the street.

Weaver shook his head. "Punk."

It wasn't long before Jack saw another familiar face, that of Gentleman Morris, a man in his 80s standing in front of his house.

"Hello, Gentleman Morris. How are you, sir?" Jack called out the window while reaching into that beer-stocked cooler in the back seat to produce a cold Coors. Morris walked slowly to the Caddy in his familiar frayed sport jacket and stained but always pressed white shirt.

"Hallo, Mr. Kellog." He smiled and accepted the brew with a laugh. He was staggering just a bit from some other alcohol it seemed from the smell of the air between them. After some talk about the Morris family, Jack asked Morris where they might find Rasp Wilson.

"If I'm not," the old man paused, swallowed a hiccup, "not mistaken, I believe he be sitting in his car with that long-faced boy that works down at EZ Car Parts. They be sitting across from the Torch Lounge."

"Thank you, Mr. Morris. You are a the gentleman," said Jack. Morris waved them off. They drove down the street. "That's a good old man," Jack commented as they returned into traffic.

Jack parked the Caddy in the pitch-black, back lot of Bain's Wire and Metal Factory. He and Weaver slipped out with their baton-sized flashlights in hand and walked quietly toward Avenue L and the Torch Lounge. Once across the street from the lounge, Jack spotted Rasp's '76 Monte Carlo and pointed it out to Weaver. Several heads turned as lounge patrons congregating outside spotted Jack and the 6'5" black giant in the white Stetson with him. The crowd rumbled, then shifted away as a disorganized, yet single single organism.

Weaver approached the driver's side from the rear as Jack ran to the passenger side. Slamming into the car's side, Jack flooded the interior with bright light. Weaver stuck the barrel of his .357 right up to Rasp's temple. Rasp's head jerked back from fear and surprise. Weaver maintained the metal-on-flesh contact. The passenger, who was indeed a long-faced fellow, stared at Kellog in sheer terror. Jack winked at him and half-smiled.

"I heard you was a bad dude, Rasp Wilson. A real bad dude," Weaver growled. He cocked back the hammer on his revolver. "Well, muther-fucker...be bad now. Be real bad...now."

Rasp refused to be bad, so he was arrested instead. Weaver yanked him out and cuffed him under Kellog's watchful eye. A Houston PD, two-man prowl car arrived and a routine check was run on Mister Long Face. He came up clear.

"You clear now," Ranger Wisdom told him, "but if you keep hanging out with the likes of these sorry asses? You will be in trouble soon enough. Go on."

Long Face moved off but kept looking back at Wisdom.

"That ain't no prediction, son. That's gospel," the Ranger added in a shout.

Rasp's Monte Carlo was impounded and a search of

the trunk, floorboards, glove box, and interior incidental to the impound process failed to disclose the famous steak knife - or any other evidence linking Wilson with the crimes. Rasp Wilson was booked into the Harris County Jail screaming for a lawyer, calling Sgt. Kellog a racist honky and Ranger Wisdom an Uncle Tom. Same old song, same old dance.

Hours later, Jack and Weaver leaned against their respective cars parked side-by-side in the West Forge PD parking lot facing each other.

"Be out on bond by morning," Weaver said.

"Maybe," said Jack. "But, I got the fix in with the D.A. No bond. If he gets some ass-wipe, liberal judge to turn him loose, Lupez will have some of his people on him. I called him. They're ready to up a surveillance operation. They hope he returns to one of his rape victims, especially Ida Bell. They said they will cover Isa's apartment if he gets out."

"What Rasp needs is a good, old-fashioned ass whoppin'," said Weaver.

"Yup."

"Twenty years ago we didn't have such cocky mothas on the streets, didn't have such crime either. Twenty years ago we had some real attitude adjustments," Weaver said.

For a moment, Jack flashed back to that arrogant, challenging black youth. The whole world had become a complex, confusing mess and getting worse.

"See ya later, big fella." Jack turned to get into the Caddy.

"Be tight, Jack," Weaver pushed off from the side of his LTD and headed around its front to the driver's side.

They pulled out of the parking lot, turned in different directions. Jack reached around to the cooler and drank a can of attitude adjustment while driving home. But Jack had one more trip and he didn't want Weaver tangled up in and branded as trouble too early. He drove to the Palawa.

It was Friday night. Message night. Jack, with a Houston Police Department Patrol Sergeant and a State Gambling Intelligence Officer, stood on the roller rink parking lot watching the HPD officers march the dog-fighting enthusiasts into a paddy wagon. The faces Jack most wanted to see - Pontecorvo, Tetro, Ira, and the Tanseeds - were not in custody, nor to be found in the building. By the service door a city animal pound crew wrestled with a variety of dogs. No fights tonight. No more fights, here anyway-not for a while.

The Diller Bailey robbery case had suddenly changed from a bag of worms to a snarl of loose rattlesnakes. Jack chuckled. The Houston Chronicle would call this a dog-fight gambling raid in the papers tomorrow. Jack called it one helluva message back to Mr. Raymond Pontecorvo.

CHAPTER SIX:
THE GREAT EAST TEXAS PLANTATION RAID

"Jack and I had...broken up. For good. One night in 1979, I was sitting quietly beside Henry my husband - he's dead now - as he was driving us home from a Republican fund-raiser. My gaze fell on, then followed, a jogger ahead of us. I felt almost hypnotized for a moment by the way he moved. As our Mercedes' headlights lit up this runner, as we got closer? I was shocked. Shocked to see the jogger was my Jack Kellog. He looked strong as a bull. He was, you know, sweating a lot, pumping right by me. He didn't notice me. I wanted to pound on the window. But couldn't, because of Henry. Obviously. I burst into tears much to Henry's surprise. Jack, my knight in armor had galloped right past me. I haven't seen him since. Not once. Read about him. Good news stories. Tough ones. But, never saw him again." - Shelia Havolick, Miami, Florida, 2003

Archie Lennox, tape interview 34

In Vietnam fashion, the chopper hovered to within several feet of the ground and Jack dropped his gear first, then leaped from the skids, followed by five other men. The state police chopper whisked off, and the six men began saddling up their backpacks for the five-mile hike through the East Texas hills and forests. Their destination - a position just west of the marijuana farm cabins owned by Baker Tanseed and Ray Pontecorvo.

Jack carried a large backpack he'd borrowed from Breasley's son. It contained boxes of ammunition, a mess kit, packaged cold cuts, a first aid kit, flak vest, Kel-light, and a down vest. Atop the back he tied a sleeping bag rolled around a flask of tequila and a red "team" ball cap issued to each member of the raid. He threw a modified AR-15 with sling over his shoulder. His old uniform police pistol belt carried a canteen, his .45, handcuffs, and some extra magazines.

Weaver Wisdom sat beside him, wrestling his equipment into place. For a brief moment, Jack and Weaver's gazes caught each other's struggles and they broke out laughing.

"You about a Noah's Ark looking motha." said Weaver. "Packed for 40 days?"

"And 39 nights. I'm leaving as soon as I can," Jack returned, as he joined in the procession of officers he had met only a day earlier at the Pine County Sheriff's Office.

Thirty-Six Hours Earlier:

"Jack Kellog, Ranger Wisdom, this is Daniel Reeves and Len Euro. I'm Willy Friedman, State Narcotics. Reeves and Euro here are Pine County's two-man narcotic wizards. They hang around us State boys a lot and pick up our leavings," said Friedman.

"Like flies on bullshit, bubba," Euro added with a smile as the men leaned over a conference room table filled with aerial photos to shake hands.

"Jack, this is our area Ranger, 'Pepper' Lawton. Pepper has done all the skywork on this project based on what your man Bailey has told you," Friedman said, beckoning Pepper out of a nearby office.

Pepper shook Jack's hand but greeted Weaver with a hearty roar. Weaver and Pepper were friends for years, well before being selected as Texas Rangers. Their relationship had started when they served as troopers together in Houston in the late '60's.

"No FBI?" Kellog asked, looking around.

"No."

"Jeez, and they promised."

"This is one of our county prosecutors, William Gayfield, who has drawn up our search warrant and has made sure we all have behaved thus far in the investigation, Freedman said'

"We plan to drop in by DPS helicopter five miles northeast of the farm, hike nearby, cold camp, and position ourselves by these cabins (pointing to an aerial shot). From there we will break radio silence, call in uniformed county units and our chopper to come in the front door with the warrants. There'll be at least 14 officers involved. I've been in on at least 30 farm raids like this here when I was on loan to California. Generally, these people are heavily armed, but there is usually little-to-no gunplay. These Cubans may be different."

"I have a question," said Euro. "Who is packin' in the Miller Lite?"

******

A late afternoon rain fell lightly on the procession in gusts and through openings in the pines as they climbed up and down the slopes, avoiding thickets and streams. Friedman, a fitness fanatic, was in the best shape of the group. He became the scout, running ahead at various distances with compass in hand to reconnoiter.

At a point they caught up to the bearded Friedman near the top of a hill, heaved off their gear and collapsed on the ground. The rain clouds had passed revealing a country-blue sky.

"We're pretty close," said Reeves while enjoying the rest. He was a balding big man with a broad face, especially heavy in his hips and legs.

"Yup" said Friedman "we're about one mile, from their cabins. If we get up just before sunrise and head in, we should be there about 7 a.m. Surely all those dope heads will be asleep that early."

Pepper, who had taken the aerial photos from a tremendous, hopefully unnoticed, height stared out over the view. Like Weaver, the Rangers had taken him many places, from the Governor's mansion to manhunts through the sewers of San Antonio. Pepper took a dip of snuff and said,

"There are two mobile homes. Also an old barn, which must have been built 80 years ago. We counted two jeeps, a station wagon, and a couple of cycles...and a whole bunch of dope growing. We never could see any lookout location."

"Pretty day," Jack said.

"Sure is," said Euro, "if we had any smarts, we'd be fishin."

"I'll settle for some hunting tomorrow morning," said Friedman.

******

Near 9 p.m. the men settled down into a semi- circle of sleeping bags with Reeves' small transistor radio playing country music quietly. The moon was bright, the conversation full of war stories, cases, second jobs (every married officer had to have one) and women. They were just getting into Jack's flask.

Willie Friedman got up and unzipped a duffle bag, pulling out wooden dowels, string and some metal handles and metal discs. While the others watched, Willie connected the discs to the handles by clamps and wires.

"Boys, these are metal detectors. Tomorrow we will be splitting up into two-man teams. Each team's gonna have one, gonna need one. One team member will work one while the other will work this," Willie said as he turned a dowel around letting a string roll off the wood till one end of the string reached the ground.

"While one man tests the ground ahead with this portable metal detector, the other will be right beside him with a dowel like this, payin' strict attention to the string. It will hang up and catch on things, maybe trip wires. Might be a bomb? Might be just an alarm, a noise-maker."

"We'll need to be in position at daybreak right near the crop. Now there are walkways, paths, in betwixt the crop. These paths may be booby- trapped. Lord knows it wouldn't be the first time a dope farm or drug lab was booby-trapped. It's like a siren alarm for them too. They're usually not set off by light touch, like by animals. Just people. At first light we move in, and when we get near the crop, we get this gear out. Throw this switch on the detector here and watch the light. Notice that it doesn't hum. Unravel this string and hold it out in front of ya. Now, we can't afford the luxury of tiptoein' on up to the cabins trying to sniff out any mines or trip wires, but we need to do our best. As fast as we can to get into position...and not get punji-sticked or blown up."

The mood of the group grew silent and solemn as they passed around one of the portable detectors. Euro ran a detector over his wedding ring and the light flashed.

"Lots of yer' mines are gonna need power bases. Look fer wires or light poles in the field that might have a line running down into the ground like it's going nowhere. That line may run right into a booby trap. Now some traps might be battery powered. Some traps don't need no power."

"I saw a mouse-trap converted into a trip-wire shotgun one time on a drug raid," continued Willie. "Some dopers stood a mouse trap up by building a bottom for it, then secured a length of pipe to the top so that when the striker of the trap landed, it would hit the hole on one end of the pipe. Next, they threaded the pipe and screwed in a shotgun shell. They aimed the pipe to where they ran a trip wire and set the trap's striker right to the wire. You hit the wire, the striker flies, hits the shell in its makeshift barrel, and boom...you're mincemeat."

A morbid silence continued for a few moments. They piled the anti-booby trap equipment into their backpacks.

"So how did you get the title 'Jumpin' Jack?" Reeves asked to break the ice.

"Well...never earned any real title. Years ago - hell, decades ago - I boxed for a while," said Jack.

"Oh, yeah?" said Euro.

"Yeah, in '63. I worked as a patrolman with Houston PD. I'd been there for about six years, but always wanted to be a fighter. Boxed in high school, even boxed while I was on the force. Finally, though, I quit Houston, found a trainer. Boxed for about two years. Never won one fight. Pretty much got an ass-whoppin' each time, but I never would go down easy. Trainer said I needed a gimmick, so 'Jumpin' Jack' was born."

"You keep Jumpin' back up when knocked down?"

"More like ricochet," Jack added.

"Ricochet Jack Kellog." Wisdom tested it out. "Sorry, no music."

"Maybe you needed a different trainer," said Pepper.

"What I needed was a left hook." Jack said.

"So, you gave it up, huh?"

"Yeah. You know when Too Tall Jones quit the Dallas Cowboys to box, at least he won once in a while - and Landry took him back. Not Houston PD, though. Some old boy in recruiting told me that since I had quit on a whim, they wouldn't rehire me. West Forge hired me in '66, and here I am."

"I've never been to Houston," Euro said.

"Ya ain't missing much," said Pepper. "Weaver and I were stationed there for about four years as troopers. It's a growing monster of a place."

"That's cause you're an ol' country boy at heart, Pep," said Friedman, a native-born Kansan. The flask made the rounds.

"Weaver and I worked Narcotics together in Houston, before he became rangers," Friedman said. "We used to live and breathe speed, dope, and cocaine. Made a lotta busts and Weaver kicked a lot of ass while I watched."

"You used to just shoot a lot of them," Weaver added, and everyone laughed.

"I didn't start no fight I didn't think you couldn't finish, Weaver." Friedman replied.

"Jack, was Mohammed Ali Clay one of 'em that whipped ya?" questioned Reeves, returning to the boxing subject.

"No. Everyone I've ever fought had their careers die graceful deaths like mine. Never have seen nor heard of any but one. Johnny Handell, who - as the fates would have it - is now bodyguard and muscle for Baker Tanseed, co-owner of all the dope we're fixin' to seize tomorrow."

"There's ya a little revenge. Is this raid really gonna help nail 'em?" asked Euro.

"If we can pull this raid off and put substance to the words of our informant - get him on the Federal witness stand and our Harris County stand, we'll hook Baker Tanseed, Ray Pontecorvo, and others into this raid and a whole bunch of other crime business," replied Jack.

"Better watch yer ass," mumbled Friedman as he settled down in his sleeping bag. "These sound like big bad boys."

"Friedman," said Weaver quietly, "if you wake up at 5 a.m. with a compulsion to do sit-ups and push-ups or some such shit, please do it quiet like."

The conversation dwindled along with the energy of the men. Reeves reached over and clicked off the radio. After a brief period of silence, Euro whispered almost to himself. "If it rains again, we're fucked." The men broke up in laughter at their shelterless situation.

Finally, sleep came to all but one. Jack stared at the sky, only partially concealed by slowly swaying tall pines. That old tightness caught his throat. His view, which overlooked the slope and a small lake, was nothing but beautiful for some, but not for Jack. It was more lonely than beautiful.

The last few days had been hectic and thoughtless, just packing and planning. He sipped from the flask. To Jack, people's lives ran normal veins of existence with some kind of basic destiny, and in those lives there came occasional cracks that flung them from their normal course. Most people recovered and returned to their destiny. Boxing was one such crack, a fault line in Jack's picture, sending him away from police work for several disappointing years, but he had returned.

He thought about the fault lines. The second major crack was the seven years he'd spent loving the wrong woman. A married woman. The one who had managed to lead him down the primrose path for years. Her name was Shelia Havolick, Mrs. Shelia Havolick. She was a buyer for a large Houston department store and married to Henry Havolick, a successful clothing salesman and co-owner of a sportswear line. Jack met Shelia, of all places, on a traffic stop when he was a West Forge patrolman in the late '60s. Jack was fresh from his boxing days, just a carved figure of granite in blue, and Shelia had accepted her speeding ticket graciously, so graciously she had invited him to dinner. Jack smiled and leaned against the side of her Mustang convertible.

"Well, Mrs. Shelia Havolick, what might your husband say about that?"

"I don't know," she replied with a saucy and irresistible smile. "He's in Chicago this whole week, and I can't ask him."

So he was, and so it went. While "he" traveled, they met and met, for sex at first, but they became best friends and watched each other's lives change as she was promoted to vice-president of the store and he became a detective, then quickly a Sergeant.

After two years, he knew he wanted to marry her and though he was quite sure she loved him, she said she also loved and admired Henry. She said that she really didn't have a bad relationship with Henry. At times she promised many things to Jack, but never did she come through. So, after seven full years of rendezvous, three-day weekend trips, lunches, dinners, clubs, movies, sex, Astro and Oiler games, so many good moments, Jack had found himself deeply frustrated and depressed. Shelia, on the other hand, seemed quite content, almost thriving, having the deficiencies of her men cancelled out by each other.

Henry was quiet and polished. Well-connected. Jack was loud and loose, well connected too, but in a negative sort of way. He was almost a local folk-hero to the legions of the night people. Taxi drivers, janitors, motel clerks, waitresses, and newspaper deliverymen. All the local thugs knew him. Though Jack might not be invited to a Benefit League Banquet, local businesspeople knew him and liked him for work he had done in investigating many of their crimes. Jack was his own benefit league. Henry had class. Jack had only color in a negative sort of way. Class was not a word or worry in his mind. Henry had money. Jack was a cop. Henry was an average guy, in a world of cloth and figures and balanced books. Jack was a fort for a lot of people who needed walls, too much of a fort at times for Shelia, just too risky a fellow. Jack would gallop. Henry wouldn't even go near the horse.

Jack should have known early on when she blurted out, after quite a number of drinks, in an Italian restaurant one night that she would NEVER marry anyone who would let himself be shot at. Or, carry a gun. That about said it all. He should have known. But he let five more years slip by.

He found himself living in limbo between Henry's business trips, between Shelia's promises and her realities. For one too many Christmases he'd driven past the huge, decorated Havolick River Oaks house, and seen her friends and family inside.

In August 1978, he reached for his office phone. A fan blasting hot air around the room clacked in the background.

"Shelia, please."

"Shelia Havolick," she said.

"Sheel, I am sitting here wondering why I should ever be with you again. Henry is your number one man, and I am your number one fan. I love you. Goodbye."

He hung up and still some 10 years later had never said another word to her or seen a glimpse of her again, despite her cards and calls and attempts to catch him at different locations. She came banging on his front door several times, and he refused to answer. Refused and dodged being spotted through the windows. She even showed up at the station, when he wasn't there.

Close friends and Jack's brother Robert told Jack he was never the same after Shelia. Jack chalked it up to age. After Sheel, no other woman seemed so attractive, so special. After Sheel, Jack bought his big house and planted flowers and monkey grass. He got a little overweight and became much more serious and intense about his work. There was nothing much else to do. But no one argued that after Shelia Havolick, he let himself become a lonely man. Sheel had taken him in his prime, kept him, flung him far from the normal relationship he might have had with another woman. Timing. A crack in the destiny, one he still hadn't recovered from. Sheel.

Two empty hours later he fell asleep.

******

"Ranger 860 to all raid units," whispered Pepper Lawton into his radio, "ground teams are in position, all raid units move in."

"10-4, 860, units are en route," a voice returned with a crackle through the ear plugs of their radios. In the unseen, unheard distance county squad cars and a state helicopter began their approach.

Jack and Weaver's position had been stealthily attained by 30 minutes of slow-motion metal detecting and string-watching through acres of marijuana to a position just south of the site's barn and the two large mobile homes.

The fields were beautiful in this quiet, chilly red dawn. With all the two-man teams in position, they now had only to wait for the troops to arrive and bask in the sunlight. They held onto their bright, red team ball caps and remained out of sight. A strong, acrid, distasteful aroma blew over them, obviously from an amphetamine lab in operation in the barn, an unforgettable, unforgivable smell.

Quite suddenly, the men heard a telephone ringing, then some hectic shouting in Spanish from inside one of the mobile homes. A front door whipped open and crashed against the metallic exterior as a partially clad Cuban brandishing a small machine gun leaped onto the porch, then over the railing, and ran into the barn. In the far-off distance there came the sounds of several bursts of automatic gunfire. The fierce yelling continued inside the homes as the other half-dressed Cubans began to pour out of windows and doors, some shooting randomly into the thick marijuana fields before them. A lookout on the road with a radio must have informed them the police were en route. The ground team accepted the frightening fact that things were not going to go smoothly and to prevent the escape of suspects and the destruction or removal of evidence they would have to engage themselves in the worst possible outcome of their mission, a small war.

"Move in. Stay low." Friedman ordered into his portable radio, and he stepped from the tree line behind the homes, rounded the end of one home, and opened fire at the Cubans who were shooting across the field. Three were hit squarely and dropped, flipping their weapons in the air on impact. Friedman's bullets had momentarily joined the suspects' bullets as they rifled through the air above the heads of the ground team until Friedman broadcast "all clear" and dropped back to his tree-line position.

Engines roared from inside the barn. AR-15 barrel first, and minus the red police hat, Jack peered over his dirt mound to see a trail bike blast out of the barn, the driver juggling a handgun while shifting gears and steering. Back at the second house, a man stepped out screaming Spanish curses and fired at Jack with a carbine rifle. Jack twisted away, while, from seemingly out of nowhere, Euro popped up to Jack's left, barking an American curse back and fired away at this suspect, causing the shooter to fly off the porch in spastic motions.

The cycle was bound to run right over Kellog. He squinted up in time to see Weaver Wisdom open fire at the armed biker, his AR-15 rounds first striking the front fender, then shattering the headlamp, causing the bike to wobble. The next rounds punched into the biker's chest and stopped him in mid-air, ripping him off the bike as it traveled on. The Cuban squeezed off one skyward round from his revolver and collapsed in a heap, much like his vehicle did some 20 feet later.

Euro and Reeves stood and shouted "Police" having to blast away at yet another armed Cuban who had just dropped from a window. They rushed the barn as Kellog and Wisdom made similar moves.

A Bronco barreled out, taking half of the barn door frame with it, and all four men fired at the vehicle. The driver cut the wheels so sharply that it tumbled up onto its side, offering only an underbelly view to the officers. A county car finally arrived, skidding to a halt, spitting up dust, near the dirt road entrance to the site. A Cuban struggled to appear out of the Bronco driver's window by bracing his foot in the steering wheel and standing. He wrestled to aim a machine pistol, clacking off inaccurate 9mm rounds everywhere. The officers hit the ground. Euro and Wisdom returned similarly desperate, inaccurate rounds into the underbelly of the vehicle. It was Friedman again, who left his position to face the other side of the Bronco roof. He ended the attack by tearing through the thin metal roof with three lines of M-16 gunfire.

A second county unit arrived, and the state helicopter hovered over a suspect in the field who decided it best to surrender under the direction of the dark-fatigued SWAT trooper who bore down upon him with both words and a shotgun. Two more Cubans emerged from the barn unarmed with hands skyward, greeted by uniformed deputies who ordered them face down on the dirt in their best Spanish.

Jack and Weaver scurried to clear the first mobile home. Weapons ready, they entered and scanned the plush, freshly ventilated interiors.

"No, please, don't shoot." came a voice from a back room. "I have no guns."

"Prove it," Weaver yelled.

A longhaired, white male in a thermal undershirt and faded jeans appeared in the hall with his hands fluttering above his head.

"Turn around, one time," ordered Weaver, which the terrified hippy did as instructed. Jack cuffed him, then searched him as the chopper landed outside, blasting wind and dirt into the open doors and windows.

"Donny Mecher, I presume," said Jack, while searching the man.

"How...how ja know that?"

"I am a student of old UTA yearbooks, bubba," Jack replied. "We have some papers to serve you... and on you."

Within minutes, all three buildings were searched and secured. A State narcotics agent, toting a portable video camera was filming the crime scene area. Other agents examined the illegal crop. Weaver and Jack stepped out of the house and turned a handcuffed Mecher over to the deputies.

Pepper approached them. "Two of our county boys, both deputies, in a marked sedan, were hit bad by a lookout up the road. Let's run up there and check on 'em."

Pepper jumped behind the wheel of a county car as Weaver and Kellog slid their equipment-heavy frames into passenger seats. One ambulance passed them in route to the site, and they spotted another parked ahead in amongst state police and county squads. One police car was completely ditched, its windshield caved in and forming a bloody mosaic of a million pieces stuck in the thick blood on the dashboard and front seat.

A sense of doom fell over Jack as they left their car and weaved through the uniformed onlookers on foot. They saw the objects of their solemn intensity.

Seeing death, the monster of it, is not new to the police officer, but seeing two bloody officers, lifeless, ruptured, mauled and red, with abandoned medical tubes and bandages visible, all between shredded and punctured uniform shirts from EMT shears and bullets, was a unique tragedy, and a nightmare mirror. Jack, already covered in sweat, felt flush and weak and leaned against the ambulance. He pushed his slipping sunglasses up the bridge of his nose.

A patrol sergeant turned to Pepper. "A look-out up there got 'em," he said pointing to a deer stand in a pine tree just off the dirt road. The Sergeant's eyes and nose were running from tears and he had only some medical gauze for a wipe, which he did. Another deputy pounded on the hood of his squad car some 20 feet away, cursing.

It was Weaver who crossed the culvert and walked over to the tree. Looking up he saw a Cuban's head and arm dangling off the edge of a metal deer stand. He could see the barrel of a machine gun. An FM radio up on the stand broadcast the trumpets of Spanish music. From him, this guard, from this hidden place, came the warning to the mobile homes by way of a telephone nailed to a branch. From here came those first few bursts of fire they'd heard. On the ground, a few steps from the tree, rested a large, soggy cardboard box that read, "Western World's Finest Deer Stand, The Ambush 12."

"Ambush 12," Weaver muttered to himself. Baker Tanseed. Pontecorvo.

"We need a photo of that box," Kellog told the officers.

After a moment Weaver turned and walked down the long dirt road by himself, all the way to the home-site where he sat alone in the chopper until Jack rejoined him and it left.

******

"Detective. Sgt. Kellog," an elderly woman in the office beckoned.

Kellog, slowly dragging all his gear into building, wiped his brow, turned to her and she handed him a message.

"Thanks," he said and over the confusing din of the Pine County Sheriff's Office, he tried to concentrate to read the note. It said, *Call me ASAP. Urgent. Jack Breasley. 11 p.m.*

Yesterday. A call long overdue, but there was much urgency here too and much to do. He shoved the note in a chest pocket. Weaver and Pepper were briefing Pep's Ranger Captain before the State Shooting Investigation Team's arrival for yet another look into the firefight. Euro, Reeves and Friedman helped deputies and jailers book in the uncooperative Cubans. A fever-pitch hostility lingered between the police and the prisoners, both groups had lost comrades. Both were ready to fight.

Jack walked into an interview room with a confused, twitching Donny Mecher. Mecher sat behind a plain, pine table.

"Mecher," said Jack to the disheveled hippy, "how'd ya wind up livin' with so many of these Castro rejects?" he asked and sat with him.

Mecher nervously sucked on a cigarette and shrugged his shoulders. His face looked pale white.

"I think I should consult with my lawyer," Mecher said.

"Consult with yer lawyer?" Jack turned real serious. "Ya shoulda consulted with yer lawyer before you went to work for Baker Tanseed and Pontecorvo. Now you need to consult with yer common sense."

Mecher stared at the floor and shuddered.

"Ya see son, people died here today. Police officers died here today. I don't give no flying fuck about some communist Cubans dying here, but they did too. You look to me like the brains behind this whole operation."

"I am not!"

"In fact, you look to me like Marilyn Monroe. Ya know, Mecher, a blond, long-haired fella like you looks kinda like Marilyn Monroe to those hungry boys in the federal pen too. What with them boys not havin' them some pussy for decades." Jack was really pouring on the simple redneck routine and it looked like it was working.

"That's of course if you first survive these local fellers. They lost two friends out here this morning. And I'm sure you realize we aren't exactly in downtown Austin out here. This is piney woods country here-abouts and you could flat disappear between here and the fuckin' bathroom. And nobody would care but your momma."

Jack let that message sink in.

"Now I have a deal fer your straggly ass," Jack continued. "So let's cut the bullshit and do some straight talkin' here man to man. AND fast."

"I think I need a lawyer," Mecher said.

"I think you need your head examined. Do you think your mafia employers want you alive talking to anyone? You are a ticking time bomb waiting to confess. What are you? French or something?"

"Scotch Irish."

"Scotch and Irish. Anything but Italian gets you dead, son. This is the Italian brotherhood, A-one, fucking New York mafia."

They were interrupted by a knocking and Jack turned, disgusted, to see the young officer's face in the small window of the door.

Jack cracked the door. "Yeah?"

"Sir, there's a Detective Breasley on the phone. He insists you talk to him," the deputy said.

"Hmmm," Jack grunted and left the room, locking Mecher in before following the officer into Euro and Reeves' narcotic office. He snatched up the phone. There were no hellos.

"Diller's gone. Maybe dead." said Breasley.

"What?"

"They got to him Jack. At the motel. Last night. Shot up the place. Shot the patrolman guard."

"Which one?" Kellog quietly asked, knowing no answer could possibly offer relief from the deep, swelling sick depression.

"Timmes, Roy Timmes from Willacker's shift," replied Breasley.

"Shit." whispered Jack as he sat on the desk. He had just spoken to Timmes on the phone about the Erma Fredrick case the day before he left for East Texas.

"What happened?"

"Somehow they found out we had Diller at the Sandust Seven. Looked like a bazooka blew the place up. Timmes was shot in the back. He's in critical right now-slug pressing his backbone-East Duchess."

"Diller?" asked Jack.

"No sign of 'em."

"Two kinds of blood in the room?"

"No, Jack. Attaway and his boys ran the whole room and there's evidence of only one blood type -Timmes'. They must have taken Diller with 'em. Diller's blood was typed at the hospital when he was beaten up. He has a different type than Timmes."

"How-could-they have-known?" Jack mumbled almost to himself.

"A snitch. An informant. A mole. A payoff to someone in our department." Breasley said.

"Like the big city."

"Like the big city."

"We lost two out here this morning, Jack," Kellog said.

"Damn,"

"Ya know, I don't think...I just don't know much about Timmes," Kellog said.

"He's got two little kids. Married. When are you

coming back?"

"Tomorrow night, I have to," Jack mumbled.

"Another motel customer, a woman heard the shooting, saw the attackers…"

"How many?"

"Two…run up to the room, heard the shots, then she took off. She said one was a big guy with black hair parted down the middle and a leather jacket. The second was almost as tall with curly hair. They pulled up in a van, a dark, custom van."

"It's Ira Tenpenny. Tenpenny and Handell," said Jack. "Can they be identified?"

"Unlikely. The woman, she was at the motel cheating on her husband with some cowboy. Well, either she's afraid to cooperate or she wasn't close enough. When the bullets flew, she ducked."

After reviewing the details over and over, they finally hung up. Jack sat alone in the Narcotics office staring past the windows and hallway, through more windows into the "book-in" room. He saw one of Castro's castaways shouting to a jailer,

"Do hue tink hue kan hurt me, mung? I had been in badder jails. Badder jails dan hue kan eber put me in mung."

A jailer shoved the man toward a hallway, and the Cuban shuffled off in a cocky strut with his elbows flaring out and flapping behind him with each step.

Jack stroked his long moustache, feeling a burn in his stomach - the kind ulcers are made of. He returned to the interview room, sighed deeply and looked at Mecher.

"Ever heard of the Witness Protection Plan?" he asked.

"Yeah," said Mecher.

"We gotta lotta death in this one. Whole lotta death, and we can get you outta jail and away from all the death. New name, new place. We give you all this for testimony and information on the involvement of Baker Tanseed and Raymond Pontecorvo in your drug operation," Jack offered point blank.

"No fucking way," was Mecher's reply.

"Suit yourself, Marilyn."

******

"Two Pine County Deputies were shot and killed today, ambushed in their squad car while participating in a daring raid on a marijuana and drug farm.

Details are sketchy at this time, but Pine County Sheriff Blockway said State and Harris County officials assisted in the raid of a farm on FM Road 1119, about 22 miles north of Milters Cove. Sheriff Blockway said several suspects were shot and at least five are dead. Several Cuban men were taken into custody.

Department of Public Safety Captain Boyce Campbell of Narcotics said that approximately 78,000 marijuana plants and a very large methamphetamine lab were seized in the operation. The seized drugs were valued at well over 50 million dollars. The murdered deputies are William Warings, age 44, married, father of one; and John L. Kerns, age 25, single. Sheriff Blockway said the particular suspect who allegedly shot these deputies was himself shot and killed by backup police units as he tried to escape.

-MILTERS COVE DAILY

******

"A West Forge Patrol Officer, 32-year-old Roy L. Timmes is listed in critical condition at East Duchess Hospital this morning after a shooting incident that occurred at the Sandust Seven Motel in the 1700 block of Biner last night.

West Forge Deputy Chief Alice Blanke would reveal only that Timmes was on an undercover assignment at the motel where he was shot and wounded when attacked by two gunmen. Suspects are being sought. The Texas Rangers are assisting in the investigation. The motive for the shooting remains a mystery and all law enforcement participants decline comment." - HOUSTON CHRONICLE

******

Scooter Gleason giggled, trying to tap in on the unwritten bond between the officers of the court, judges and prose-cutors, even in this country, county courthouse miles from home turf in Houston. His overdone, obnoxious, good-ol'-boy manner was over-extended even in this East Texas District Courthouse. Gleason had filed a motion to reduce Donny Mecher's bond to $100,000 from the original one million. The court was crowded and noisy and not at all formal. Lawyers, clients and witnesses seemed to shuffle about while the hearing and proceedings went on up by the bench. Gleason tried to mingle with all of them.

Ranger Wisdom walked in and sidled up beside Kellog.

"Well looky here. It's your ol' buddy Scooter," Weaver said.

"Who else?" Kellog detested the Harris County attorney and an almost juvenile rush of disgust poured through him at the very sight of Gleason. Even his physical appearance was irritating. He had the long red bushy hair of a clown bunching out under his cowboy hat. He was tall and thin but with an unusual protruding potbelly. His face was pale and sickly, the pallor of an alcoholic.

Jack had encountered Gleason many times, first as a prosecutor with Harris County, then when Scooter resigned to hang out a private practice shingle. As a rags-to-riches defense attorney, Gleason lost his pants, then got unbeliev-ably (and questionably) rich, then no pants again. During these up and down times Gleason was suspended from the state bar twice. During one suspension he lost his home to the West Forge Savings and Loan. He lived in the back of his brother's hardware store. The storeroom became his office when the suspension was lifted. He defended drug dealers, bikers, thieves, and old political cronies. Pontecorvo made the obvious choice by retaining Scooter Gleason and establishing a "hometown" legal connection.

Judge Samuel S. Grants lowered Mecher's written bond by half to $500,000.

"Jack boy. Jack." Scooter blurted out when he saw Kellog in the back of the courtroom.

Kellog smirked at him.

"Donny, catch ya at the Sheriff's office in 10 minutes you'll be out. Just some paperwork," Scooter said over his shoulder to Mecher as a jailer escorted him away. Scooter approached Kellog as though he were Stanley finding Livingston.

"Heard you called my client Marilyn Monroe." he said.

"What are you doing here?" Kellog asked Scooter

"Well, ya know, Baker Tanseed called me late last night and asked me to get on down here and get Donny out of the hoosegow." Scooter had a way of conversing out of one side of his mouth with a protruding bottom lip.

One would think it was an obvious legal mistake to mention Baker Tanseed's name, but Scooter so loved dropping names, especially influential ones. Perhaps it wasn't a mistake at all. Jack had spent many hours wondering how smart Scooter Gleason really was. To underestimate him was certainly a mistake. Then at times a babbling, almost insane personality easily presented itself, surfacing undiplomatically to diminish all the smarts previously displayed. Jack often thought Gleason was crazy. Or on drugs. Or both.

But crazy or not, Scooter was a popular guy. Jack had, years ago, arrested a federal fugitive in West Forge's Ramada Inn. The criminal from Indiana came to town for one night only to conduct business with a local organized auto theft ring. After his arrest, in the book-in room, the man offered up Scooter Gleason's phone number from memory to the jailor as his one book-in, phone call. Scooter then fumbled his "aw shucks" way into the station and bonded the stranger out. The fugitive jumped bond and the county had yet to punish the attorney for the forfeiture. How did this organized crime, out-of-stater know to call Scooter? From memory?

"Quite a little dope haul, isn't it?" said the attorney. "These guys, Jack, I tell ya, boy - very big. They never learn. Can a cowboy get a beer around this city?" He looked over the crowded room like he was looking for a waitress.

"I'm leavin' real soon," Jack said.

"Well Jack, maybe we'll raise a few back home. Catch up a little," suggested Scooter with his head tilted back and his jaw jutting out toward Jack's face inches away. Part of Scooter's act was to be a space-crowder. Get right up close in your face.

"Hmmm," replied Jack, as Gleason sauntered back to the defense table, cracking a stale joke to the bailiff.

"Scooter Gleason," whispered Weaver watching him walk off.

"Bozo the Clown," Jack added.

******

Jack strolled out into the fresh, cool afternoon, sucked in some of the air the Pine County seat offered, and cleared some of the hostility in his chest. He spied a new gold Mercedes with a personalized license plate "Scooter" sitting in a parking space marked "handicapped only." Jack shook his head and bounded down the steps past the car. In amongst the cardboard boxes of forms, the loose stacks of papers and books, Jack noticed a ball cap on the dash. It read, "Lawyers make better lovers." and on it a cartoon of a man and a woman horizontal with the usual lines suggesting motion about their bottom halves.

"Scooter is a real class act," Jack muttered to himself.

******

Rain again. It blurred the dark interstate highway. Weaver slept sound, snoring in unison with the Caddy's windshield wipers. If at all possible, they would return to Pine County for the funerals of the two deputies.

The monster runs loose. It commits everything hideous it can think of doing. It breaks fingers one by one. It beats, it marauds it kills over much more than weed and greed. It's hooked up to the entire nation, breeding on every single thing, in every single crack that is wrong with our system of justice. It sells drugs to our children that strip them of their personalities, turns some into prostitutes. It feeds burglars and robbers with drugs and fences and money. It controls jobs and contracts and destinies. It controls politicians and corrupts police officers. It vomits out insignificant things like Diller Bailey - deputies - Timmes. It is everywhere, like the rain.

Jack felt suffocated and lowered the power window a crack. Howling, whistling wind blew in. Tanseed and Pontecorvo were just hydra-heads, a small-town outlet, a branch office, easily replaced, and Jack could do only so much, handicapped by a vanished witness and an obvious traitor in his department. Jack would still throw his best punch.

Things were not always this bad. The fresh air and early morning sun at the marijuana farm made him think of his family farm in Yoakum. Warm days when he and his brother Robert would jump from their homemade bunk beds and run to the kitchen for breakfast. He could almost smell his mother's biscuits and gravy. See a blurry vision of her face. Blurry was good enough. He could see the sleeves of her dress folded up past her wrists. And he remembered the exact smell of his Dad's pipe.

"Where the hell did all that go to?" he said to himself.

He did not feel like himself lately. Couldn't concentrate. He suddenly thought of a Sunday morning in the Austin Hyatt Hotel some 15 years ago with that same blurry sun beaming in through a crack in the heavy curtains. He lay in bed with Sheel, on one of her business trips. Sheel's face was blurry too and blurry would have to do. He felt happy then. It seemed like he hadn't smiled in years, not since he was a dumb kid on a farm, or since he was dumb enough to stay with a married woman. "Dumb." he grunted out loud to no one. Weaver slept right through it.

"Something must be wrong with me," he thought to himself. What is it? All these people shot? Must be it. Has to be it. But really he knew that was only part of it. Only cold rain streamed in through this thin crack in his world and the pressures blowing on his eyes turned into sharp pain. That pain for all the things he knew, the living and the dead, and the near dead and the missing. And the death that was sure to come.

"Harris County attorney, Scott 'Scooter' Gleason arrived this morning in Judge Samuel S. Grant's court representing Donny Mecher who is charged with the manufacture and possession of illegal drugs.

Gleason made only this comment to reporters. 'Well, boys, and ma'am, it is more than obvious that my client, Mr. Mecher, is an innocent victim of overzealous police work. Police who act like soldiers in Vietnam or some such place. He happened to be visiting that farm that morning when these, these here shock troops dropped from the sky and everywhere else just a killin' and a maimin' as they went. This is a disgusting display of police brutality and unlawful arrest. Really just a butchering party. I'm positive every officer involved will be indicted shortly.'" - Milters Cove Daily

CHAPTER SEVEN:
GONE DILLER GONE

"When Kellog got back from Pine County that morning, he came to see me first thing. I told his captain to assign the Timmes' shooting to him. I asked Jack if he wanted a partner, or a team even. He told me Ranger Weaver Wisdom would help him, but he didn't want any other help. You know at the time, we thought we had us a damn snitch in the department. We didn't know who. But it was a possibility. Jack Kellog was...you know... tenacious. I mean he wasn't a genius or anything. No Sherlock Holmes. But the boy was tenacious. I felt comfortable assigning him any case back in those years. He'd pull it through for us. Then, years later? Well, all that's history now. Times change. But we had us a snitch. We had an officer shot and damn near killed. We had a key underworld informant missing. We had the New York Mafia setting up shop in our city. I mean to tell ya, there was knives being sharpened everywhere." - West Forge Police Chief "Shrewdy" Collins (ret.) Galveston, TX 2004

Archie Lennox interview tape 49

And the note from Timmes read,

"Jumping Jack, I questioned every resident on the block and one person saw the Fredrick's mugging. They all felt like the suspect was a local resident. One witness, John Willis, saw the suspect again at the neighborhood Kroger in the checkout line. He's certain it's the mugger. Willis got the suspect's car license plate from the parking lot, BCF-802, which comes back to a Roger Pommett.

Pommett has a record for theft, is on probation currently under charges of theft of lawn furniture and shoplifting household items. Pommett's apartment manager thinks Pommett is setting up his apartment with stolen merchandise. A small pine tree sits right now in the sunlight in his front window. Bet that's our boy. Attached you'll find a statement from John Willis and one from me about seeing the plant. Sorry I can't do more, but I'm going on special assignment to bodyguard your "boy.""

Kellog found the note stapled atop a stack of reports and statements Timmes had collected the very morning he was later shot. Jack spotted the note first thing on his desk when he walked in.

Right beside it he found a copy of a West Forge PD offense report with R. Timmes' name on it too, this time in the victim's block. The charge block read, "Attempted Capital Murder (Police Officer)." But for the crack EMT crew and East Duchess Surgeons, the charge might well have had the "ATTEMPTED" dropped.

Jack flopped into his wooden swivel chair as Breasley filled him in on all the local happenings. Breasley carried the full workload until Jack shook free of the "Western

World" investigation, which now included the shooting of Officer Roy Timmes.

Breasley dashed out for a courtroom appearance, leaving a solemn Kellog to analyze the casework on Timmes' shooting. Jack's mind wandered to the leak. Who in hell was the leak, the mole, the snitch that tipped off Diller's location? He thumbed ahead to the overtime guard duty list. Twelve men had rotated turns watching Diller. Twelve officers with wives or girlfriends, families, friends and other overtime jobs. A city secretary typed the overtime work list and who knows how many other people processed the overtime pay slips. The building crawled with janitors in the evenings, some of them more than nosy.

Through the years, small change, stamps, and pens had disappeared from his desk and others. Through the years, janitors had asked him for favors for friends and relatives locked up for countless reasons. What loose tongue led to a bullet in Roy Timmes' back? Would Diller's body float up somewhere in the Gulf? Would they unearth his remains 10 years from now? Picking up and questioning Tenpenny and Handell without indictable evidence would prove worthless at this point. Somebody the likes of Scooter Gleason would bond them out in a New York minute. Damn.

They could polygraph. At least starting with the 11 surviving officers on down. Department policy required officers to take the test, but what about civilian personnel? Weaver could arrange for a state poly examiner to do the testing.

******

Jack coasted into the jewelry store parking lot and killed his Caddy lights as four empty beer cans rolled to the front passenger floorboard. It was 2 a.m. Depressed, Jack had thrown on his jeans, a blue sweater and windbreaker, boots, and a .45 and took to the streets. His two car radios, the FM and the police scanner, quietly spoke.

He stared across the avenue at Western World from the jewelry store lot. Western World, a huge, modern, sprawling store on a parking lot the size of a football field. Western World's windows displayed a high-class western fashion look, as well as huge windows of camping gear and horse accessories. The main window contained a stuffed golden Palomino horse, a regular Tanseed trademark. Jack sipped his beer as Merle Haggard's voice filled the Cadillac. He pulled binoculars from the glove box and studied the magnified layout.

Through the lenses, his gaze followed the asphalt road up the gradual hill to the massive, three-story mansion near the top, where he could see lights and movements from within.

"A bug, a bug, a bug," Jack mumbled. What a precious thing a microphone would be in that house. Years ago Jack would have planted one, warrant or no warrant, but he'd been tempered by the times, even paranoid about some of his own "legal" decisions. No such rules tempered Pontecorvo and Tanseed. Nothing. Weaver had already filed papers in court for electronic surveillance and phone wiretaps. Surely enough probable cause existed since the Pine County drug raid and the motel incident.

An array of foreign cars, glistening pickups, and a horse trailer adorned the circular brick drive. Beyond the expensive iron fencing, cattle grazed by day. Jack caught some movement and light from the modern stables, three-quarters of a mile east of the house. He sighed and put the binoculars down. He was as far away from the words and actions in that house as he was from filing a case on any of them without Diller Bailey.

They were as...

"Jack, Jack, are you all right?" came a voice from Jack's left.

"Yeah, aaah...Willie...I guess I fell asleep..." Jack said to the patrol sergeant at his window. Blinking his eyes, he checked the clock on his dash. It was 3:15 a.m. He had been asleep for almost an hour, passed out in the middle of a thought.

"We got a call about a suspicious car on the jewelry store lot," the sergeant continued. Jack eyed the squad car some 15 feet away. It had pulled up, and he'd never heard it.

"I'm sorry, Willie. It was just me. Sorry." Jack started up his car.

"See ya, Jack, get some sleep." Willie stood back from the car, and Jack pulled away.

The sergeant walked back to his squad car and looked at his rookie.

"That is Detective Sergeant Jumpin' Jack Kellog," Sgt. Willie Willacker told his trainee, Dale Cunningham, after he climbed into the squad car. "He was sitting out here on a stakeout or somethin' and fell asleep. Remember, when you see that white Caddy out, it's Jack and more 'n likely he's a workin'. He's the one that shot those two dudes that broke in his house a month ago."

The rookie acknowledged with a nod of his head.

Willie pulled out on the avenue and followed behind Jack at a great distance. "Jumpin' Jack never shuts down," he continued. "He works by day, works by night. He drinks some. But if the drink has affected his work any, it's affected it to the better. I think maybe he's had a few tonight," Willie said, watching Jack's taillights.

"You mean he's driving while intoxicated?" questioned Cunningham while zeroing in on Jack's unswerving, steady car.

"Maybe," said Willie. "Let's make sure he makes it home. Listen, let me tell you something right now. Jack will back up the patrol units at night if he's out and got the chance. If you're in a bar fight gettin' your ass whipped, or some punk is shootin' at ya? There ain't nobody in the world, none you'd rather see coming - than that man right there - coming through the door. He is the right stuff."

They followed Jack until they could see he turned safely up his driveway.

Jack unlocked his back door and reset the new alarm system. He guzzled the last of his Miller Lite and shook off that paranoid feeling he'd had of late since he was attacked in his house. That Lincoln wasn't even parked down the street tonight. The Continental's absence meant he was even less of a threat to Tanseed and Pontecorvo. Why should they care about him now? Without Diller, there would be no more raids, no more arrests. He collapsed on his living room couch, dreaming quickly that he was on a cruise ship with Diller. It was a ship lost at sea.

******

"I'm Sgt. Kellog, ma'am, with the West Forge Police Department."

"Ow, ah, yes?" said Mrs. Fredrick.

"I wanted to stop by and let you know, ma'am -that we are building a case on the man that did this to you," Jack said.

"Please do sit down, Sergeant," Mrs. Fredrick said in such a sociable manner that Kellog knew it could make for a long visit.

"No, I just can't," Jack refused. Mrs. Fredrick propped herself up with a hospital pillow.

"Why me? Why did this young fellow do this to me? Why? You know, my hip needs an operation now, and my doctor doesn't think-well, my age and all-that I should have one."

"Yes," said Jack amiably. They talked for several moments, and he answered the routine questions with memorized answers, all the while thinking of Roy Timmes upstairs in the intensive care unit.

Finally, he left for ICU. The unit was always a pathetic sight for Jack, as well as a bad memory. His father had died in one in Houston eight years earlier; his mother, one in Yoakum. Everyone in the unit felt desperate, on edge and uncomfortable, even the workers.

Jack approached Timmes' room. A multitude of wires and hoses held the officer captive. Periodically, Timmes regained a delirious kind of consciousness, then passed out again. The doctors told Jack this was a good sign, but then, so was a beating heart at this stage of the game.

Jack stared through the glass window and into the room where Timmes lay and his wife sat beside the bed, holding the all-hours frightened vigil of a true loved-one. Jack's silhouette caught the corner of her eye and she regretfully rose and left the room, feeling obligated to greet all well-wishers as though it were her assigned duty.

"Hello," she said quietly to this new well-wisher.

"Hello," he replied. They both stared at Roy. Though strangers, the disturbed woman mumbled a troubling thought.

"Every day they deliver flowers to this room. At first, I thought they were from people that cared. Regular folks or maybe the police department. But you know what? They aren't. They're not," she said almost into her own reflection in the glass an inch away.

Kellog eyed the many roses in the room. She continued, "What I think is? Whoever did this to Roy is sending these flowers to him. Why? Why?" she began to cry softly.

"I don't know," said Jack. He realized it was a bad time for him to come, but then, when is it a good time to visit the wife of an officer in ICU?

"What do you know, detective? What did Roy know? What do any of you know?" she chanted harshly.

Kellog remained quiet and turned away from her tears. No pat, memorized answers came to him this time.

"He was stupid. STUPID to do the STUPID job in this STUPID world." she growled and, with her initial attempt at being sociable gone, she shook her head and resumed her place back in the room beside her husband. It was the same message from Sheel years ago. Stupid to do a job where you got shot at. Stupid to carry a gun.

"I understand," he said.

"I'm sorry, who are you?"

"I'm Jack. Jack Kellog. A detective at the PD."

"Oh, okay. I…I haven't heard of you."

"That's good to hear."

Jack fondled some of the "get well" florist cards, noting the initials "T.T." on almost all the sets of flowers.

"These roses." said Jack softly holding up a card, "they mean that they are sorry for you and that what has happened was nothing personal. It was business. Soon you might even receive money."

"Business? Money? Why, why, why?" she kept whispering to no one in particular.

Jack stepped from the room, keeping one grieving card signed "T.T." No doubt from Tony Tetro, the one-time "cop's cop" from the great city of New York.

******

Cold, gray and misting. A cold front had blown in a northern, dropping the temperature some 25 degrees. Jack turned up the long driveway to the Tanseed/Pontecorvo house past the Western World store. To Jack, investigation had several formulas and one such equation read, when all else fails, when all leads burn up, go and rattle the cage of the suspect. He and Weaver had planned such an expedition on this blustery day.

They parked amongst the Western World fleet, stepped out into the wet cold and mounted the huge front balcony porch.

An attractive Mexican woman in her 40s answered the doorbell.

"Jack Kellog, West Forge PD, ma'am, and Weaver Wisdom, Texas Ranger. We'd like to see…well, a number of folks here will do," said Kellog.

"Yes," she nodded perfunctorily and shut the door. Jack and Weaver exchanged glances when the large carved door flung open again. Johnny Handell stood there grinning in a V-neck sweater, jeans, and boots. He chuckled then leaned against the doorframe.

"Collecting for the newspaper, boys?" Handell asked. Jack's lip curled. Weaver never had taken to being called boy. "Or are you just here to collect other kinds of money?"

"We're here to talk to you, Ira Tenpenny, and Pontecorvo," Jack said.

"Well, then, come on in, just wipe the cow shit off yer boots, boys. Carpet here's worth more than the two of ya," Handell remarked as he strutted away.

Weaver grumbled, "Ten years ago, they'd be wiping him off my boots."

They followed Handell through the western-styled mansion. The back of the place was U-shaped with the surrounding backyard containing a Spanish-styled garden, patio, and an Olympic-sized pool that rippled under the wind and rain. The three filed into a huge, expensive den that offered this same back-window view, to include one Raymond Pontecorvo at a desk and one Tony Tetro on a leather couch reading the sports page through bifocals. Both were casually dressed.

"Well," said Pontecorvo with his head bobbing up and down.

"I need to speak to you, Handell here, and Ira Tenpenny," said Jack.

"Oh, this is PO-lice business," said Pontecorvo, mimicking the southern pronunciation. "Only lawyers speak to the PO-lice, Sgt. Kellog."

Jack gave him a long stare and sighed. He snapped his head over to look in Handell's direction.

"Where were you on the 4th of October. Nighttime?"

Tetro hummed a few bars of the Dragnet theme, never looking up from the newspaper.

"Fuckin' yer Mama," Handell said indignantly with his eyes wide open and a smirk on his face.

Jack smiled, then chuckled. "Where's Ira?" he asked.

"Don't know," Pontecorvo said.

"Don't know?" repeated Jack while running his hand over his face. He grunted another short, deep breath and walked up to Pontecorvo's desk, sitting on the corner. His leg purposely shoved things out of place by at least eight inches. Ponty's eyes flashed to Tetro.

"On 4 October, a PO-lice officer was shot - may die. That officer was with Diller Bailey and we ALL know Diller. We ALL know where it happened, fact is, we all know WHO'S responsible," snarled Kellog to Pontecorvo.

"Oh, oh. Lemme throws these fuck-ups out," groaned Handell.

"You touch me once boy," barked Weaver, "and I'll handcuff your neck to an express train to Huntsville."

That unique sort of remark took Handell completely by surprise. His shock registered clearly in his expression. Handell knew Huntsville was the location for the Texas Penitentiary, but...

"This is Texas Ranger Weaver Wisdom," introduced Kellog.

"All my men, da men yous guys want ta tawk to were all playin' poker with me that night-yeah, yeah-five card, cowboy stud. Ya know nosin' around my business is fuckin' suicide, Kellog. Fuckin' with my dogs, fuckin' up my east Texas deal is TROUBLE." Pontecorvo was still pretty frisky with Kellog looming over him.

"Trouble. Trouble is...," Jack interrupted between gritted teeth, "...poking around my city, shootin' my officers." Jack violently swept the desk clean and the blotter, clock, pens, etc. flipped through the air and crashed to the floor. Handell and Tetro wanted in, but the monstrous presence of an agitated Weaver Wisdom held them at bay. They both still had a giant nightmare vision of the 6'5" Huntsville Express in action.

"Trouble is..." Jack continued, "...you don't know who YOU are dealin' with here." He reached across the desk with both hands and snatched Pontecorvo by the head hair and shirt, then actually yanked him up from his seat. Jack almost lost his self-control.

"Trouble is...ME, mister. I ain't one of yer Yankee mongrel cops. You had a man shot...may've killed another. Who the hell knows what else? Fact is I'm just a goddamn hair away from blowing yer fucking brains out all over this veranda." Jack flung him back into his chair as if he were a leper. The chair rolled three feet until it hit a throw rug and almost flipped backward. Pontecorvo struggled to regain his balance, looking truly astonished. He tried to make a remark but could only stutter.

"My lawyer..."

"Fact is I'm about to throw the law book in the trash can and come after you and these pieces of shit you got here in an O.K. Corral you ain't seen the likes of yet," growled Jack.

Over his bifocals, newspaper in his lap, and steadfast to his seat, Tetro watched Jack and Weaver strut out of the den. His eyebrows were up and he was almost smiling. No one followed the lawmen.

"Senora," Jack beckoned to the lady who first responded to the door. "Have you seen this man?" He offered her a mug shot of Diller. She shook her head rapidly with great fear in her eyes.

"Thank you," Jack said solemnly as she shut the door behind them.

Tanseed and Tenpenny emerged from another room and as Tenpenny watched them drive down the road past the store, Tanseed rushed into the study.

"What? What?" Tanseed quizzed Pontecorvo, perplexed to find him stroking his hair and repositioning his shirt. He screamed tirades at Tetro while Tetro returned things to their place on the desk.

"I pay you - RIGHT. I pay you to fucking sit there while that son of a bitchin' bastard pulls the goddamn hair out of my goddamn chest? Right? Right?"

"Easy, Ponty, easy," said Tetro calmly. He hid a smile, "Jeez, da black bastard had two big fuckin' .45's on his cowboy belt and he was breathing fire down our necks."

"I guess they don't have Diller either." said Handell.

"Could be a bluff," said Tetro. "Kellog's pretty smart. Dis coulda' been for show." Tetro said.

"Shit T, did ja' see his face? NAAA. NO SHOW. They don't have the little scumbag because if dey did, we'd be all out on bond right now already. Dey got nothin', nothing but to fuck with us," said Ponty.

"If Diller got away, he would run, maybe never come back," said Tanseed sternly, quite familiar with his old running "podna."

"Get me Scooter Gleason on the phone." barked Ponty to Tetro.

"I've a ...I've a seen guys like dis Kellog before," Tetro said. "Too gung-ho. Ya know, I worked Narcotics with Serpico years ago. Kellog's crazy like dat kind of guy. Crazy," Tetro added while dialing Scooter's number.

"Snuff 'em." said Handell.

"Na, na, naaa. Always hold off killin' a cop, always," Pontecorvo said. "Look at da heat now with di Timms thing." He glared at Johnny Handell. "Too much trouble. Naaa. We'll call our man tomorrow, right Tony? Call our man at the PD to see if they really have Diller or not."

Tetro nodded.

"You mutha fuckas have shot a cop already and look at the heat. LOOK AT THE HEAT you brought down on me and he ain't even dead yet." He repositioned his shirt again as if the heat was still present on him. "And ya still let da little scumbag Diller get away."

"We need to follow Kellog," said Tanseed, even though he had already secretly ordered the tail weeks earlier despite Ponty's "hands off the cops" decree. Pontecorvo always felt that police officers were better seduced than reduced. Tanseed thought they were better off shot in the head.

"Gleason," bellowed Ponty into the phone, "Kellog was just here. Right here in my house. He grabbed me, roughed me up. I wanna' press charges against him. File a citizen's complaint." He clicked on the intercom for the room to hear a calm, soothing, almost musical, country voice.

"Ponty. I know the police chief here, Shrewdy Collins, from years ago when I worked in the DA's office. Shrewdy would do nuthin' but laugh at any such complaint you might file on Jumpin' Jack."

"File it." shouted Ponty. "He is still responsible to da people. I'm da people. He is still responsible to rules."

"We'll try, but..." said Scooter, as Ponty interrupted him by slamming the phone down. He knew Gleason was right. Back home if some dumb cop even looked at him funny, he opened up his list of Lieutenants and Captains and Aldermen and would request, even order retribution. But here, these traditional, perpetual connections were just not available. Not yet.

"If there's one ting we need, one ting we need da cops ta play, is by the fucking rules so we can figure out what dere gonna do next, and how," he said waving his finger at Baker Tanseed.

It just killed Tanseed to be the object of that finger. He would sooner bite it off.

"Do you hear that, Ira Tenpenny?" Ponty yelled to the adjoining rooms, "You do not shoot da' cops. Mustn't blow them away. Cops go crazy when dat happens. You ain't seen heat like dat. Look at da heat."

Pontecorvo was still carrying a grudge against the "unauthorized" shooting of Roy Timmes, something unnecessarily done by Tenpenny and Handell while trying to kidnap Diller Bailey from the police.

Fact was, Ponty wasn't even aware of the mission until well after the shooting. Baker Tanseed had overheard the tip-off on Diller's location before Tetro told Pontecorvo. Tanseed acted reflexively by ordering the motel room assault. Ponty and Tetro would have done things differently. To make things worse, Diller was not to be found in the room after they shot Timmes.

"Put some men on dis Shrewdy Collins tomorrow," he told Tetro, "I want his life story, as thick as a Britannica, on my desk in a week."

Tony continued resetting Ponty's desk clock. He nodded his head.

"Ya know," said Tetro, "I put da' word out all over the country, coast ta' coast that Diller Bailey has a price on his head, I told some boys in Mexico and Canada too."

Tenpenny entered the room, and he and Tanseed exchanged glances, with Tenpenny receiving some kind of secret message. Then he left again.

"Never believed dat story," Tetro mumbled.

"What story?" asked Handell.

"That after the Knapp Commission, Serpico left for Switzerland. It was just a cover story, a trick. I tell ya, Ponty, we might oughta take dis Kellog out right now." Tetro concluded.

"Be happy to oblige," chimed in Handell.

"From now on, you will be happy to oblige to do what I tell you to do. ME." said Ponty. He glared maliciously at Tanseed.

Baker Tanseed stood and left the den, marched upstairs into his suite of rooms whereupon he shoved his wife aside and punched a huge hole in a bedroom wall.

******

"Didn't accomplish a damn thing but blow off some steam. Just hot air," said Jack, turning onto the boulevard.

"Oh, I don't know." said Weaver, "No one's probably touched Pontecorvo like that since he was 10 years old. You still have some of the greasy bastard's hair stuck to your fingers. We know one thing for sure now."

"What's that?"

"He don't wear no wig. We rattled his cage." said the Huntsville Express with a smile.

CHAPTER EIGHT
TIME WILL NEVER MEND CARELESS WHISPERS

"Harris County Crime stoppers is offering a $1,000 Cash Reward for information leading to an arrest and indictment in the following police investigations. In the last three months Harris County law officers investigated a professional truck-hijacking ring operating in the area. Armed and masked bandits forced truckers off the road or kidnapped truckers during their break, stealing entire shipments of items like stereos, TV's, kitchen appliances, VCR's, and clothing. Co-operating truckers were released unharmed, though one driver was critically wounded when he resisted. If you have information on these or any other crimes, call Crime Stoppers at HOT-TIPS. All calls are confidential." - HOUSTON CHRONICLE

"Houston PTA officials declared an emergency meeting Tuesday night to discuss plans to combat a recent rash of drug use by grammar, junior high and high school students. The rash became evident after marijuana laced with a dangerous animal tranquilizer caused the hospitalization of at least 20 *students. This same substance has also been found in recent cases of amphetamine induced seizures according to the Houston Police Authorities." -HOUSTON CHRONICLE*

Sec.5. Control of Intercepting Devices.

(a) Only the Department of Public Safety is authorized by this article to own, possess, install, operate, or monitor an electronic, mechanical, or other devices. The Department of Public Safety may be assisted by an investigative or law enforcement officer in the operation and monitoring of an interception of wire or oral communications, provided that a commissioned officer of the Department of Public Safety is present at all times.

(b) The director shall designate in writing the commissioned officers of the Department of Public Safety who are responsible for the possession, installation, operation, and monitoring of electronic, mechanical, or other devices for the department.

Sec .6. Request for application for interception.

(a) The director may, based on written affidavits, request in writing that a prosecutor apply for an order authorizing interception of wire or oral communications.

(b) The head of a local law enforcement agency or, if the head of the local law enforcement agency is absent or unable to serve, the acting head of the local law enforcement agency may, based on written affidavits, request in writing that a prosecutor apply for an order authorizing interception of wire or oral communications. Prior to the requesting of an application under this subsection, the head of a local law enforcement agency must submit the request and supporting affidavits to the director, who shall make a finding in writing whether the request and supporting affidavits establish that other investigative procedures have been tried and failed or they reasonably appear unlikely to succeed or to be too dangerous if tried, if feasible, is justifiable, and whether the Department of Public Safety has the necessary resources available. The prosecutor may file the application only after a written Positive finding on all the above requirements by the director.

> - CHAPTER 18, TEXAS CODE OF
> CRIMINAL PROCEDURE. 1985

"This is Buster Simmons and Ralph Liggensworth. Boys, this is Jack Kellog," introduced Weaver. All four crowded around the nightclub table. Buster and Ralph were electronic specialists employed with the state, traveling in a four-county area setting up electronic surveillance and bugging devices per court orders.

"The state narcotics division has rented an empty office in the shopping center across from Western World. That's where Buster and Ralph will do all their monitoring," Weaver advised Jack.

"The Court has authorized us to record all the phone lines to the mansion and the store plus, from that vantage point, we can use zoom lenses to photo all the cumin's and goin's at the mansion. We'll have mug shots of every swinging dick that goes in and outta there," said Buster.

The men were quiet while a waitress came and took their order.

"What about the cars?" Jack questioned.

"Nix on the cars. The judge wouldn't include bugging the cars, and anyway, there would be a range of problems with the equipment we have. If it weren't for the Pine County drug haul you scored, we would never have gotten these taps," said Buster.

"Despite all the probable cause y'all got together, the judge will only allow this much. I think the disappearance of the informant weighed heavily with his decision. A lot of probable cause went down the commode when Bailey disappeared," Liggensworth added.

Jack tipped back and stared at Weaver's sturdy, intense profile. For the first time he seriously wondered, just wondered about the corruptibility of a local judge. He knew some were inept. Some were about half-crazy. But on the take?

"State narcotics agents will be coming in to cover the post on weekends and some nights when Buster and I are off. This is gonna kick the state's overtime budget in the ass," said Liggensworth "The feds just won't commit yet."

"Yeah." said Buster while lifting his coffee. "We're eight-to-fivers."

"Eight to five." quipped Jack, "What in hell's that?"

CHAPTER NINE:
WHAT HAPPENS IN VEGAS SOMETIMES GETS HACKED UP
AND BURIED IN A SHALLOW GRAVE OUTSIDE VEGAS

"I'll tell you what now. We always had some kind of shit going down in Sin City. But I was never more glad to see that cowboy Jack Kellog and that speed freak Ding-Dong Bailey leave Las Vegas. They turned our place into a Quentin Tarentino movie with body parts, shoot-outs and corpses." - Homicide Detective Gregory Catelli Las Vegas Metro (ret.) Henderson, NV – 2004

Archie Lennox interview tape 60

"Where in hell are you?" Kellog pleaded into his office phone.

"Vegas. Las Vegas," said Diller Bailey, "and hey I'm scared, man. Where have you been? I call prob'ly five times a day - yer out - yer out - yer out. I ain't leavin' my name with nobody. I trust you, Kellog. You. These otha mutha fuckas gonna get me killed."

"Wait. I don't want to talk on this phone. Where are you right now? A pay phone I hope? Er what?" asked Jack.

"I'm in a Casino. Yeah, a pay phone," Diller returned.

Jack collected Diller's number and darted through the department, out the lobby, and across the street to Pickle's Cafe, neglecting his blazer jacket and displaying the badge and .45 on his beltline, but Jack was just too well known in the neighborhood to cause a stir about an armed man running on the street. Al Pickle let him use the phone in the cafe office without hesitation. Jack called Diller.

"What happened?" asked Jack, "how did you get away?"

"I left the motel room, right? Before the shooting. Just fer five at the pool, taking in the night. That laws ya know, what's his name?"

"Roy Timmes."

"Yeah, is he dead?"

"Not yet," said Jack.

"Well the laws let me sit out by the pool every night. Timmes was sittin' on the bed in the room with the door opened a crack to spy me. I could see into the room from the far side of the pool, sittin' in the dark. The lawsman was watchin' L.A. Law on TV. Then, I seen the van pull up and Handell and Tenpenny jumped out carrying artillery. They runs straight, I mean straight, to our room, shoved the door and opened fire. The laws didn't stand a chance. Like I got outta there. Over a fence. They never saw me at the pool. They never saw me leave. They split. I split. I crept back and got the rest of my money, the money you gave me and well, you know, I got into the law's wallet and got what he had, too. I split. I shagged me a ride to Vegas. I've been knowing me a little Keno girl named Felicia in the MGM here and..."

"Alright, Diller, say no more. I'll be there. Will you be safe?" asked Jack.

"Yeah, I guess," said Diller slowly.

"You ever go to Vegas much?" asked Jack reluctantly, afraid of the answer.

"Yeah, Tanseed and I have a lot."

"Diller, going to Vegas was not too bright," Jack said understatedly.

"Busy place. I'm just one face," sang back Diller.

"Yeah, the place is just crawling with fuzzy- headed, Fu Manchus with earrings in their ears and a cast on their hand. Yer lost in the crowd. Whatever you've been doing? Quit it. Wherever you've been going? Don't go there. Felicia? Don't see her. Call me at LVPD detective bureau on Thursday morning at 10 a.m. We'll meet. I'll get you to a safe place," said Jack.

"Where?" Diller asked.

"With the monkeys and zebras."

Jack hung up Pickle's office phone and sat calmly. This time no one would know where Diller was bound. As he walked through the restaurant, he slid money across the old Formica counter to the elderly man clad in starched white.

"Long distance call, Pick. Two-dollar call, five-dollar bill."

"Take care Jacky," Pick said as he slipped the fiver in his pocket.

Diller hung up the Bally's Hotel lobby phone and clapped his hands together. Ever since the night Ira Tenpenny and Johnny Handell opened fire on officer Roy Timmes, Sgt. Jumpin' Jack Kellog's stock had gone up dramatically in Diller's eyes. He started across the chaotic casino toward the coffee shop. Through Jack, he could transform into a new person, hidden away from the Tenpenny's and Handell's. A new escape, a fresh score? Money would be involved. How much? All details to be worked out through Jack.

He shuffled past the coffee shop hostess and sat at an empty table.

"D'ja get through?" A small, thin Keno girl asked him.

"Yeah. Yeah-finally. Tomorrow I'll know somethin,' Felicia." He smiled. She smiled. He knew Kellog wouldn't be smiling if the detective knew he'd ignored his advice and continued staying with Felicia. But it was Vegas.

"Yo. Over here," shouted a man while stuffing his face and filling out a Keno sheet. There ought to be a Vegas law against thin women with boney legs like Felicia's wearing those showgirl-style, derriere-revealing outfits. Still, Diller, with his varied taste, stared after her lustfully. Wistfully.

"Gotta go, babe," she said over her shoulder, continuing her route through the breakfast crowd collecting Keno sheets before the next game.

People kept getting in Kelly "Piggy" Banks way as he strained to see around the waistlines and beltlines of circulating slot machine players. Though Piggy was disgustingly obese, his arms were as strong as a professional boxer's from 20 years of hauling his heavy, paralyzed-below-the-waist body around in a wheelchair. Pulling the arm of a slot was his only other exercise. "Piggy" abandoned his one-dollar machine and rolled clear of the immediate crowd to stare into the coffee shop. AHA! It was Diller Bailey sitting right there. It was. And through Diller, Piggy's stock went up dramatically. Banks' new score. Word on the floors was Diller had a price on his burr head. How much? When? Details to be worked out with one Al Tanno, a friendly neighborhood freelance hood.

******

Luella rested a hand on Jack's shoulder as she leaned over to set a cup of coffee on the table. She left to wake up her sleeping giant Weaver. Once again, Weaver'd worked all night on another case. Jack eased back into the kitchen chair. Weaver soon emerged from the hallway and sat with Jack.

"Weave, Diller is alive and well in Las Vegas." Jack

detailed his phone conversation. "That Lincoln is back, slow-trailing me again. I just lost 'em before I got over here tonight, but I can't chance them follerin' me when I leave for Vegas tomorrow. I need 'em taken down. I need you to run interference fer me. Can you and a trooper meet me on the east side of the Preston Barnes Turnpike at 8 a.m. tomorrow? I'll be in my pickup."

"Can do."

******

"Here's the body bags, look, here dey are." said Al Tanno, shoving cardboard boxes aside to show his lifelong friend and partner, Victor Shafrin. The men were scrounging around in their mini warehouse on the east side of Las Vegas.

"I knew dey were here," he continued, as he yanked one out and handed it to Vic.

"I'm not driving all the way to Houston, Texas, with a body in the trunk, fa Chrissakes, Al." complained Vic. "Dats' old school. Too. Old. School. Come on. It's da fuckin 80s!"

But Al wasn't listening. Al hadn't listened to a word since his phone conversation with "Piggy" Banks two hours earlier. When he hung up, he'd turned to Vic. "Dat was Piggy. He was playin' the slots at Bally's. He saw Diller Bailey in the coffee shop, actin' up with a Keno girl named Felicia."

Vic could tell then and there that Al's adrenal was pumping that same old lunacy through him again.

Al Tanno and Vic Shafrin fled Chicago back in the '70s to escape angry wives, vindictive girlfriends, pissed-off cops and insane working accomplices. Al and Vic were once streetwise hoods with a string of successful wheels and deals. They had hijacked, stolen, burglarized, robbed, and even, occasionally, killed, but they were "unaffiliated" hoods, unprotected by larger gangs and families with political support and power. They hired-out. Freelance. This often left them out on a limb, often a scapegoat in the Shakespearian ploys of crime and criminals.

In 1974, there was trouble with the Bolichi brothers. Chicago business people paid them to fly to New York and collect loan shark money from a couple of brothers who'd borrowed cash to open three topless clubs in the Big Apple.

Unbeknownst to Al and Vic, however, these clever Bolichi brothers had quickly affiliated themselves with the Gallanti family as soon as their titty bars opened by offering all the Gallanti street hands free drinks, drugs and girls. Gallanti people partied there regularly, and they had even killed an informant in one of the club's back offices. The brothers became even tighter with this crowd by completely cooperating in the resulting cover up. In a world of favors, the brothers were in the Galant-plus column. Girls. Booze. Drugs. Murder.

Chi-Town Al and Vic showed up in New York doing their best "I am a crazed-mobster" routine on the brothers. The Bolichi's were scared to death of the routine at first, but one phone call to the nearby taxi stand brought instant remedy to this most uncivil suit. The taxi stand was the area headquarters for many of the neighborhood Gallanti wise guys. They responded, in taxis, and Al and Vic found themselves unable to collect, roughed up and spit out of the Big Apple, their reputations soiled, their careers stained enough that they semi-retired to Las Vegas. To be employed only when Al's adrenaline bursts pressured them into some kind of illegal scheme.

Vic remembered well the last time Al's glands had so activated. Two years earlier, a gambler from Dallas owed a medium-sized, Vegas Casino a very large sum of money. The casino asked Al either to collect it or cut something off of the gambler's body as a lesson. Seeing the fee and hoping for similar future contracts, Al prodded Vic into the trip to Dallas. They met the gambler, who readily admitted his inability to pay.

"I'm sorry guts. I'm sorry. I don't have it. I can't pay," the man said.

Facing death, the gambler knew something had to go, like the hand. They hacked off his left hand with a chain saw. At least he was right-handed. Fearing for his life and feeling lucky to still have it, the gambler paid a doctor to quietly treat this crude amputation. He never reported the incident to the Dallas Police. Al and Vic took the hand back to Vegas.

"This is his hand?" the casino asked looking at the Poloroid.

"Yeah."

"He still alive?"

"Yeah."

"He gonna be a problem?"

"No."

Simple, one might think. Not so. As fate would have it, a City of Dallas sanitation worker found the left hand in a dumpster. Dallas Homicide officers, fearing a "cut-up killer" might be loose, opened an investigation on the garbage can discovery, printed the fingers on the severed hand and found a match-up in the FBI files. Astounded, they located the gambler alive and well, except for the cast and bandages. Though the gambler refused to press charges, he did reveal the overall nature of the loss and the local Dallas papers carried the story in headlines, then the AP, embarrassing the casino businesses in general for such barbarism. Al and Vic were not mentioned as the man wanted to retain his other hand. But, the they never worked for any casinos again. They still hustled scams a plenty in Vegas, and they were certainly capable of doing what dirty deeds needed to be done.

"Are you listening to me, Al? Earth to Al? Earth to Al?" chanted Vic. Vic was 56 years old, though he looked 66. "I do not want to drive a body to Houston," he repeated in a steady rhythm. "In. A. Fucking. Bag."

"No, no," disagreed Al. "We're not gonna take the body, just da head."

"What? What's dis, a head?" barked Vic.

"A head."

"A fuckin' head."

"A head. We cut his fuck's head off, put it in dis bag, roll it up in a suitcase or somethin' and go. You know, an ice chest or somethin'. I don't know. I leave you in charge of the head department."

Vic stood there dumfounded. His jaw dropped as low as it could go. Then adjusted his lower dentures. "I need some Polygrip on the way home."

Al took the bag from Vic's hand and put it in the trunk of their Cadillac. Vic locked the door of their warehouse, a place where the warehouse office manager knew them as Peter and Ralph, traveling jewelry salesmen. Al really looked the part. He kept his black hair slicked back, his shirt never buttoned above the navel, a medallion always present in a mangle of wiry, grey, chest hair.

"I wanna look into Pontecorvo's face, Vic," said Al, "open the bag and let dis fuck's head roll out on his carpet." The fuck they referred to was Diller Bailey. Vic stared out the car window at the flat, bleached Nevada landscape. He thought back about "Ponty" Pontecorvo. The name Raymond "Ponty" Pontecorvo meant a lot to him and Al. A lot. In 1974, it was Ponty, a nephew in the Gallanti family, then just a "street lieutenant" at the taxi stand who'd thwarted their New York collection mission. It was Ponty who had sent them back to Chicago with their bruised tails between their respective bruised legs.

"Gonna set a price foyst?" asked Vic, finally condescending to the plan.

"Foyst? Foyst, I want in fuck. Then we'll call Ponty. We'll say, 'Dear Raymondo, do you by chance remember Al Tanno? Remember Victor Shafrin? Guess what Vic and I have?' I'm not gonna call till after we find in fuck. I wanna' make sure Piggy is right. We get 'em then we call."

"Mmm," hmmed Vic in agreement, pressing his false teeth together. 'Foyst, I need some Polygrip."

"We find Miss Keno girl, ya know, Foyst." said Al.

"Da Polygrip."

******

Morning. Jack opened his garage door at the back of his house to reveal the "War Wagon," his nickname for his 1975 Ford pickup truck. Through the years he had used it primarily for surveillance, and the large metal toolbox held more police equipment than it ever held tools. In the confines of the garage, Jack threw a suitcase and a duffel bag into the bed, climbed into the cab and drove down the driveway beside his house. He stopped to set the alarms. He saw three men in the Lincoln sitting way down the street. He ignored him and started off, en route to extract one Diller Bailey from Las Vegas, Nevada.

******

Al and Vic scanned the late morning casino crowd, looking for low-flying objects, i.e., Piggy Banks. They didn't wait long. Soon Piggy wheeled around the corner of a wall of slot machines and bumped into Vic's leg.

"Diller Bailey's a short, thin guy with black hair-a crew cut-one star earring, and he's got a Fu Manchu moustache and, hey, he's got a cast on one hand."

"Okay, okay Piggy, who's the Keno chick?"

"That's her. Right there. Felicia," said Piggy while pointing into the coffee shop.

"Dis woiks out Piggy," Al said, "and ya got a couple a grand ta loose in dese machines," Al told him. Piggy smiled broadly. Al and Vic were to be good payers.

Al and Vic took a few steps forward and converged together by a talking blackjack video machine that beckoned gamblers to try its odds. Their gazes remained fixed on the distant figure in the Keno outfit.

"Felicia, baby," Al mumbled into the smoky air.

******

"210? 210 this is 101," Kellog said into his CB radio mike.

"Go ahead 101," replied Weaver.

"I've entered the Turnpike authority now, passing through the booths. About 10 cars behind me you'll find subject vehicle, a black Lincoln."

"10-4," said Weaver, who rode as passenger in a marked state police sedan. Trooper Glenn Dalhart drove. Weaver saw Kellog drive by in his old pick up, then saw the Continental with three white males inside.

"That's the car," said Weaver, and Dalhart pulled in behind them, throwing on his red lights and flicking the siren. The Continental pulled over, and Dalhart and Weaver got out and approached the anxious men.

"Good afternoon, sir," said Dalhart, "May I see your driver's license?"

Weaver looked ahead as Jack's truck climbed the bridge incline and drove out of sight across the long snaky structure spanning the Temple River.

"Good luck, good buddy," Weaver whispered to himself as he stood looking into the Lincoln's passenger window.

"Sir, this car is not registered in your name. In case it's reported stolen, I must ask you to accompany me to the

Turnpike Administration Building just back near the toll booths where we'll confirm your authorized use of this car," said Dalhart with a smile, ignoring the cursing men inside.

"What da fuck?"

"This the fuck," Weaver Wisdom said.

******

When Tetro heard Kellog had left via the turnpike, and further that a DPS trooper and the "Huntsville Express" had detained their tailing Lincoln, the seasoned and clever ex-cop formulated a plan to locate the vanished detective. He called several state police agencies surrounding the state of Texas.

"Yes, I have a problem," said Tony Tetro pitiably to the Arizona State Police Dispatcher on his telephone, "I have an emergency message for a relative of mine, a Jack Kellog. He's driving through your state on business. A black 1975 Ford pickup, TX TB-1497. A close relative of his - a Chester Festus died." Tetro continued to lie to the police dispatcher, telling the same tale he had told state police in Oklahoma, Louisiana, New Mexico, Missouri, and Colorado, requesting what is called an "emergency message" BOLO (be on the lookout) to every station in their respective states. If a trooper saw Kellog's truck on their highways, it would then become the trooper's duty to contact Kellog about this emergency message.

"One udda ting," added the somber Tetro, "should ja men find 'em, please have them cawl me back ta let our family know that you notified Cousin Jack. My name is Tony Tonto."

"We'll do so, sir," said the dispatcher. "We'll add a request for a return call to you to the teletype."

"Yous people are simply wonderful. Tank you so much," finished Tetro. Even if Kellog could convince a trooper not to place this return call and tip off his location, Kellog would at least be psychologically harassed.

Pontecorve pursed his lips and nodded.

"Dis, dis right here, is why I pay you ta be my pally," he said.

******

Diller Bailey gulped down his last free casino drink and left The Shadows. He climbed into Felicia's Camaro and turned down Las Vegas Boulevard, delighted with the thought of receiving a nice large government "subsidy," a welfare check if you will, a reward for information simply in his head. Since the Camaro's radio didn't work, Diller began to happily sing a Led Zeppelin tune. He'd spend one more night with Felicia, then abscond to a safe place with the monkeys and zebras, wherever that was, and begin to get his own hustle together.

While Diller considered himself priceless, Raymond Pontecorvo thought he was worth about $75,000 - tops.

*****

The harsh pounding on the motel room door rattled the security chain and the dreams from Kellog's head. Jack rolled from the bed and cautiously peered out the window seeing first a New Mexico State Police sedan in the parking lot, next the stoic figure of a State Trooper at the door. Jack cracked open the door.

"Mr. Jack Kellog?" the trooper inquired.

"Yes,"

"Mr. Kellog, I have an emergency message for you from West Forge, Texas. A Mr. Tony Tonto requested our agency locate you by way of your vehicle. I spotted your truck on this lot."

"Hmm?"

"I have some bad news for you, sir," said the deadpan officer.

"What?"

"Mr. Tonto's message said a friend of yours, a Chester Festus, is close to death or possibly deceased back in Texas, sir."

The two men stared at each other.

"Chester. Festus." repeated Jack.

"Yes, sir."

Jack almost laughed despite his predicament, then said, "Tell me Trooper, will you routinely notify Mr. Tonto that you located me and delivered this, this emergency message?"

"Yes, sir. My dispatcher was in the process, when I reported in that I located your motor vehicle."

"So, Mr. Tonto will know his message was delivered to me, here? Here in Paraden, New Mexico?" asked Jack.

"Yes, sir," the trooper touted proudly.

"Hmm," hummed Jack. "Fine work, trooper, fine work."

"Thank you, sir. Ah, I'm sorry, sir," added the officer.

"Sorry?" quizzed Jack.

"About Mr. Festus," the trooper finished.

"Right, Chester, right," winced Kellog.

Jack shut the door and chuckled again. Only an ex-cop could have manufactured such a little coup and had police officers duped into doing his bidding. Only an ex-cop. But Paraden was far from Vegas. Really, Tetro only knew that Jack had turned west after the turnpike bridge.

******

What can you say about Vegas? It's flat and gaudy and it hasn't rained there in a million years. A year for each light bulb. A million people walked the streets. All from somewhere else. Kellog stopped about a million pedestrians trying to find the location of the police department. All tourists, none could help till he found a local who directed him five blocks this way, three blocks that, landing him in the visitor's parking lot.

Jack badged the duty officer, explaining only that he awaited an important call. He quickly found himself among brethren in blue who invited him back behind the desk for coffee and conversation. The station buzzed with activity. A land surveyor had recently discovered a freshly severed female torso. There were one million traffic accidents and a drunken brawl at a motel. At 11:39 a.m., the phone rang. A call for Jack? No, not Diller Bailey, but Buster Simmons, the State Police surveillance tech, back in West Forge, Texas, who was sitting in his makeshift headquarters in the shopping center across the street from Western World.

"We've been intercepting a lotta phone calls on our wiretap about you, Jack. Finally, we had to get Weaver to tell us where you were. Tetro called six state police agencies trying to trick them into running you down for him. New Mexico returned the favor telling Tetro Tonto Tony you'd received his bullshit message in Paraden."

"Yup," said Jack, curious whether this was Buster's only dispatch.

"Well, there's a helluva lot more," continued Buster. "Listen to this tape we recorded, and you may want to write part of it down. We recorded it only this morning."

After a pause and static:

"This is Al Tanno. Do you remember Al Tanno? Do you remember Victor Shafrin? New York? The titty bars?" Said the scratchy voice on the tape. Kellog still felt puzzled, then he recognized Pontecorvo's voice saying "Yeah."

"Guess who we are fucking looking at, big shot? Guess?"

"Don't know," Ponty said abruptly.

"I am looking at Diller Bailey. He's tied up in my living room chair." Returned this sarcastic voice.

"Ya need to cawl back," said Pontecorvo calmly.

"No fucking way."

"If you'se want a fuckin' deal," Ponty's voice escalated,

"ya hafta cawl back and ya give me a numba of a phone booth. I don't want any of dis on my phones or you'se phones. I don;t know nutten about nutten. Just call back with a numba." The tape ended.

Buster came back on Kellog's line.

"About five minutes later Jack, this Al Tanno called Ponty back and gave him a number. We got the number, but we thought we were through, that they would never call on the house phone. Then our window camera man shouts to us that Tony Tetro runs out the front door of the mansion, into a Jag, drives down the road and you'll never believe this, drives across the street, right into our shopping center here and pulls up to a pay phone two stores down from us. Ralph walked casually out to our van parked outside, got in and aimed our boom mike right at him, recording Tetro's half of his conversation with Al Tanno. We couldn't believe the luck. Here is as much as we could get from Tetro's half of the phone conversation."

"(static) yeah well, you guys are a pair of fuckups. We want dis ting done properly ya unnerstand properly? We will meet ya in Vegas - Ya will not take Diller anywhere. (static) Dat's right. We will call ya at dis numba you are at right now tomorrow morning at 9 a.m. Hey, hey, you ain't shootin' the guy. Dis ain't no hit. Ya ain't gettin a hit man salary. Yeah, $75,000 tops. Tomorrow. Nine o'clock. Be at this phone."

"Next thing he does at the pay phone, Jack, is book three airline tickets to Vegas for 6 p.m. tonight," Buster finished.

"Vegas. Al Tanno. Victor Shafrin. Diller Bailey tied up," mumbled Jack. "Shit." Depressed, he stared blankly at the ceiling.

"They's comin' atcha, bubba," said Buster.

After some quick plans with Buster, Jack hung up. Somehow Diller had landed himself in yet another bind.

Jack marched past a startled secretary and walked into the detective captain's office. A Gregory Catelli looked up from his reports, his face clearly showing he wondered who this gruff looking stranger in a leather blazer, starched white shirt, jeans, and boots might be.

"My name is Jack Kellog, Sergeant, from the West Forge, Texas PD. I need some good help, fast."

******

Kellog and Captain Catelli, along with Detectives Rick Can and Fred Tolier had a 30-minute think tank session in the division commander's office. Can and Tolier were summoned in from the torso crime scene. Six other investigators organized a ground search of the area. Their presence in the office, armed with the latest info from the murder scene, also helped with Reed's constant barrage of telephone inquiries from the press concerning the unidentified chop-suey, female victim.

"Well, Captain," said Can as Reed hung up from the fifth interruption, "it is a conspiracy, a criminal conspiracy. Kidnapping. Somebody kidnapped this Bailey character and three Texans are coming to get him with money."

"If they get Diller Bailey," Kellog said, "they will rent a car and drive him back, or kill him on the way and leave him in the desert somewhere. Thy can't fly back."

"Yeah," Can said. "typical mob maneuver. Buy shovels, dig a hsallow grave in like…New Mexico… or someplace."

"Yeah," agreed Tolier.

Kellog busied himself scrutinizing the thick, organized crime, intelligence files on Tanno and Shafrin, reading all about their backgrounds in Chicago, their occasional shenanigans in Vegas, and their hand amputation fiasco in Dallas. The press rang yet again. Reed again answered. It was the Los Angeles Times wanting information on the torso murder.

Impatient, Kellog proposed his own solution.

"Why don't I call Texas and set up a surveillance to find out who boards the flight, so we know whose landing in Vegas tonight for sure? Why don't we arrest whoever these three males are fer conspiracy or whatever? Hold 'em incommunicado overnight and call Tanno ourselves. Hell, I got the contact phone number on tape."

Captain Catelli held the phone, but his eues and ears were on Jack, as were Can and Tolier. Kellog continued.

"Why don't me, Can and Tolier here pretend to be these Texicans comin' in fer Bailey. Go meet Tanno. Get Bailey out alive and arrest these kidnappers. These murderers."

"Murderers?" questioned Tolier.

"Boys, I just betcha," said Jack as he stood and straightened his gun-toting basket-woven, western belt, "that yer torso out there belongs to a little Bally's Keno girl named Felicia."

"Huh?"

The three men stared at Jack.

Can finally dialed Bally's hotel. Ad yes, a certain Felicia Summers had missed her breakfast shift at the hotel cafe. No, she hadn't called in sick.

*****

Ordinarily, only family and friends tend to converge with newly arrived travelers at international airports, but only plain-clothed and uniformed LVPD officers surrounded Tony Tetro, Ira Tenpenny, and John Handell upon their arrival. The trio found themselves looking down the business ends of several automatics and revolvers in baggage claim. They were placed under arrest as Tetro busied himself searching the serious faces of the official crew for Jack Kellog. He didn't find it.

"What fer-WHAT FER?" yelled Handell as a patrol woman yanked a briefcase out of his hands.

"You three men conspired to commit kidnapping," said Detective Can as he clicked open the briefcase. He found it chocked full of money.

"You better have search papers to look in there." protested Handell, while submitting to handcuffs.

"That's our gambling money," Tetro said. He knew that if they were slick enough to intercept him at the airport on kidnapping charges, they were slick enough to have a search warrant too.

"Who were we supposed to have kidnapped?" Handell asked.

"A Mister Chester Festus," Detective Can answered.

Tetro had to smile at that one. The three were carted away to the city jail where police held them without bond and without phone calls. Further, all three men possessed stolen identification and credit cards adding a few extra charges and extra potential, bond fees. In fact, one of the three had purchased all the three plane tickets with a stolen card. One thing that never ceased to amaze Can and Tolier, who possessed significant skill and experience with hustles of organized crime, was how cheap criminals were. Despite having millions, and often carrying tens of thousands in pocket change, they still traveled, ate and bought with stolen credit cards. They found the "get-over," the "hustle" made the transactions sweeter. Their actual bond hearing would be delayed for as long as possible.

"I demand my phone call!" Handell yelled.

Ira Tenpenny and Tony Tetro said nothing.

"You'll get one when we properly identify who you are. Who are you?" a booking officer asked.

"Moe, Larry and Curly," Tony Tetro said.

*****

It surprised Kellog to hear about such a valuable catch

- three big players in the organization. He had expected Tetro and two middle-muscle men not Handell and the icy Tenpenny. At 9 a.m. he dialed the number Buster Simmons recorded for him, the contact number of the infamous Al and Vic, Vegas kidnappers and lady killers.

"We're here," Jack said.

"Good. Suite 945. Classics Hotel. Thirty minutes." Click.

Al and Vic weren't dumb. Thirty minutes hardly constituted enough time to set up and sufficiently cover a hotel room on the 9th floor of a 40-story hotel and, to make matters worse, kellog had the sick feeling Diller Bailey would be the only one not there.

*****

Knock, knock, knock.

A great deal of speedy preparation took place before these knocks. Plainclothes officers dressed like tourists disbursed throughout the hotel lobby and casino. Tolier, Can, and Kellog stood anxiously out in the plush hallway in front of Room 945. Kellog carted a very valuable and very heavy suitcase.

"Who's dere?" came a voice.

"Texas is here. Open the door," said Kellog.

The door did open, and Kellog recoiled at the sight of a bulbous, fat man in a wheelchair rolling back away from the opening. He stepped in to see this handicapped bald man raise and aim a sawed-off shotgun at him. Kellog smirked, shook his head and walked right by him. Across this huge room of multiple couches, chairs, tables, and a wet bar, Al Tanno stood. Behind him, the west wall stretched out entirely of glass, offering a nine-story high view of Las Vegas. The room contained everything but a bed, and Diller Bailey. But through a door slightly ajar leading to another room lay another room that might contain both.

"Who are you?" Al asked.

"Ira Tenpenny," said Jack. Can and Tolier followed in behind Kellog.

"How much ya got?" asked Al. "Seventy-five thousand," Kellog said dramatically.

"Open," said Al, strutting across the room with a big shot gait.

"And Diller?" asked Jack portentously.

"New plans, Tex. Ya boss Pontecorvo and I go back some yeahs -10 yeahs maybe -to Noo Yawk. He owes me, and ya see he also owes some pursons in Chicago $60,000. Need anodda 60 G's, Tex," said Al, "to settle an old Chicago score. Tell Ponty it's from the Bolichi brothers."

"Ain't got it," shrugged Jack with an uncaring resolve, giving Tanno a cold, dead stare.

"Get it," quipped Al. He walked to one of the room's six phones and punched in the Western World mansion's number, "Heah," and handed the ringing time bomb to Jack.

"Where's Diller?" asked Jack while the phone rang. Tanno only smirked.

"Don't see 'em. Don't call," said Jack simply as he hung up the phone. "First thing Pontecorvo will ask is if I've seen 'em." He felt lucky to postpone the conversation.

Silence.

"If he's dead, yer not gettin' shit," added Jack.

Trouble brewed behind Jack's back. Piggy Banks set his gaze on Tolier.

The streetwise Banks had seen him somewhere before and he now aimed his shotgun sight at Toiler's chest.

Al pounded out the number again and asked for Pontecorvo himself. This time he did the talking.

"Ray. Al. Al from Chicago? You owe people in Chicago because of the Bolichi brothers. You kept me from recovering 30 grand for them - now with interest it's 60 grand."

Al quickly handed the phone to Kellog. Moment of truth. Kellog hoped the Indian spoke as little as he looked like he would. In a low voice he said, "Tenpenny."

"Ira, dat choo?" asked Ponty.

"Yup," said Jack.

"You OK? You sound funny," asked Ponty suspiciously.

"Yup," muttered Jack. Then he proceeded to act as though he was engaging Pontecorvo in a conversation about Al Tanno' s latest developments. This drove the crime boss back in Texas crazy and confused, but convinced Tanno on the Vegas end that his deal had been cut.

"Who the hell is this?" Ponty shouted, storming around the room the length of the cord. "What the hell is going on?"

"I know him." Piggy blew up like a bomb, just as Jack hung up. "I know him. He's a dick." Piggy screamed at Tolier. "I've seen him in the casinos. He's a Vegas dick."

Al Tanno almost pulled his pistol, but Kellog ripped out his .45 and turned on Tolier and Can first.

"Som-a-bitches." Kellog barked. "These were my contacts in Vegas. They met me at the airport. Som-a-bitches," he said to Al over his shoulder as if he too realized for the first time that Toiler and Can were actually cops.

Tanno pulled his semi-auto - and aimed it at Tolier and Can. Tanno looked wide-eyed and confused, but Kellog had "Texas" written all over him so Tanno believed him so far.

"What in hell is going on." screamed a tiny metallic voice from the phone receiver still in Jack's left hand. Jack pressed the phone tightly to his ear hoping Tanno couldn't hear the angry, pleading voice of Pontecorvo.

"Ray. Tenpenny again," Kellog continued, "two undercover cops. The two guys I met at the airport - my connection - undercover cops. I need to get Diller and fast. The cops are on to us. I need this other 60 thousand. Look here, we need to give Tanno even more now. They're gonna be on the run from the local cops now. Yeah. Okay." Jack slammed down the phone and turned to Al.

"Ray says you got a deal, but ya got to show me Diller."

Al nodded, never once taking his eyes off the two cops. Kellog followed Tanno into the adjoining room where they saw a tightly tied up, gagged, wrinkled, filthy, bruised Diller Bailey attached to a chair. His eyes bugged out when he saw Jack. Jack stared at him and sighed. For the first time he actually felt something toward the hustling hippy, but he quickly returned to his business-like gangster role.

"How'm I gonna get this som-a-bitch outta here?" he barked, while looking around the room.

"The trunk," answered Tanno, pointing to a huge travel trunk sitting empty and open on the floor by the bed. "That's how we got 'em in here."

"Right." drawled Jack as he scanned the spacious layout. "Wheels?"

"Two on the bottom. Roll em right outta here."

"Right," Jack said. "Count yer first half of the money," and he threw the briefcase on a sitting table. The bedroom contained elegant and huge furnishings. It also contained a hot tub area, elevated one step up and his and hers dressing rooms and toilets. As Al popped the latches, Jack headed for one of the bathrooms. He looked for Victor Shafrin, the backup. He knew he had a 50-50 chance to find him in one of the bathrooms, but turned out, the one he strutted to didn't contain Vic. Jack shut the door behind him and rested against a wall contemplating his next move. He took in a deep breath. Judging from his gagged face and popcorn eyes, Diller looked as confused as Raymond Pontecorvo must have been when Jack hung up the phone.

In the other room, a scared, bald, cripple held a pump shotgun on two detectives and although Tanno hadn't impressed him much as yet, Tanno constituted an armed and experienced killer indeed. Jack had yet to find Victor Shafrin. Jack flushed the toilet and left the room.

"Where's yer podna?" Jack asked. "We oughta tell 'em about these cops."

"You always piss in the dark, Tex?" mumbled Tanno.

Jack hadn't realized it, but he never flicked the bathroom light on, apparently evident from a space between the carpet and the bathroom door.

"Just when I'm pissin' and thinkin' about an ambush from yer podna," Kellog said calmly, "more thinkin' than pissin'."

"Uh huh," said Al while counting the bundles of money.

Al began to impress Jack. This whole situation unfolded touch and go. Tanno shut the suitcase, glared at Jack, then picked up his pistol and pointed it at the detective's chest.

"Just who are you, anyway, Tex?" he asked coolly.

Jack sighed, nodded his head once and said, "Don't matter much, does it?

Ya got the drop on me and the drop on them out there. Ya got 75 thousand in yer hand. I think you need to complete this deal, leave Diller and get the hell outta Dodge City while ya can."

"Put that pistol on the floor," Tanno ordered.

"Uh uh, think not. See I never NEVER...give up my gun. Fraid I'll be killed by my own gun in somebody else's hand. Rather die in a gunfight than die unarmed by my own pistol. You push that issue? Well, I'll jump-you'll shoot. I'll draw. I'll shoot. We'll have us a helluva mess in here," said Jack.

Tanno smiled. Jack made a respectable and tough argument. He pulled the phone wire out of the wall, went to the adjoining room door and shouted to Piggy. "Bring them in heah," which Banks did. Tolier and Can filed on in, dismayed at seeing Al Tanno in control of this room, too. Banks had already disarmed the Vegas detectives.

"Don't worry," said Al. "We have an understanding in here, don't we, Tex? Piggy and I are gonna rip out all in phones and walk outta here. My 'podna' you are lookin' for is down in hall with a shotgun. If he sees yous guys in hall, he'll blow ya away. Got it? When Piggy and I are safe, we'll send a message to this room, den he'll leave. If he gets stopped. If he gets stopped. I'll kill the foyst Grandma I see in casino on the way out. I'll blow her brains out. Bye bye, Grandma. Ya unnerstand?" Piggy wheeled around in a frenzy ripping out phones.

"Dis ain't your money, is it Tex?" Al asked while snatching up the briefcase.

"Nope," said Jack.

"It's Pontecorvo's, ain't it?" he asked.

"Yup," said Jack.

"Good." Al said nodding his head up and down. "We both fucked him didn't we, Tex. You got your witness. I got my money."

"Yup," said Jack.

As they proceeded out the room door, Al turned and remarked, "Remember, one less Grandma." Then they left.

Can untied Diller's gag and Diller spat, coughed and sucked in air like he'd paddled underwater for three full minutes.

"They killed her, Kellog. They killed her," he yelled.

Tolier unbuttoned his own oxford shirt and pulled a small undercover microphone out he'd had taped to his chest. He began methodically relaying the latest turn of events into it, and into the ears of the police officers elsewhere in the building.

"Where is Victor Shafrin?" Kellog asked Diller.

"In a car on the street. He ain't in the hall. I heard 'em makin' their escape plans, the motha fuckas," cried Diller.

Kellog and Can continued to strip the ropes from Diller's arms and legs. They were sadistically over-tight. Diller's pent-up captive emotions burst out in sobs and tears,

"It was there at her apartment when they killed her. There was blood everywhere. It was horrible, man."

"Felicia?" Kellog stopped and asked him softly.

"In front of me. Right in front of me. They took us out in the desert, took a chain saw and hacked her up. Right in front of me. Thought they might hack me up too."

As soon as they untied Diller's hands he reached out and grabbed the detective's shoulders as Jack knelt beside him to untie his ankles.

"Okay, Diller, stay with these men," Kellog said as he stood and jogged for the room's front door.

Gun in hand, Jack dashed for the elevators. He saw no sign of Victor Shafrin. He boarded an elevator lobby bound. When the doors opened on the first floor, he did not hear the customary gambling crowd, the rumble of machines, the live floor performers. Instead he heard screams and gunfire from the large casino.

Jack ran down the hall to see the casino floor in chaos. Al Tanno, still clutching his suitcase, blasted his gun away at the crowd. Two plainclothes LVPD officers dropped for cover. Customers leaped and dove, screamed and ran in every direction. While Tanno's heavy magnum slugs pelted into coin machines, the LVPD men were hesitant to return fire because of the people. Tanno ducked in and around the machines en route to the casino's front doors. No Piggy Banks in sight. Sirens howled from the streets. Tanno looked like a trapped and dangerous rat.

The crowd had dispersed enough for some of the pursuing officers to fire a few shots at glimpses of Tanno as he maneuvered between the aisles. It became apparent to Jack that Al had given up on his front door escape and now bounded for the downstairs shopping mall. Unencumbered by tactical maneuvering because some 200 feet separated him from Al, Jack ran straight along the wall for the stairway and mall escalators. Just as he reached the open area before the stairs, Tanno appeared in a dead run 30 feet from Jack.

Tanno saw Jack and fired a wild shot at him and Jack dove to the tile floor, sliding sideways some 10 feet and crashed into newspaper racks in front of a gift shop. Tanno did some diving of his own. He went airborne over one of six down escalators, flying 20 feet before grinding, chest first, onto the already descending metal steps.

Police bullets hit the thick metal sides. Al's adrenaline told his body to ignore his cut, bleeding chest and knees from the impact of landing on the serrated metal steps. His adrenaline told him to pick up his body and run like hell when he got near the bottom. He didn't just wait the ride out either; he crawled down the descending stairs like a slithering snake, pistol in one hand, his future in a briefcase in the other.

Now Jack became part of the pursuit, allied with four other officers leaping down the stairs beside the escalators and dashing through the underground shopping mall, a place where random, calm customers, unaware of the action on the casino floor above them, strolled the large halls. The shoppers all froze in shock at the vision of a bleeding, huffing, shredded Al Tanno barreling past them. Between gasps for breath, two officers shouted, "Police. Police. Go for cover." to alert the crowd.

Jack, who always prided himself in pursuing suspects strategically, even if it meant cutting off the chase to second guess where the suspect might end up, found himself without any other option than a 100-yard dash. To stop and fire a shot would put him out of the race. No problems for Al, though. He spread wild and dangerous rounds over his shoulder every 30 or so feet, exploding massive sections of window glass and splintering stone, wood, and plaster on each side of his pursuers. Worse, with briefcase squeezed between his arm and torso, he was reloading.

Daylight. Al saw daylight. His adrenaline got a taste of hope as he turned into the hall by an ice cream shop, and he spotted mall doors to the street. Sixty feet, forty feet. He was flying. Thirty feet. Black and white and red. It flew into that picture-perfect opening, skidding to a stop. The red light threw reflections on the wall. The black and white car doors opened and two tan uniformed officers got out pell-mell and darted across the sidewalk and ran through the first set of his doors to daylight. They held silver guns.

Al jammed on his brakes. Jack Kellog and the other officers rounded the corner by the ice cream shop, spotting their backup team disappearing into the hall decor for cover and Tanno caught in the middle. As Al turned, Jack scrambled in amongst the 10 white, wrought iron tables in the ice cream shop, flipping over some in hopes the metal patterns might weave some cover for him. A florist's booth became a wall of defense for one sliding officer as the female arranger clasped her head and screamed. The other two, unable to stop from their run, slipped on the floor like racing ice skaters might fall, rolled but managed themselves into prone firing positions.

Then things didn't happen so fast for Al anymore. It all became slow motion. The LVPD officers raised their pistols. Jack raised his. He stood too. Al squeezed off a shot. Two of the plainclothes men fired, and Al looked like two baseballs hit him square in the chest. They slowly knocked him down. The precious suitcase flipped in the air over Al's head. He never saw it land.

The lawmen remained on the floor. Jack rolled over on his back, sucking wind. The sudden absence of combat sights and sounds allowed normality to seep in around him. People off in the distance gasped. A woman cursed. An officer spoke on a radio. The low sound of mall music permeated the air:

"Time will never mend.

Careless whispers of a good friend."

Jack got to a knee, then stood. He saw the ice cream clerk pressed flat against the wall in the shop. Eyes wide under the white hat. Jack limped through the wide-open doors up to the glass counter.

"How about a single...dip...vanilla...in a cone." He holstered his gun.

"You want an ice cream cone after all that?"

"I don't see no whiskey."

Detective Tolier appeared in the doors and Jack gave him a thumbs up, then he ran to the entrance. The boy scooped the vanilla and dropped it in a cone.

Jack left a whole dollar, winked at him and walked off.

The two uniformed officers from the street approached Tanno cautiously. Jack strolled up beside Tolier.

"You think Shafrin's outside?" Tolier commented, more than asked.

"Wrong doors. He's a long-gone daddy."

"That fucking Piggy Banks. I knew we had trouble when I saw that skunk-fuck in the room. Aiming a shotgun at me. He'd like to cripple me too."

"Reckon so," mumbled Jack, busy with the cone. Jack up righted a chair and sat down.

"Piggy Banks," Kellog repeated. "He can't roll to far."

"No he can't. They are already looking for him.

"Garages and parking lots," Kellog said between licks. "Handicapped van."

"Yeah."

Safrin gone. Tanno dead. He'd defecated and urinated in his clothes. Three hours later, morticians from the Gephart Funeral Home would deal with that cleanup. Mall janitors would mop up all that adrenalized Al Tanno blood from the cracks in the floor, the same juice that once powered Tanno through his criminal schemes and drove Victor Shafrin crazy.

In the next two days all sorts of dominos fell. A concerned Vegas doctor prescribed Diller some powerful tranquilizers, but Jack knew with Diller's tolerance for drugs, he'd need enough to knock out two racehorses. Can and Tolier completed an 18-page statement with Diller. Arrest warrants would be issued for Victor Shafrin and Piggy Banks for the murder of a little Keno girl named Felicia, whose only mistake in life came down to knowing a man named Diller Bailey. Somehow, in all the confusion, Piggy Banks had escaped from the casino along with Victor Shafrin.

A team of detectives scoured Tanno's mini warehouse and home, as well as Felicia's house for forensic evidence. They would find a weapons cache, cocaine and blood, flesh, hair and bone in the bathtub drainpipe where their post-Felicia tools had been washed.

Weaver Wisdom called and tipped off Kellog that Scooter Gleason had jetted to Vegas to bond out the big three-Tetro, Tenpenny and Handell. Their bonds were soon set at one million dollars apiece. After a few arrangements, Scooter reappeared and paid the bonds…in cash. Someday, these men would have to answer to the Clark County conspiracy charges, though two unrelated Las Vegas mobsters had actually committed the kidnapping and murder. Scooter had already prepared the defense arguments on how these legitimate businessmen from Texas tried to rescue one of their prior associates from vicious kidnappers.

"Something," Gleason told newspaper and TV reporters, "even H. Ross Perot his own self would do."

CHAPTER TEN:
ACAPULCO DREAMIN' ON SUCH A WINTER'S DAY

The guy looked majestic. Even Baker Tanseed was impressed. The guy resembled Gilbert Roland, Ricardo Montalban, and the Cisco Kid all rolled into one. They called him Rex Antonio, at least the movie people did as no one knew his real name. He'd become one of Mexico's famous movie stars in the late '60s. Action flicks. Vaquero flicks. He was also a closeted homosexual and a killer. A killer of killers. Some he did himself, some he hired done.

In reality, the real Rex who-ever-he-was, also became one of his country's largest marijuana exporters, a kingpin in a violent kingdom, good for a take of several million dollars each deal, just about each week. He had so many people on his payroll he functioned like a mini government. Outsiders thought he ran a major movie studio. But motion pictures only constituted the very tip of his iceberg, and a great cover.

"Senor Tanseed," he greeted the Texan graciously.

"Senor Antonio," replied Baker, respectfully. The

balmy Acapulco air, the Pacific sun and displays of fresh fruit and Australian and German bottles of wine surrounded them. The two men sat upon splendid furniture on a marble balcony of Rex's west coast home overlooking the ocean. Within moments, the wine drinking commenced, and their bodyguards faded to the doorways and hallways. Rex Antonio did most, if not all, of the talking.

"What do jour country and my country no longer... hmmm...care about? Eh? They care much about the heroin. Yes. About the cocaine. De cocaine. De cocaine, madre mia. And de crack is a very big American concern. Now what is on de bottom of this concern list? Marijuana."

There is a special way an eloquent Hispanic can say marijuana. Baker recognized it because he imagined how Ricardo Montalban would pronounce it in a TV commercial. Breathy. Exaggerated. Rex knew how. The...leather... the...mar-JAUN-a.

"Science, aahh botany, has enabled me to grow the richest, finest, strongest marijuana in the blackest of our Mexican soils. I have hundreds of tons of it. I have my own boats, my own planes. HA. Me amigo, I can have my own starship someday. We lease docks, airstrips, fleets of trucks. We can move it all around the world. Senor Tanseed, we have set up a tremendous chain. An outlet system. Even border guards are on our payroll. We pay dem thousands a truck to let them pass. Now de beauty is this, too. Once we know our marijuana customers, we make it known that we can supply other pleasures for them. You know. Cocaine. Heroin. Crack.

"Now, you must not forget, the real day-to-day money to be made is from marijuana. The street marijuana dealer is everyone's friend is he not? Ahh...as they say in the United States...a hippy. And the friendly neighborhood hippy also now has access to coke and heroin."

Baker nodded while sipping his wine. Outside, imported monkeys from South America ran up and down the nearby trees.

"Marijuana is de essence of my empire, the foundation of your dreams. Jou see? I hab an island. It's in the beautiful Caribbean. I have 80 soldiers guarding it. Haaah. With guns stolen from your country's armories and Costa Rica. Of course, in my empire I produce movies. Colossal movies. Sometimes I am in them, sometimes I am not."

A monkey leapt from a branch onto the wall of the balcony. It sat near the men with a pensive poise for a moment. Then it lunged across the table and snatched a piece of pineapple, in doing so knocking over a bottle of wine.

"Look. A scavenger." Rex cried with delight.

Suddenly no less than 15 monkeys, emboldened by the first, swept in and ravaged the tables. Tanseed, who'd been standing with a foot on his chair seat, pushed his chair toward the monkeys in defense. A male and female servant dashed into the room swinging hand towels and shouting. The raiding party vanished over the wall and into the trees.

Rex never moved away from the table throughout the attack.

Tanseed slowly pulled his chair back toward the table and sat down and leaned back reluctantly.

"Sometimes my men here shoot the monkeys because they do not like them. Is no problem. I jus' buy more. But I like them. I would never shoot a monkey. They are like hairy children, jou know?"

As the hours wore on, Cuban cigars flared in the darkness. It had been a rich, long day. There were final points to get to, some very sharp points.

"What you must do next is free yourself from this Gallanti family." Rex said

"Pontecorvo, the Gallanti family, have a pride about their business. They will kill as a matter of right and wrong, of business, of lessons," Tanseed said, staring at the dark seascape from the patio.

Rex nodded his head up and down. "Then there must be some death, Senor. Death. But it must look like it does not come from jou."

"Yeah. Pontecorvo and his man Tetro, too. Tony's a smart one, both must be killed but by somebody else. For some other good reason, so New York won't take any revenge on me."

"On us, mi amigo."

The men conversed long into the night. Tanseed listened while Rex relived his climb to power, interwoven with philosophy and murder. They smoked marijuana and then snorted some cocaine at 3 a.m.

At daybreak, a hoarse, tired Rex said, "If jou only had just come to me first, amigo, flown south instead of north to New York, you would be such a rich, independent businessman. Now we must work so hard for you to become this way."

"There's a crazy cop, a detective up there. If I play my cards just right, if I set things up right, I might get him to kill the yankees," Tanseed said.

"Si, senior."

Baker and his two sworn-to-absolute-secrecy Texas henchmen drove up the sunrise coast, picked up his bored wife at their plush hotel and then cruised to the airport for a private jet back to Houston, Texas.

The Tanseeds arrived fresh and tanned from what was advertised as a weekend getaway in old Mexico. On the mansion's back patio, when Ponty told Baker about the abduction of Diller, the payoff trip to Vegas, and the strange call from a substitute Ira Tenpenny, the cowboy seemed calm and distant. No one could really tell just how distracted Baker Tanseed was. He had tropical islands to dream of and the clever murders to plan for the men who stood right there in his way. He wouldn't hire an expensive killer or a redneck hitman. He would figure out a way for Jack Kellog to kill them. If only he could reach his ol' buddy Diller Bailey. Talk to him. Offer him enough money, maybe Diller could help set it all up...

CHAPTER ELEVEN:
WITH THE MONKEYS AND ZEBRAS

"West Forge and West Houston experienced a series of arson reports last evening when fire-fighting units of both cities responded to eight fires, all in area businesses. West Forge Fire Marshal Larry Scott Craig, using the very latest investigation methods, said his investigation concluded arson, as in a firebomb-type device. It is unknown at this time whether these were acts of vandalism or sparked by another motive.

According to our preliminary investigation, we have found similar incendiary devices in all the West Forge fires and the Harris County fires. We've collected some materials to be tested for further results,' said John Sharp, assistant West Forge Fire Marshal.

'The list of businesses includes three dry cleaners, three restaurants, and two hardware stores. This is Becky Kaffy, Eyewitness News."

'Thank you, Becky. Violence erupted elsewhere in Houston today when three Illinois businessmen were shot and killed while they sat in the back seat of their chauffeured *rental car in the 700 Block of Lamar. Bob Martinelli has that story."*

"Jeff, three visiting businessmen, all reportedly in Texas on a merger deal between corporations and staying here at the Clusters Inn, left for a meeting at about 4 p.m. in this car. Suddenly, two men in suits, armed with automatic handguns, approached the vehicle and opened fire, shooting some 150 rounds into the vehicle. Driver Jesus Garza is listed in critical condition while the three backseat victims, whose names are being withheld pending family notification, are dead. Ricocheting bullets struck three innocent bystanders. All three are listed as stable at Houston's McNaulty Hospital."

"What we believe we have at this time is a gangland-style triple homicide; the motive remains a mystery. Bob Martinelli, Eyewitness News. Back to you, Jeff."

- Eyewitness News Houston

Kellog's War Wagon rolled over the Arizona miles.

"Still can't figure why we didn't fly?" asked Diller.

"Well, there's a whole lotta' roads and just a few airports. Tanseed and Pontecorvo could flood the airports with men watching for us, but they could never cover all the roads. I figure that they figure, there's no way in hell I'll bring you back to Harris County. That by now, the Feds will ship you to Canada or some such place. But even the Feds don't know I've gotcha' yet. And when they do, they ain't gonna know where I'm keeping you. Only you and me, Diller, and..."

"The monkeys and zebras, right?" interrupted Diller.

"Yup," nodded Jack.

"Yup, sheriff," mimicked Diller.

"You know, I just don't know what it is. These last few weeks I've been called Marshal, Sheriff -and Tex a whole lot."

"Still wished we'd fly," replied Diller with a smile and that familiar bob and weave with his head. Jack noticed that it was the first normal expression Jack had seen from Diller since Vegas. Since the death of the Keno girl.

"Riiiight," said Kellog. "You are severely detached from reality."

******

The War Wagon crunched up the secluded caretaker's rocky drive to the bungalow-style house. A strong wind carried the sound of a distant elephant roar. Diller grabbed the satchel of toiletries Jack brought for him, and he followed Jack up the wooden steps to the front door. A man in his 60s let them in.

"M.J.," said Jack. "Here's one each, Diller Bailey."

M.J. nodded his head and shook Diller's hand. They sat down in the dimly lit room. An open book entitled, *Hippopotamus,* rested by the only lamp. By this light Diller got his first good look at the man charged with keeping him alive until a grand jury appearance. M.J. appeared overweight and short-legged, dressed in a blue jump suit, quite worn at the knees. A patch on his left chest read, "Falthom City Zoo", and under it "Warden", a fancy title for a man who repaired fences, fed animals and hosed down bears in the hot summer for a little city zoo.

No one would ever guess that another insignia once rested on that chest for 27 years, that of a Houston PD badge. No one would know or barely remember that M.J. had served as Jack Kellog's training officer decades ago. On disability and retirement now, Warden M.J. Benjamin lived alone in the zookeeper's house with only animals and some rarely seen cops for friends.

"Kept by a warden," Diller commented. "Somehow that gives me the Willie Nelsons."

"Think of me as Dr. Dolittle," M.J. said.

"What's fer dinner, Dolittle?"

"Kangaroo pie."

"Oh shit."

Jack made for the door. "I'll leave you two magpies alone."

"See ya around, Sheriff." said Diller as Jack left the two silent men in the kitchen, an odd couple for sure. Jack felt relieved because only he and the Warden knew the whereabouts of the precious informant, an informant who would testify soon before Federal, Harris and Pine County grand juries, not to mention Las Vegas now. The agenda? The attempted capital murder of Officer Roy Timmes, the brutal murder of Felicia, drug smuggling, kidnapping, gun-running, and general racketeering of the Pontecorvo, Tanseed crime confederation.

Visions of multiple indictments danced in Jack's head, and the end of numerous enemies danced at the end of the proverbial rope. Too bad they quit hanging folks.

CHAPTER TWELVE:
MR. KELLOG GOES TO WASHINGTON

"At 9 a.m. that morning, my field director handed me a sub-poena with Jack Kellog's name on it. I was informed that, in no uncertain terms, Kellog was to appear before the committee in 48 hours. Mine was not to ask why. But just to do. This had never happened before. Never without preparation. Never without the witness having time to obtain a lawyer or consult with the committee staff to bring support documents or evidence. This was a sudden emergency." - Agent Nathen T. Kussler FBI (ret.) Bethesda, MD

Archie Lennox interview tape 13

Drenched by rain from his mad dash from his Caddy to the station door, Kellog peeled off the damp windbreaker and made for his office, the only lit room on the second floor. Summoned in by a worried-sounding Jack Breasley, he found Breasley and a young West Forge officer waiting for him in their division office. Kellog tossed the jacket on a chair and sat at his desk. He looked at the two men.

"Jack, this is Dale Cunningham, a new officer. He also had the distinction of failing the polygraph test yesterday about revealing Diller Bailey's location at the motel where Roy Timmes, was shot," Breasley uttered in a sharp tone.

Kellog couldn't even recognize the new face, which wasn't uncommon for most of the vets, with the hiring and firing and quitting that went on in the patrol division.

"You know me, sir. I was riding with Sgt. Willacker the night we found you asleep on the parking lot across from Western World," Cunningham said.

"Hmm," Kellog acknowledged.

"Last week, you know, we routinely tested every officer working overtime, at the Diller Bailey motel," Breasley continued, "Cunningham flunked his test, and I questioned him for several hours. He wouldn't admit to anything. Then an hour ago, he called me and wanted to talk. So, I called this meeting."

"Well, what is it, son?" Kellog asked.

"Well, Sergeant, it's hard...hard...to find a beginning... ahh, two years ago I used to work on a quarter horse ranch. I trained and worked horses with Adel Peterson for Baker Tanseed. Drinking and talking with the guys, they all knew I wanted to be a police officer someday. I talked about it a lot, but never took any of the tests or anything until I made this deal."

"Deal?"

"I met a man who called me on the phone, who asked me to meet him at Steak and Ale for dinner. His name was Anthony Astramodo..."

"What he look like?" Jack interrupted.

"A tall husky man with black hair and a beard. He told me he was a retired Boston cop, and oh, what a life he'd had. What stories."

Jack rifled through his desk files and selected a color photo and tossed it in front of Cunningham.

"That's him." the young man declared.

"That is not Anthony Astramodo from Boston. THAT is a Tony Tetro, a slimy low-life, punk som-a-bitch, ex-cop, turncoat traitor yankee hood from New York," Jack said intensely.

"Well, he asked me if I wanted to be a police officer. I said yes, I would. Then he said he worked with a group of people that were, you know, supportive of police. Like rich people? And they would support new people they liked, if they would join local police departments. He said that the group knew the police pay and the benefits were bad and the group wanted to support good, new people. If I passed all the entry exams, they would give me $1,000 a test. If I got hired, they would give a $5,000 bonus. This group would then pay me, secretly, $500 a month to remain a police officer."

"Secretly," Breasley said.

"Secretly," Cunningham said.

"And that didn't sound suspicious to you?" Jack asked.

"Well I ...no. No it didn't. I thought it made sense. He said that a police department, any police department, would not like outsiders paying officers any money, but secretly, that this was...the only way to help support good people to stay on the job. Alls' I'd have to do was report to them about my job, and things like - well, how good a job I was doing, you know, so that they would trust me, believe in me, so that I would be worthy of the group's support. I have been here eight months now and I have seen Mr. Astramodo six times."

"Tetro."

"Ah, yeah, Tetro. He mentioned that I am not the only new man on the force he works with. I told him a lot of things about our department. He's always asking questions about what improvements could be made, where we need help, who I think are bad cops, who are good," he hesitated for a moment. "I have even given him our personnel list with home phones and home addresses."

"You did what, boy?" Barked Breasley.

"Well, he said his group, this pro-law enforcement group, wanted to contact the better officers, quietly and offer them this extra support, too."

"Shit." growled Jack. "Ya know, now they know the homes and…and the families of our people. Their kids. These people, this group will blackmail and threaten and kidnap and kill. Just to have their way."

"I also told him about the good work you were doing to fight crime and you were working on a big kind of mafia case…and we were bodyguarding a big witness, too," Cunningham finished quickly as though to get it over with.

"He asked where it was, and it just came out."

"I oughtta crack you right across the face with the back of my hand, you little dumb-shit." Kellog growled.

Then he sat back and studied this fool. He could easily see why Tetro had selected this young man, the same reason West Forge had picked him. Squeaky clean. He was also immature, naïve and easily influenced, like so many of the new recruits Civil Service obligated the West Forge Police Department to hire. A rare few caught Jack's eye with promise of a career-long potential. A lot of the streetwise, people-wise common sense that police officers needed to excel could not be taught at the academy or even in the field. Recruits must already possess the core savvy of it. The Cunningham kid didn't have it.

"His line sounded so great, Sergeant. I mean-so professional. He said they could only support a select few, a new breed of cop, that I should never tell anyone because then everyone would demand the $500 a month, and the group would go broke. I believed him at first. Hell, I'm just a country boy."

"Well, I'm a country boy too, son. That's no excuse fer ignorance, though. If only ignorance was painful," said Kellog. "What did they say their group was called?"

"The Coalition of Law Enforcement Progress."

"There's a mouthful of shit," Breasley said.

"CLEP," Gunther said

"I love police work, detective. I am working out around here. Just check my training records." Cunningham pleaded. "When I really started working, when I learned what was going on, well, sir, I became troubled over this coalition. No one else ever heard of such a group or such an idea of one."

"Well they got something like it up north. They do got 'em up there. Boston. New York. Chicago. And they twist the life outta young men and women like you. And then you wake up one day and find yourself sawing a body in half for some skunk-fuck in a disco suit. Or, you wind up dead in a ditch ya own self, for not doing their bidding. I just left Las Vegas and saw a young girl spread out and cut up like a barnyard chicken just so's she'd fit into a suitcase. It's called the mafia, son. Not the Coalition of whatever-the-fuck Progress. It called the Coalition of Anything Goes - Into My Wallet. And what went in this time was your soul. Your very own…fucking…soul."

The room got real quiet. The rookie was pale, scared and wide-eyed.

"I saw and heard about you, how hard you work for what you believe in, and some of the other guys and gals, and - well I had to come in and tell you what happened. After a while I knew it just wasn't right. I even knew Roy Timmes."

"It's know Roy Timmes. It ain't knew. He ain't dead yet," corrected Kellog.

"Yes, sir."

"Well, ya did the right thing by comin' up here and telling us this. It's the right thing. All the police academies and training officers in the world really can't teach a man what he needs to know about life in this job and that is just to do the right thing. And you did it by telling us."

"Will they fire me, Sergeant?" he asked anxiously.

"Don't hardly know. You failed a polygraph like the one you did. Lie like that."

"I didn't hink I was lying about anything."

"You said you didn't tell anybody about Diller in that motel," Breasley said.

"That's a firing offense right there. Ahhh don't know. We might need you. We might just need your help in nailing these boys. We just need to know first, though, whose flag are ya flyin'? Ours er theirs?" said Kellog.

"Ours, sir. Our flag."

"You type?" Kellog asked.

"Huh? Yes, sir."

"You sit yerself down out there by that typewriter and type out this whole story. I mean the whole one. I want every detail in there like a Harvard lawyer, not a...country boy. I wanna know everything you ever said to Tetro, everything he said. Everything."

"Should I ...should I get a lawyer?"

"Lawyer? You're beyond lawyer, son. You get a lawyer now, and I'll kill you myself."

"Yes sir."

Breasley guided him to the typewriter then returned to the office. The two Jacks stared at each other in a depressed state of amazement.

"He'll have to be wired and worked by pros. Coached," Kellog said.

"He's like a communist spy," said Breasley, aghast.

"Like a spy seduced by a bearded Matahari," added Kellog. "And communism ain't got nothin' to do with."

*****

"Report to the Chief's Office" was the morning message.

Kellog's raised his eyebrows after seeing the cold stares of the two men in three-piece suits in Chief Collins' office.

"Jack, these men are with the FBI, Washington office," Shrewdy explained in a calm voice.

"Sgt. Kellog," the solemn black agent spoke up, "consider yourself formally served with this subpoena, to appear at the special Senate, Sub-Committee hearings on organized crime."

Astounded, Jack took the papers, trying to find the pertinent information amongst the jargon.

"Tomorrow, sir," the agent continued. "Here you'll find your travel voucher, hotel arrangements, and airline tickets. We took the liberty."

"Where to?" asked Jack.

"The Capital, sir."

"Austin?"

"Washington, D.C., sir" said the second agent.

"Tomorrow," repeated Jack, still unfolding the form and trying to comprehend the idea behind it.

"What's it about?"

"It must be information you hold on organized crime."

"Other than that, we know absolutely nothing," the second agent added. "we're just travel agents with badges."

"You will find the details on the subpoena," the first agent finished. "Here is my card for when you get there. Call us. Thank you, Chief," he said, and both men stood in unison and left the room.

"What the hell's next?" Jack muttered.

"Pack, Jack. Just pack," said Shrewdy. "Listen, Scooter Gleason came in yesterday. Wanted to file a complaint against you for Ray Pontecorvo. Harassment. Said you...

touched him. Grabbed his chest. Pulled his greasy hair. Shoved him around. I ran him the hell outta heah. He laughed and left. Invited me to go fishing."

Jack growled.

"You know, half the city council is made up of yuppies from Boston and California now. You know...I can't fade heat like this forever. These people don't know shit about the cowboy mafia or the Yankee mafia. Or that sometimes a good ass whippin' can change a man's life."

Jack found himself too preoccupied with his subpoena to respond. He turned for the door, scanning over the voucher.

"Jack." Interrupted Collins. "What you got planned for this rookie boy?"

Jack dropped his hand with the papers down to his side in sudden disgust. "If it were up to me, I'd kick his pale little ass and fire him. He's a little boy and we're not in the business of raising children around here hoping they'll turn out to be mature ladies and gentlemen. It's a tough enough job for grown men and women as it is. But fer now, I want him just as he is. I'll wire 'em for his next meeting with Tony Tetro. I want him in case we need to feed a line of bull into the Pontecorvo organization via Mr. Tetro. When all these sons-a-bitches are roasted on a spit, then you fire the little shit for lying, fer being seduced into being a traitor. Fire 'em for being damn dumb." He turned for the door.

"We were young once too, Kellog," said Shrewdy as Jack disappeared down the hall. The chief had already ordered polygraphs for all officers with two or less years' experience to weed out other possible spies. He contemplated running the whole department through the test.

*****

Marble and more marble. Statues and oil paintings. Mahogany and brass. Jack purposely left his Stetson in Texas, but his suit still had its western flavor right down to his bolo tie and Tony Lama boots – the heels of which, announced his arrival at the Senate chambers. A uniformed guard stood in front of a group of news reporters and cameramen who'd been congregating outside the congressional, closed-door meetings daily for nearly two months.

"Sgt. Kellog," came a voice from Jack's left. Jack turned to see a man holding a briefcase standing by himself.

"Hello Bob," Jack said to the FBI agent Bob Pellen, the one from the first Texas meeting in the Government Building with Diller. It looked to Jack like Pellen was standing there waiting for him to show up.

"Bob, would you have some insight on what's going on?"

"Sgt. Kellog, my congratulations on your successful drug raid," Pellen said, he stepped over to Jack to shake hand. Pellen looked tense. As the reporters overheard Kellog's name they turned toward the men and headed in their direction. Noting the approaching crowd with some dismay, Pellen leaned in close to Jack. Pellen's hot whisper on his cheek made Jack flinch.

"Do not tell the committee members where Diller Bailey is," he whispered.

"Huh?" Jack looked at Pellen's white stern face. He thought it held the expression of a man who had just seen a ghost and went back for a second look. Pellen didn't respond. Instead, he spun around and walked away, just as the media engulfed Kellog like a wave.

"Sgt. Kellog, why have you been subpoenaed from Texas?" questioned a newsman.

"What do you expect as a result of today's session?" Another reporter asked.

Jack watched Pellen step into the elevator turn back

and return his stare.

"Are you involved as a suspect or as a police investigator?"

The elevator doors slid shut, interrupting their hypnotic trance. Jack found himself staring at the metal doors.

"Do not tell the committee members where Diller is," echoed in his head. Do not tell. Do not tell. Was it possible the corruption and payoffs had infiltrated a congressional committee?

"Sgt. Kellog, there have been gangland shootings in...," a reporter shoved a mike under Jack's chin, "...your city. Do you think..."

Giant doors opened before Jack into an adjoining room. A man in a tan uniform called out his name.

"Yeah. Right here."

"Are you armed sir,"

"For most of my life. I am a peace officer for the State of Texas."

"Okay sir. Sure. Follow me in please."

The room was huge and packed with people. The man clutched Kellog's elbow and led him across the room to a table. Another guard shut the doors behind them.

Nine preoccupied senators sat in a semi-circle about Jack, a level above and some distance away.

Jack took his seat almost unnoticed by the members at a table before them. He pondered Pellen's warning. He knew what Pellen meant, but he had difficulty digesting the implications.

A gavel struck a table hard.

"I am Senator Tayfield, Chairman of this Committee. We are investigating organized crime in these hearings, Sgt. Kellog." He went on to advise Jack of several legal prerequisites and gave Jack the oath.

"State your name for the record."

"Jack Daniel Kellog."

"Your age, date of birth, place of birth?"

Jack answered each.

"Your employment."

"I am a Sergeant for the West Forge Police Department, Robbery Division, have been so fer nine years. Before that I was a West Forge Patrol Officer for six years."

"Prior to your West Forge employment you worked for severally years with the Houston Police Department, is that correct?"

"That is correct, as a patrol officer," answered Jack.

"Our records show, you were involved with professional boxing in the '60s, Sgt. Kellog."

"Yes, I was a boxer for a few years."

"Did you, at that time, meet anyone, or become involved with anyone in any form of organized crime?"

"No, not that I know of then," sighed Jack.

"Never threw a fight?" interrupted a senator from the right, through a microphone. His nameplate read "James Dru." The other members shifted nervously in their seats knowing this was an undiplomatic, bold question.

"No," said Jack, leaving his lips pursed after his reply.

Tayfield continued, "You have recently contacted the Attorney General's Office and the FBI in Houston, Texas, with information about organized crime activities in Harris County. Is that correct?"

"Yes."

"For the record, I shall read the minutes of a meeting, your meeting with U.S. Assistant Attorney General Bob Pellen, other law enforcement officers, and one Diller Bailey. Then I will read highlights of Mr. Bailey's informal testimony from that meeting." Tayfield continued by reading portions of the transcript, which took 35 minutes. "To the best of your memory, are these words accurate?"

"Yes."

"This Diller Bailey tells a long-scattered, rambling story, not in any real chronological order," said a Congressman whose nameplate read Tass Lidell. "Did you find him credible?"

"Diller has a shotgun style a tellin' a story, but all the pieces do fit in the end. He came to me when he felt desperate. I find 'em to be entirely credible. And I don't like that you've read his account aloud here."

"This is a closed hearing, Sargent. Our records indicate a drug lab and marijuana farm raid in East Texas, based on Diller Bailey's information turned out quite successful," said Tayfield.

Jack shifted in his seat and mumbled, "Two police officers died, if you want to call that very successful."

"We already subpoenaed the police reports," interrupted Dru unnecessarily impatient, again.

"Sgt. Kellog, several Cubans were arrested in this raid in East Texas. There was a reference to a Cuban meeting between Castro and Raymond Pontecorvo made by your informant. Do you recall these statements?" asked Senator L. Lontanio.

"Yes, I do."

"Sgt. Kellog, are you aware, from your conversations with Diller Bailey that there is a conspiracy, a Cuban...a Communist plot, to infiltrate this country with their agents, secreted in through the Cuban flotilla during the Carter administration. These agents have several functions. One is to support the drug flow, to slowly decay a portion of our population, in particular the upper middle class with the so-called, rich man's drug, cocaine. How do you feel about this plot, and does your informant know any particulars about this?" questioned Lontanio.

"Well, there are tremendous profits in these cocaine deals tempting to anyone, any Cuban refugee, agent or otherwise. Picking out communist plots and plotters is very difficult.

Diller Bailey knows details about a meeting between Pontecorvo and Castro. I am not just gonna say that the Cubans arrested at the marijuana farm are some kind of secret agents. They do need to be questioned by DEA officials, or the FBI. I believe they have. As far as I am concerned, I am just working criminal cases from my city."

Tayfield took over the questioning. "Justice Department investigators have gathered intelligence from your local police agencies and news media. Do you, as a local officer, feel an increase in what we would traditionally call 'organized' crime in your home region?"

"Definitely," said Jack.

"We understand there was a gangland-style shooting in which West Forge officer Roy Timmes was critically wounded while protecting Diller Bailey after which Bailey was either missing or dead. Now then, as of two days ago, your local District Attorney's Office was notified by you that Bailey is, in fact, alive and well and in your protective custody again," said Tayfield.

Jack sighed. A few Texas phone calls and in two days here he stood in Washington, D.C. The AG's office in Houston, Bob Pellen's group, must have called D.C. immediately after Jack called Rye Edleson.

"Sgt. Kellog." Barked Dru, impatient for an answer.

"I have located Bailey," Jack admitted. "Only I know where he is. He is ready to testify before grand juries and courtroom prosecutions," Jack said. This caused rumblings amongst the members.

"Where is your man?" inquired Dru as an order.

"I know where he is," Jack replied.

"Where is he?" Dru demanded.

The face and words of Pellen haunted Kellog.

"I can produce him anytime," he said.

"Mr. Kellog, I am not asking you about producing him.

I am asking you to testify before this committee about, WHERE the informant IS." shouted Dru. "Our agents can offer him superior protection and custody."

"There has already been and attempt on his life. Now he..." Jack began.

"This government is in control of these hearings," Dru interrupted. "This government..."

"This government," it was Jack's turn to interrupt, and loudly, "has been investigating organized crime for one hundred years. This government can't seem to do much about it. This government has leaked to the press, leaked even to organized crime. Things like money and influence and promises have leaked INTO THIS GOVERNMENT from organized crime-FOR ABOUT ONE HUNDRED YEARS. I am not going to reveal Bailey's location. He. Is. Safe." Jack turned quickly to Tayfield. "And I will produce him to you at such time as you desire in the company of Texas Rangers."

"You are under oath." growled Dru. "Are you insulting this committee, its members? Each of us here have..."

"DON'T MUCH CARE..." roared back Jack, then he quietly and methodically continued, "...what each of you has done. I know what I have to do. Now you can...you can put me in your jail here for contempt, you can do whatever you think you can do, but I am not telling anyone where my informant is."

There was a moment of stunned silence while Dru silently steamed. His anger was reflected in the lowest minority of the board members.

"Sgt. Kellog," said Tayfield calmly, "One week from today, Tuesday, the 11th of November, at 9 a.m. we would like to see Diller Bailey. At 11 a.m. we will have him appear before a Federal grand jury. The next step, following any indictments, will be an appearance before a task force for the U.S. Attorney General. Can you serve the subpoena?"

"Yes. I can along with a handpicked company of Texas Rangers," replied Jack.

"Thank you, sir. I hope you will stay in contact with the FBI agents you've met and appraise them of your progress. You are dismissed. Of course, you know not to reveal any details of this secret session," Tayfield concluded, but Kellog was not through.

"I'll say this one thing-fer the record. It is my intention to make detailed video tapes with Diller Bailey before he leaves his current location. Anything happens to Bailey, it is my intention to make these tapes public."

"Then you may find yourself charged with the contempt of this committee." declared Dru.

Jack ignored the remark and left the room.

"Kinda horsy ain't he?" whispered one of the southern senators to another.

"Can you reveal to us any information about the hearings?" A reporter asked Kellog as he left the chambers.

"Yeah. I can reveal that these people hauled my ass all the way up here from Texas to talk to me for about 40 minutes. I guess the telephones ain't working 'round here?"

He strode off, leaving the reporters in his wake. And they all loved his answer.

*****

Intently, Tony Tetro listened to his long-distance caller from Falls Church, Virginia.

"The sub-committee on crime has rescheduled to convene at 9 a.m., 11 November," the caller said. "Now, some of the senators and their aides are scrambling to reschedule for that day. They must cancel other important meetings. This thing has to be very important. All the members will be in attendance."

"Keep tawken'," mumbled Tetro, the phone enveloped in the side of his neck as he scratched out the information on a motel pad.

"Word from the aides is a big informant, maybe bigger than Valachi, will be there. They are saying 'Kefauffer' all over again. Big press. Big action."

"Say a big hello to your stock broka' and check your latest, new investments," finished Tetro, his way of promising payment for the tip.

"Thank you, sir," said the caller.

Ten minutes later, the phone rang again. This time it was a local call.

"Secretaries from the Harris County District Attorney's Office are preparing indictment casework against y'all. An emergency session has been called fer the grand jury for 10 November," the caller reported.

"Thank you," said Tetro.

The New Yorker gathered up his handwritten notes, shoved them into a small piece of luggage and left the motel, climbing into a Mercedes for the 20-minute drive back to the mansion. An indiscriminately chosen motel, paid with cash, was always the best, coolest, untapped place to comfortably make a series of important phone calls, especially if one isn't followed, as Tetro was assured from his precautions. Big Tony knew being followed would mean someone could discover his room, check the long-distance phone numbers, etcetera. T.T. had done that himself many times when he busted hoods up north.

*****

"What cha got fa me, Big Tony?" asked Pontecorvo, when Tetro arrived in the den at the mansion.

"Action on da hill, action on da hill. Sgt. Kellog must have Diller Bailey ready. Got a call too from Harris County and the DA's office is scrambling for an emergency grand jury meeting here on the 10h. Woid is, from da nation's

Capital, Kellog started all dis. Senate hearing called for the 11th. Outside woid from da news reports, ya know... investigation dis, investigation dat. Inside woid, Diller Bailey is ready to squawk to everybody, about everybody and only Matt Dillon Kellog knows where he is."

Pontecorvo ate another pistachio nut. His fingers, lips and teeth were stained red. "Bring me Kellog," he said, slapping his hands together to rid them of the red dust.

CHAPTER THIRTEEN:
AN ACLU NIGHTMARE

This afternoon, a Police Sgt. Jack Kellog of West Forge, Texas, a suburb connected to Houston, testified before the Senate Committee investigating organized crime. This comes as a result of Sgt. Kellog's investigation into a crime problem in his city, a problem both he and the committee refuse to comment on after their closed-door meeting. Recently, a police officer was shot and critically injured in a gangland-style ambush at a West Forge motel. Kellog has also participated in one of the largest marijuana farm seizures in Texas history. Police agency spokespeople refuse to comment on the connections between these events.

Following today's meeting Committee member Tass Lidell made this comment about Kellog's appearance: 'At this point it's obvious that Sgt. Kellog is involved in an investigation with national and perhaps international ramifications that involve this committee. I can say that ah...that Sgt. Kellog is a tough talking...ah...Texas lawman who intends to see some justice, whether through this committee, or not.' Other members declined to comment.' " - Washington Post

"Yup, yup, yup." Jack and I go way back. He was always a hard-working investigator. One of the best. This mafia prosecution. Whew boy. This was one of the biggest things that ran through my office, even the whole DAs office. We had a lot riding on this character Diller Bailey, and lookin' back I just couldn't see it all work through. I spent a lot of hours with that squirrel, and I thought he'd surely run like a rabbit first chance he'd get."- Rye Edleson, Retired Felony Prosecutor Current Attorney at Law - 2003

Archie Lennox interview tape 39

Several days later...

"How are you two getting on?" Kellog asked M.J. the Warden as they walked to the hill overlooking the three old lions.

"Ahhh, he's a fuckin' weirdo. Watches cartoons on TV all the time. He brings up the Keno girl, Felicia, all the time. Seeing her murdered left quite a mark on 'em."

"Hmm," said Jack, scanning the distant preschoolers and their parents visiting the bird sanctuary.

"But we're gettin' on. Gettin' on. I'm wonderin' if he's needin' some dope. He sure seems squirrelly like he does."

"That Vegas trip didn't dry him all the way out. The doctors prescribed more drugs to calm him down."

They leaned atop a fence by the petting zoo.

"Okay, listen here now. I have arranged for Weaver and his company to come out here and pick Diller up at midnight. I'm set to call Weaver at his DPS office and tell them where Diller is."

"Midnight."

"Now, M. J., they'll be comin' in police sedans. They'll be armed to the teeth. Well you know Weaver, and you know what some of the other Rangers look like. Shouldn't, but if somethin' happens to me and I can't call Weaver, and no one shows up here by 2 a.m.? You call Weaver at the DPS. Tell him who ya are, and where Diller is. He'll remember you."

"Oh yeah."

"They're gonna carry Diller to the courthouse in Houston for the special grand jury. Then, Weaver's got a plane ready at an airport. The whole team will take him to D.C. for their hearing. After that he's a federal problem, he belongs to Uncle Sam. Witness protection."

"Witness protection. What must that be like? God." The Warden smiled. "We may be getting on, but I'll be glad whenever he's gotten gone."

Jack chuckled.

"Dja' talk to anybody about what Pellen said to you in Warshington?"

"No," Jack replied in one of his patented breathy sighs. "I haven't, M. J. and I just don't know who the hell to tell what. Who to trust? I trust you. Weaver. It kills me that I'll be losin' all control of Diller after the Feds get 'em. No other way, though."

The men slowly strolled to Jack's car.

"Lots of folks are successfully on that witness protection plan though," Jack continued. He shook off the depression with a reminder, "Thursday night. Weaver. Rangers." He climbed into his Caddy and said though the open window, "If they don't show by 2 a.m., you call Wisdom at the DPS."

"Right on," said M. J.

Kellog drove off. In the passenger seat, the briefcase beside Jack contained a new batch of cassettes and video tapes the content plucked from Diller's brain about names, dates, places, vehicles, and times. Diller was a bewildering source of both important and trivial information. He opened the briefcase and hit the play button on the cassette player to listen to one of Diller's rambling dissertations again.

"Diller, what did they do with this Demally's body?" Jack heard himself asking on the recording, following up on but one of the confederation's hits.

"Took 'em to the pig farm."

"Pig farm?"

"Yeah... pig farm right chere in Harris County. Pigs'll eat any damn thang ya know. You want to get rid of a body, just turn it loose with some hogs. They'll eat the flesh, the bones, the hair. Pigs. Yeah. All registered bad guys gotsta have 'em a good pig farm. I hear up north, they raise minks. Minks are like pigs...eat any damn thang. They also paid poachers to get them some alligators from Louisiana. They got 'em down in a man-made lake on the mansion grounds. They haul people down there and scare the living shit out of them by saying they'll feed 'em to the gators. Them gators now...they're scarier than shit. Ira Tenpenny tends to them. Feeds them every day. He swears he'll make a pair of boots out of one them someday. They're perfect pets for a cold-blooded bastard like him."

(fast forward)

"...Welder, Wisconsin. Someplace like Welder, Wisconsin, er...er, Bumfuck, Montana...that's where they's sendin' me, huh? Gimme a phony name like, like Peter Richardson. 'Hi. Hello. My name is Peter Richardson the Third from Dungberry, Kansas.' I am a pet rock salesman. I was a roadie for Barry Manilow. What the fuck? I wonder what these federal boys will do with me? Who will I be? And where I'll be? Don't know if I can live a straight life. No dope. No deals. Shit. Will the laws be watchin' me all the time?"

(fast forward)

"...Al Tanno had her down, split her head open with a hammer..." Diller's voice changed drastically in this segment to which Jack had randomly stopped on. It sounded low, solemn, monotonous, zombie-like. Not the cocky, infectious resonance he usually rambled in. Diller's voice continued. "Felicia lay on her kitchen floor...lots of blood all over. It was all stuck-like matted in her hair. Tanno and Shafrin were confused, pissed at each other.

"They had me tied up tight. I don't think they would have killed her if they had got me out of the house before she came home. I don't know. They carried her to the bathtub and cleaned up the blood. They waited till dark, till after midnight, watched television, game shows, then comedy shows, then news. They even ate some food from the refrigerator. I knew that Felicia was dead. She had to be. Just bled to death in her own tub. Right where she used to like to take hot baths and read. Right beside all her knick-knacks of trolls and dragons. Colored towels. I had to piss, but I was tied to the chair. I just peed in my pants; I didn't even care no more. It didn't matter anymore.

"After midnight, Vic pulled the car up the drive, and they put me on the floorboards of the back seat. They put Felicia in the trunk. Vic spent some time in the house, then we left. We drove for a while. Then we were out in the desert. No. No first we stopped at their warehouse. That's where they got the chain saw. Then we wound up in the middle of nowhere, way away from Vegas."

"'Okay, fuckface,' Al Tanno said to me, he saus like... 'Dis is what will happen to you if you'se fuck up.' Al cranked up the chain saw, and they cut Felicia up like a butcher, like she was never a real person. Like a dummy. They cut her up. I tried to look away, look at the sky full of stars, but the sounds of the saw, working through the tough spots...damn it, man. Goddamn, man. I can't look at the night sky anymore, man. I think like I hear that fucking chain saw. How could people be so fucked up, so like animals, to do that shit, and not even care, not even think about it twice? Ya know, Kellog, when we were in Felicia's house, they had me tied up and she was dead in the tub, Al and Vic just watched reruns of "All in the Family" and other shows and they were laughin' at 'em. How could those twisted motha-fuckas do what they had done and still laugh like that?" Diller was sobbing.

"I don't know, Diller," came Jack's just as solemn voice on the tape. "I think about things like that sometimes too."

(fast forward)

"Back in the middle '70s, me and two of my buddies met this pilot, an ol' boy by the name of Norman Kerr down in Austin. Norman was a smuggler. Now this is the same Norman that later introduced Tanseed to the Pontecorvo clan. Well, me and my two podnas figured that we needed to run some appliances down into old Mexico. Mexicans with some money were dying to buy U.S. of A. washers, dryers, TV sets. Stereos. Shit like that. What a mark-up we charged. But we couldn't run those big bastards over the border crossings. We started buying 'em, loadin 'em into Norman's plane and shuttling it across the border. Well, shit, we soon realized that we were flying back empty. Right. What a waste. Nature whores a vacuum."

"Abhors..."

"Yeah, well. We started pickin' up coke and pot, flyin' right back into Texas to an airstrip near Austin. One time we had dropped off a load of microwaves in old Mexico and started loadin' up bales of dope. Here come the Federales, YEAH. Mexican polices runnin' over the top of the hill shootin' pistols all up in the air and around at us. Shit. We dropped the load and flew that bugger off with bullets a flyin' everywhere. Ya know, years later Norman met that Federale Captain and together they worked many a damn drug deal. Ya know that load of dope they chased us off from? This Cap-e-tan seized it and sold the whole load to some other Texas boys to fly over the border. If ya ain't connected, your gonna wind up in the Mex jail house."

"Diller, someday somebody's gonna write a book about you."

"The *Life and Times of Diller Bailey.*" Diller said proudly.

"Or...*Nature Whores a Vacuum*," Jack added.

"You know, that ain't a pretty picture when you actually come to about think it."

"No, it ain't."

"How about – I'm not a crook – that's a good title. Who said that first anyway? Bruce Lee? Einstein?" Diller asked.

"Richard Nixon."

"Figures."

*****

Kellog pulled up in front of his Ramada Inn motel room. He had been there a week, under a false name, visiting his house only two times, after which he took great pains to shake any Confederation tail that might be following him. Not only did he personally feel safer at the Inn since his whereabouts were unknown, he felt better about driving to the zoo for Diller's interviews, knowing that he could not be picked up and followed from his house. Rarely did he appear at the station of late, spending most of his time at the zoo or in the inn preparing casework on the Ponte-corvo/Tanseed operation. Each night he collapsed in the strange bed with exhausting headaches to awaken feeling unrested and anxious. It was all too, too consuming.

The phone rang.

"Jack," said Weaver. "Got news."

"Good or bad."

"Depends. I was asked to help out and identify a body found on Dowl Creek in Liberty County last week."

"Okay, okay, heard about it."

"The face was bashed in, body nude. Shot 11 times with a 9mm. The face was probably bashed in by gunfire. The corpse's hands were intact. We sent prints off to the Feds and guess who it is?"

"Who?"

"An old hippy boy we knew named Donny Mecher, our Pine County drug cook and cultivator."

"Hell, he wasn't gonna talk to us," said Jack.

"But, I guess somebody didn't know that for sure," replied Wisdom.

"Good news, one bites the dust. No more work on him. Bad news, he didn't talk and turn anybody. And now, won't ever."

"I'm not going to tell Diller this," Jack said. "It would just scare the living shit out of him."

*****

"Great amounts of shit are gonna hit a very big ass fan tomorrow, Rye," Jack told his friend, Rye Edleson, at the Assistant DA's office. "Diller begins grand jury testimony tomorrow, and that's why I would like for you to look at these."

"What's this?" Rye asked as he watched Jack pull files from a box he'd laid on the floor and slide them across the desk.

"Arrest warrants," Jack said.

Rye, as still as a discontent statue, glared at Jack looking very unhappy.

"Arrest warrants. Who ya arresting? The Houston Astros? How many got-damn arrest warrants do you want?"

"Probably more than ever before. Probably more than anybody has asked for before from your supreme highness."

"So, you want arrest warrants even though there will be grand jury warrants in just a few days? Then federal warrants a few days after that? AND, you want probable cause arrest warrants...TOO?"

"Yup," Kellog said.

"Oh, if I was that high and mighty, you'd be carrying this shit somewhere else. That's the trouble with being a pissant around here. You have to deal with all the ants." Rye hauled a stack over.

"Quit whining and read."

"I have often thought about bringin' my ol' ball an' cap, Colt revolver up heah and positionin' myself at my door at the end of the hall, right heah', and shootin' police detectives that wander my way carrying boxes with giant stacks of papers like this...heah," Rye said dryly.

"Good God," Jack said. "That's extreme. I want to have these probable cause warrants up my sleeve right away in case I need 'em real fast."

"Fast? Kellog, Diller will be testifying before the grand jury tomorrow morning, so we'll have grand jury indictments in three days." Rye snapped.

"Three days. Maybe four. Maybe next Monday if Angelina has an office birthday party or baby shower. If the judge goes fishing. Lots could happen in two or three days. I want to have some probable cause warrants to serve if I need 'em before then," returned Jack. "They all may scatter to the four winds inside two or three days."

"They'll just bond out on these PC warrants."

"Rye, they'll just bond out on the indictment warrants, too. Hell, they could be in Monte Carlo before the court clerks are through preparing the indictment paperwork. If I see any of them leaving? I'll arrest them on these PC warrants. Stop them. Delay them. Mess with them. Get 'em down on the books. They may be carrying guns and drugs..."

"Then Scooter Gleason will bond them out with cash," continued Rye.

"We'll let him bond the som-a-bitches out. Then if they go to Monte Carlo, they'll be bail jumpin' fugitives, too. Maybe then some judge will finally get disgusted and have the balls to hold 'em WITHOUT bond if they're caught again."

Rye continued with the icy stare.

"Anyway, some of those cases in that pile in front of you, are unindictable at this time, too incomplete for the grand jury, but there is plenty of probable cause in them for a judge to issue an arrest warrant. Grand jury will have to wait on those cases. I want to arrest them all on anything I can, if I need to, right away. I want to pepper their criminal histories with arrests. I want to punch 'em hard and every way I can."

Still the arctic stare. Jack smiled.

"Might not even serve the warrants, Rye. Might just keep 'em right up here." Jack pointed up his sleeve.

"Mites are on a tick's ass. MIGHT not serve 'em," barked Edleson. "If any judge in the State of Texas signs any warrant fer anybody, you have a duty - an obligation - to serve it. By law, not at yer damn convenience."

"Convenience has nothing to do with it. Strategy does," said Jack. He'd had these arguments with prosecutors before."

"May not serve 'em..." mumbled Rye while looking through the first folder. "Jack, you are an ACLU nightmare."

"Well, you know Rye, if any member of the ACLU had their daughter raped or murdered, they'd damn sure want me on the case."

Rye leaned back in his leather chair hauling the first stack of reports with him. "Yeah, Jack," he agreed. "I'll bet they would."

Diller was a proven, road tested, credible witness and the files had statements and reports on a multitude of crimes committed by a multitude of confederation characters, many with corroborating affidavits and evidence lists. In absolute silence, Rye studied the reports for a full 40 minutes while Jack worked on his third cup of coffee and stared at the big, brash, sprawling Houston skyline through a window.

"Oh, got an affidavit of non-prosecution the other day on a case of yours," mumbled the Assistant DA.

"Oh?" asked Jack.

"Yeah. Rape case. Ida Bell?"

"Ida Bell dropped charges? What in hell for?"

"Don't know," answered Rye, "Just got the affidavit."

"Say anything special in it?"

"No sir. Boilerplate form."

Kellog stood and began to pace and plan the time he would next be free to see Ida. This was not right. This was not good.

"Sgt. Kellog, pick up line eight. Sgt. Kellog. Line eight," came a feminine voice over the intercom interrupting Jack's thoughts.

"Kellog," he said into Rye's phone.

"Jack, this is Betty," said one of West Forge's communications officers. "Hate to bother you, but there's a man who says he urgently needs to talk with you. He won't give a name, just a number."

"O.K., what is it?"

She gave him the number.

"Thanks." Jack dialed the number. A man quickly answered.

"This is Sgt. Jack Kellog. West Forge PD," he paused for some reaction, then continued, "Can I help you?"

"My name is Blue Boone, Sgt. Kellog," and Jack instantly recognized the name of Tanseed's old dirty, dealing horse doctor. "I've heard about you. I must see you. I must talk to you. But it's got to be alone. My life is in ...I am ...in...no one, NOBODY must know I am meeting with you, Sgt. Kellog, and I know there are spies in your department. I must see you alone. Complete secrecy. Can you come?"

"Yeah," said Jack.

"Can you meet me tonight at 7 p.m. at my old vet's office, alone?"

"Yes, I can come." Jack hung up and beat his thumb on the phone wondering why Ida Bell had dropped charges, what in hell did the vanished veterinarian, Doc Blue Boone wanted, and how the hell much longer would Rye Edleson take approving those reports.

*****

Ida wasn't surprised to see Jack's face at her door.

"Ida," he said softly.

"Come in Sgt. Kellog," she said in her usual humble manner. He stepped inside her apartment, the home of more than one tragedy. Jack had called her day job and discovered Ida had taken two weeks emergency leave. Very unusual.

"Ida, what happened?" Jack asked.

"Sgt. Kellog." She lowered and shook her head. "He beat...he beat my...let me show you." She led him down the hall of the railroad style apartment. There, lying in bed beside an open window that let in the city street noises of traffic and sounds from kids playing was a small nine-year-old boy. He had a cast on his right arm, casts on his left knee and right ankle, and his face was bruised and bandaged. Ida had the room dark. The boy's eyes looked searchingly up at Jack's.

Kellog felt his skin crawl and tingle and he rested against the doorframe. Weakened, he couldn't help himself and sighed deeply.

"He beat my Bobby, Sgt. Kellog. Rasp caught him and beat him up. Broke his little teeth in his mouth, his face, his arm, and his little legs. Then he left him in a dump. Then he called me at my job and told me where I could find him. Told me it would happen again if I didn't drop charges. I found Bobby in the trash, Sgt. Kellog." Tears came from her eyes. "In a big trash can."

Jack looked back at the boy for half a minute.

"Bobby, do you like the Houston Oilers?"

"Yeth," he said quietly and with a new lisp.

"I do, too." Jack wanted to reach out and touch the boy. Instead, he turned to Ida and pulled his checkbook from inside his leather blazer.

"Ida, I want to buy a color TV set fer inside this room and you get cable TV for it, the sports channel, movies, everything. I want you to pay some bills, too." He handed her a check for $1200. "Don't worry about Rasp Wilson anymore." They stared at each other for a moment. Ida was silent. Jack told Bobby goodbye and let himself out.

He walked down the stairs and made for his Cadillac. He seemed to want to sob or cough, or something like that, but he knew if he did, he would start an uncontrollable, blubbering, steering-wheel-pounding fit. He climbed in behind the wheel of his car and gripped it tightly with clumsy hands and couldn't turn the ignition on. Then he did start to cry, for little Bobby Bell, for Roy Timmes, for Pine County deputies, for a Keno girl named Felicia. He cried for other things he could not list or understand specifically, for his own heathen, ungodly soul that had no believable answers for any single thing. There on Placker Street, in front of the kids who moments before were playing street football, he cried uncontrollably. Some couldn't help but stop and stare at him.

"You okay mister?" A young boy cautiously asked, outsie the closed window.

He swallowed deep, pinched off all of it.

"Ah, yeah, sure. I stepped on a nail."

"You'd better get that fixed. My uncle stepped on a tenpenny nail and it went clean through his foot. It turned all colors and they had to cut his foot off at the hospital. He shoulda gone to the doctor. My auntie told him and told him. You need an ambulance?"

"Come on Raymond." Other kids shouted to him from afar.

"Jesus had a big nail in his feet," the kid added.

"That he did. A big one," Jack said.

"A real big one and...and he died too."

"And I recken he came back, too."

The boy smiled.

"Thanks to your advice, I'm a headin for the doctor right now." Jack said, starting his car. It was nearing seven p.m. and time to see Doc Boone and put a nail in somebody's coffin.

*****

Doc Blue Boone's old empty horse clinic had log walls. It looked like a cavalry fort, right down to the tall walls that surrounded the main office, small living quarters and barn. The place looked dusty, barren, and in minor disarray. Jack pulled onto the small complex and stopped to size up the scene. On the far right, he could see an older model Suburban by the largest of the stables, bearing the personalized license plate "Blue."

Doc went out of business two years before and, though Jack had never graced the place himself, he could well remember its prosperous years when horses and cattle were trucked in from miles around for treatment at Doc Boone's hands.

Jack slowly drove up beside the Suburban, recalling Diller's tale of how Doc had fallen from the good graces of

Baker Tanseed and how Tanseed slit all of the veterinarian's prize dogs' throats when Doc had failed him in a crime.

It was against department policy and, for that matter common sense, to meet an informant without first notifying someone, a dispatcher, or supervisor or fellow cop, but Jack had been making clandestine informant meetings for decades and he heeded the secrecy warnings of Doc Boone. He knew he and the PD were under intense radio and visual surveillance by Tanseed's and Pontecorvo's henchmen whenever possible. So despite common safety sense and PD policy, Jack ignored his radio and procedures, stepped out of his Caddy and walked slowly into the dark barn.

"Doc," Jack said softly into the duskiness.

"Yes," came a voice and Doc Blue Boone's wiry frame appeared some 30 feet before him. True to his old image, he still had that huge black hat and broom handle moustache. To fight the November chill he wore a long, tan Australian, rain jacket. Ostrich boots completed the fashion picture.

"What can I do for you?" Kellog asked.

"I have to tell you something about Baker Tanseed," he said.

"And what might that be?"

"He will kill you," his voice lost control like an immediate and deadly warning. Crazed. Reluctant. "He will KILL YOU."

A baseball bat bashed across Jack's back and like a marionette whose strings were suddenly cut, Jack crashed face first into the cold ground. Two huge hands, then two knees crushed him into the dirt. A hand groped over his body and yanked his .45 from his beltline. Then the weight left his body. Stunned, Jack rolled over and tried to look up.

Tony Tetro stood before him with a huge grin, brandishing the baseball bat, a loan shark and mob muscle's favorite tool.

"Jack-Off." Johnny Handell yelled. He stood behind Tetro twirling Kellog's gun in his left hand. It had been this curly-headed skunk that had disarmed him.

Jack slowly got to his feet, not yet fully feeling the whelp across his back. He stutter-stepped and stumbled for a second.

Ira Tenpenny appeared next. He stepped within eight feet of Jack and with a monstrous, hateful sneer, instantly exploded into a twisting blur. Ira's right boot blasted into Jack's face before Jack could react. With his perfect, spin-kick complete, the Indian returned into a perfect fighting stance. Waiting. But, waiting for nothing.

Jack assumed the perfect loser's stance, spread eagle on the ground in a cloud of sawdust and hay and disintegrated horse manure. Large quantities of blood flowed readily. Jack's. Then he saw Baker Tanseed.

Tanseed strutted up beside Jack, and Kellog's good eye rolled to look up at him.

"Ya know pig," Tanseed said, "ya been to Warshington, Vegas. Ya been raidin' our drug farms, buggin' my house. How did ja think ya were gonna get away with that? How'd ja think ya were gonna do all that? And get away with it? And stay alive, boy? How?" Tanseed leaned over. "We gonna break up some pig bones. I'll piss on yer grave after YOU dig it. PIG." The cowboy gestured Tenpenny, "Bring HIM in fer questioning."

A smiling Tetro leaned on his bat as though he was posing for a baseball card photo, Handell and Tenpenny hoisted Jack to his feet. Then Handell maneuvered Jack into a half-Nelson, driving his chin deeply and painfully into his collarbone, while Tenpenny searched his body, extracting his car keys and flipping them to Tetro. Then Handell let loose like Jack's body was a punching bag.

It all got real gray. Closed in. Hazy for Jack. Crazy. Best he could see or understand, they hauled him outside...Ida

Bell's boy...to a Lincoln outside, he...the boy's in bed...and what...he was being punched again and ...Ida cried. No, it was Diller crying? No. Who? What? His boot heels dragged across the gravel parking lot. That wouldn't do. Scuffing up those boots. Tetro laughed. Did he say "home run?" The boy was in the dump. Jack's consciousness faded in and out. Like an LSD trip. They tossed him in the back seat. He could see outside on the lot. The farewell party stood there stoically. Ida Bell. Her boy stood there too. Diller Bailey and even Felicia stood there. She only had one arm. Al Tanno was there. And Piggy Banks in his wheel chair...and... Randolph Scoot shook his head in disgust.

And then finally he passed out. Or was he already? He dreamed deeply of Ida Bell's boy. He dreamed he sat in a corner of the boy's room in the dark. The boy screamed and screamed for his mother, but Ida wouldn't come. She couldn't come. She was at work.

Back in the barn, Tanseed glared at Doc Boone, an intentionally intimidating cruel look, like a drunk in a bar waiting to fight. The ex-friends exchanged no words. Doc looked ashamed. Ashamed of being Tanseed's henchman one more time. Doc had killed a man in New Mexico with Handell for Tanseed. Something he had to do. Business. Doc now had little doubt of Kellog's fate. Tanseed walked past him aggravatingly close and disappeared from the barn into a waiting Jag out back. Tomorrow there would be $10,000 deposited into Doc's bank account. Ten thousand badly needed dollars for his rented apartment, his small new vet business in Conroe and well, maybe just a little coke. Just a little.

Doc Boone stepped outside and watched Tetro drive off in Jack's Caddy. He saw the limo and Jag leave. And he saw his own ghosts standing there on the parking lot, too.

CHAPTER FOURTEEN:
GUNS AND AMMO

Jack knew Ida had to be home soon. Or would she? Would Ida report to yet another job? Then another, then another, then another...

"Jack. Jack. Jack, baby."

How could the boy scream for his momma much longer?

"Jack baby."

Slapped awake, Kellog discovered himself stretched out on the tile floor of what appeared to be a small storeroom. His hands were cuffed behind his back. He realized he had dreamed the bizarre, thick nauseous dreams that most times come when one is knocked out. Boxer's dreams. The room's fluorescent light caused him to squint. He felt cold, stiff, and beyond disoriented until he realized that Tony Tetro loomed over him.

"Come on babe, get up here," Tetro said while lifting Jack to his feet and guiding him to a folding chair. Jack collapsed into the seat.

Tetro sat back in a second chair with a huff, crossing

his formidable arms across his ample chest. "Boy, da older ya get, da tougha it gets to come outta one, don't it Jack."

Jack barely had feeling in the left side of his body, even the left side of his tongue felt numb - laying like a golf ball in his swollen mouth. Tetro was right. It got tougher.

"Da older I got, da tougha it got fa me to come outta a good knockdown."

Jack drooled, then hacked up a little blood. His ribs. Then he remembered Handell punishing his torso with rabid fists. Some of his ribs were broken. Where was I? Jack wondered. What happened? Doc Boone. An ambush. A damn ambush. Handell. Tetro. Tenpenny. Tanseed. He'd strutted his damn macho head straight into...some kind of hell. Stupid. Fucking stupid.

"Babe, listen, ya know why you'se is here, right? You is the only one in da woild who knows where Diller Ding-Dong Bailey is. You. They are going to find out from ya where he is."

Jack noticed that Tetro wore a tuxedo.

"Ain't no stopping them, Jackey. Shit, I learned that many years ago. If you want to beat them, they'll just beat you back. They get what they want. If ya do beat them, they will order your death from their very plush prison cell. No win deal."

"Back in ...oh, 1973, when I worked for NYPD, they promoted me into the Organized Crime Task Force, the whole city became ours to investigate. And I was a real ball-buster. Hey. I busted mafia chops. We caught the Gallantis in dere heists, dere smuggling, dere wheels and dere deals. I had a million Diller Baileys telling me all dere moves. They had no choice but to pay me off. Such a sweet deal. Marone!" Tetro kissed his fingertips. "Could be very close to your predicament here. Close but...ya pissed off a lot of people."

Tetro stood and walked around Kellog. Jack's head couldn't follow.

"They will fuck you up, Jackie. They got guys that will beat you up professionally. They'll torture you in such a way you won't be able to pass out. They got drugs that will rip your brains out. They use electricity on your dick. There are no secrets, Jack, just the easy way and the hard way to reveal them," said Tony. "The one-minute secret and the two-minute. No one-hour secret. You can't last."

Jack's head fell forward. His throat grew tight. He was dizzy. A gurgling groundswell punched in his stomach. His head lurched forward and he vomited.

"Whoaaaaa." Tetro yelled, dodging the fluid.

"Concussion city here. You need to be in a hospital. Take some fuckin' money, Jack. When you take the money and tawk, they got something on you. You're in the middle. And you might live. Might."

"How much?" Jack mumbled.

"Not as much as the first offer. You blew that one." Tetro laughed, then got serious. "But, babe, ya ain't in a position to deal, you know what I mean?"

"Well, Diller's where...you can't get to him... anyway," said Jack.

Tetro slid his chair before Jack and he sat in front of him, inches from his face, ignoring the vomit on his chin and the threat of another eruption.

"Ha. Where?"

"He's in an army base. He's under guard. The Feds set him up."

"Oh," said Tetro calmly, "don't underestimate us Jack. Anyone anywhere can be contracted. Army. HA. The Army is just people. We do know he's goin' to the grand jury tomorrow."

"That's what the money is for, isn't it?" Jack replied.

"Not really. Where is he NOW? Well, Jack," said Tetro as he stood. "We'll have to run some truth serum through you before we'll buy that story. This Army line? Dat dere's a line I would make up for a stall, a bluff."

"What are you gonna do about me?" Came a third voice from the corner of the small room, startling Jack. He painfully turned to see another man, bound tightly to a chair a few feet behind him. Jack shook some more cobwebs loose from his head and refixed his eyes on the man. He was in his mid-30s, clean cut and in a pinstriped suit. Tetro approached this man.

"You." He barked. "You owe us some money little pinhead, and you're very, very late." Tetro reached for a pole-like object in the corner. It was excruciatingly difficult for Jack to look over his shoulder, so he stared blankly at the floor in front of him.

"Whizzzzzzzzzzzz"

Jack's head spun impulsively toward the noise, pain or no pain. Tetro made a monstrous, insane grin. He had a weed eater in his hand, and he stuck the cutting edge right up against the bound man's shin. The cord slashed through the cloth and cut into the man's ankle. Strings of flesh flung about the room. Tetro released the trigger and smiled; the man's face reflected sheer terror.

The man tipped over his chair howling and begging for mercy.

"Rip ya a new ass," Tetro said and cackled heartily. He walked around to Jack.

"It gets way worse dan dis, Jackie, much worse. They'll cut cha' dick up with one of dese tings." Tetro unplugged the extension cord.

Kellog knew then, that the "they" Tetro kept mentioning, this "team," this intrepid "pool" of professional mind crackers, was undoubtedly the skilled and veteran investigator and interrogator, Mr. T. Tetro himself, and he was capable of anything. He could hear the man still babbling in the corner.

"You're crazy. Crazy!" the man yelled.

"Dere's a party up on da' hill tonight. Oh, gotta make sure I don't got any strips of skin on my tux. Or puke." Tetro looked over his tux. "Big Party. Some local politicos. A nice, smart judge. We make campaign investments. Big ones ya know. Den dere are a lotta guests. Guests like Mr. Pinhead here. That's how he started out with us. Guests that are not doing so well in life anymore. Guests what need some monies to play with. Some drugs? We offer 'em money and drugs. When all frivolities are over a bit later tonight, we'll come down here and we'll tawk some more, just you and me. Tawk, Jack." He began coiling up the orange extension cord.

"Tawk and maybe I can do something for you. You know deep down we are a lot alike, Jackey. Dere's a brotherhood in policing dat don't go away no matter what."

Tetro made for the door, then turned. "Oh, by da way. I haven't had a chance to tell you. Love the dogfight raid. You're like me, Jack. Ya got moxie. Ya got style. Maybe we can work out a deal. Later, babe."

He reached for the doorknob and turned back yet again.

"Oh, yeah. After this Vegas thing, we figured our phone lines are bugged, too. So, we ran the house and phone lines under some high-tech equipment and found your little bird's nest of troopahs listening in on us across the street over dere. As a matter of fact, we now got them under surveillance you might say." He left, locking the door behind him. The lights went out. Blackness.

The man was still sobbing in the corner. Watching the weed eater attack had caused Jack's body to flush with adrenaline, killing some of the pain and numbness. He immediately tried stretching his cuffed hands down his back and under his rear then around his feet to the front of his body. He accomplished this after some extremely awkward and painful maneuvering.

*****

"Did he tell ya anything?" Tanseed asked Tetro after weaving through the high-class party guests to query the specialist.

"I talked, he coughed up blood," said the big ex-cop while scanning the crowd, "I talked, he moaned. Puked. Like dat."

"What's next?" Tanseed inquired. He also wore a tux, but with a black string western tie and boots.

"Next? After this party, I'm going down there and talk some more with pliers and hammers in my hands. Ray wants to see him again, too. That little cellar room he's in is a good spot for some wet work."

Tetro spotted Pontecorvo fraternizing with a couple and broke away from Tanseed, never once having looked the Texan in the eye during the brief encounter. Tanseed backed away to a wall and rendezvous with a solid and stern Ira Tenpenny. Their heads bent together conspiratorially, and they began whispering.

*****

Hands up front, Jack tried standing but couldn't yet. He crawled to the overturned, crying man.

"Hey," Jack growled and grabbed what he thought were binding ropes. They weren't. They were plastic covered chain, woven through the chair and the man's limbs, then connected by a padlock, a rig akin to a bicycle chain.

"Damn." Jack barked, then hauled the man's chair upright. The move exhausted him and he sat down on the floor, head throbbing. He wiped the vomit off his chin with his forearm. The only light came from a thin sliver beaming in from the space between the door and the floor.

"We're dead." The man gasped. "Who are you?"

"Name's Kellog. I'm a detective."

"Private detective?"

"No. Public. I'm with the West Forge P.D."

"Francis Allen. Are the police going to rescue us?"

"Fraid not, Francis."

"Where are we?"

"We're in Western World. The basement." And, Francis Allen began telling Kellog his rueful story. Jack groped around the room finding nothing but some small, thin, soft boxes of packaged shirts, shoes, and hats. He sat back in his chair and patted his bruised face with his clasped hands. The air smelled stale and he felt sweat trickle down his back. Based on what he could find in this room, he could create only the most temporary stand-off, not worth the effort of only befuddling Tony Tetro or whoever else might soon come for them.

"I met this man at the country club. I played golf with him. Seemed a nice guy. Said he had lots of money, offered some to me a lot of times, like a real rich guy. My dad and I are co-owners in a construction business and business had dropped off, not bad, but down."

Jack barely listened. Instead, he pictured Weaver Wisdom and his company of Rangers awaiting his call at DPS Headquarters. Ready to pick up Diller at the secret location and hide him for several hours, then sneak him into the courthouse before dawn and delivering him to the grand jury. He pictured Diller and M.J. sitting at the zoo house, bags packed and ready. He crawled over to the tiny sliver of light that barely beamed through the space between the door and the floor. He maneuvered his watch into the beam to catch the light: 11:30 p.m.

Still early. Weaver would expect the call at midnight and would pick Diller up shortly thereafter in an armed convoy. Jack cursed himself for his own pig-headed obstinacy, for not wanting to burden Weaver with Diller's secret hideaway. He was one phone call away from pulling it off. One. But there was a failsafe. If M.J. didn't hear from Weaver or Jack by 2 a.m., M.J. knew to call the Ranger. Jack wouldn't know where Diller was after three a.m. No matter how they tortured him, no matter what they did with weed eaters and electricity, he simply wouldn't know.

Jack moved to the door, laid on the floor and strained to see under the door but couldn't get much of a view. He rolled over on his back and interrupted Francis Allen.

"Ahhhh." Jack moaned suddenly and loud.

"What? What's the matter?" Allen asked rapidly.

"My back. Guy hit me in the back with a baseball bat."

Allen continued his tale, "They told me if I would sign over half the company to them, they'd leave me and my family alone. Can you imagine? Can you imagine them walking into my father with these papers, telling him I sold out and now he had the mafia for his new partner?"

Jack began to calculate timetables. The later Tetro came for him, the closer to three a.m. it became, the less pain… or drugs… he would have to withstand before he could reveal Diller's location.

"Francis Allen," Jack interrupted again, "if we could break that chair, we could make some slack. Maybe you could shimmy outta those chains."

"The chair is metal."

"Shit."

Then came the sounds of approaching men.

Keys.

Door opened.

Harsh light.

Three men poured into the room. Three cowboys in casual western clothes, no tuxes or suits. One wore a cowboy hat, the other two wore ball caps advertising a local feed store. Jack saw the time as 12:05 a.m. on his watch. They said nothing, only hauled him to his feet, unconcerned that he now wore his handcuffs around front instead of around back. They ignored Francis Allen completely.

They shoved Jack out of the room into a large basement. Bound for a narrow staircase, Jack knew if he followed them all the way, he'd come out a dead man, knew he would either die like a tortured dog or die fighting.

The one in the western hat walked in front of Kellog and began ascending the stairs. Kellog followed and the other two came up behind him in a single file. The steps were tiled and clean, the walls painted plasterboard, the stairs steep. About eye-level in front of him, Jack could see the back of the western belt of the man as they climbed. Tooled into the belt he saw the name, "Aubrey."

Jack suddenly recalled something he'd seen a prisoner do to several Houston Patrol Officers just "routinely transferring" another prisoner. Since he now wore his cuffs around his front and on stairs, too, as this prisoner had, he decided to try it.

Jack reached out and grabbed the "Aubrey" part of the belt in front of him, stepped sideways to the wall, and pivoted as he yanked Mr. Aubrey back down and past him with all the strength he could muster. He flung Aubrey down on his two unsuspecting partners below on the stairs. He didn't wait to watch this tumbling heap as he dove through the doorway at the top of the stairs. He knew his trick would work. He'd been that third careless Houston officer at the bottom of the heap some 23 years ago.

Western World! Jack rolled to his feet on the floor at the top of the stairs, and with his cuffed hands tucked under his chin, he dashed down an aisle. An aisle. He really was inside Western World, flashing through the occasional low watt security lights. Near 10 long rows of new saddles he hit the floor to catch his breath.

"Kellog!" shouted an angry voice.

"Kellog!" growled another.

Guns and ammo. The entire southern wall of Western World contained guns and ammo. He slowly raised up to take in the layout and saw the three men near the store front some two hundred feet away, splitting up for their quiet search.

No one left the store to get help? Jack thought they might fear losing face with their boys, letting him escape the way he had. Surely they'd try to recapture him first. Jack saw the south wall just beyond the tents and camping gear. He crept past the tents, narrowly missing detection. The heating system came on and the hum camouflaged the periodic scuffing sounds he so desperately needed to detect the location of his pursuers.

"Kellog…" ordered one, "give it up."

Jack slithered near some leather products and saw weapons only a few aisles away, but he froze to avoid a nearby searcher. Jack saw that if the man continued in the same direction, he would inevitably walk right up on him. He reached for a thick raw leather strap destined for tooling as a belt and flung it toward some plastic barrels, hoping the noise would halt the approach and cause the searcher to circle around the row of shelves and away from him. Instead, the man continued to move in Jack's direction and in seconds would appear at the end of the aisle where Jack cowered.

Kellog pulled another thick belt from the hook. The man almost charged right past him, but his gaze zoomed in on Jack's crouched form pressed against the leather goods. Jack "caught" his eye, this time with a crack of the belt. The man's head whiplashed back, the baseball cap spinning off in its own orbit, and a slicing eyebrow wound immediately opened. Jack followed with another slashing swing, snapping across the enemy's face. He dove on the stunned man, pummeling him downward, his cuffs and fists striking repeatedly, but not quickly enough to silence a last gurgling gasp for help.

"Auuuuubrey."

Aubrey, creeping around in Men's Wear and his partner in Boots both sprinted to Camping Goods. Jack found a 2", .38 revolver on the floor beside his unconscious victim. He dove for the gun, struggling to grip it properly, and once his finger landed on the trigger, he instantly fired it into the shelves ahead, hoping the blast would slow the rush of his enemies. It did. Fearing an ambush, Aubrey and his associate dropped to their knees, their run interrupted.

Jack scrambled straight for the gun area and came to rest in a pile of soft "gun boots," a mountain of rifle bags stacked up for a sale. He held his breath to better listen for other sounds, hearing only the moaning and gasping of the man he left on the floor. Jack quickly checked the cylinder of the small revolver to make sure it was a six-shot and not five. It was a six, so he had five very precious bullets left. He peered over the top of the pile.

Aubrey and his friend had made it over to their downed partner. Silently, they helped the wounded man to his feet and they tugged him off toward the front of the store. In a moment they were near the front doors and, to Jack's surprise, they fumbled with some keys. All three men abandoned the store! They carried their wounded man into a truck on the lot. They drove out of sight. Jack stood in amazement. They left him all alone in Western World.

Confused and suspicious, he sprinted for the gun counters. Did they have a fourth man hidden in the store waiting to kill him? Make him look like an armed burglar and kill him? Did they realize Jack now had a gun and they planned to bring back reinforcements? If so, they left him with enough supplies to fight off an army in the Alps for three years. Jack snatched up four Colt .45 Combat Commander handguns and frantically studied the shelves for bullets for .45 ammo. He shoved about 10 boxes to the floor, ducked down, opened them and frantically loaded four magazines.

A nearby glass counter held an array of extra mags for sale. Using a gun butt, he smashed the inside door glass, raked out two .45 mags and loaded them too, a tedious process with handcuffed limbs. But, he had no remedy for this cuffing problem. Then looking around he noticed some 15 feet away a display case of police supplies including Kubatons, nightsticks, whistles and ...boxes and boxes of Smith & Wesson handcuffs. He shattered a second case and ripped open a box, extracting a universal handcuff key. With a little awkward finger work, he freed one hand, then the other.

Every few seconds he glanced through the front store windows out onto the parking lot. It remained empty. Did they have an execution squad hidden outside? What the hell was going on here?

With a pistol in each hand Jack ran for the camping area and grabbed a suitcase-like knapsack. He dashed back and filled it with his loaded mags, boxes of ammo, boxes of handcuffs, and two .45's. He stuck the third .45 in his belt line and kept the fourth in his hand.

Then he made for a spot still behind the long counter, by a register near the front of the store. He saw shelves behind the counter containing miscellaneous office supplies and a phone. The clock on the wall said 12:40 a.m. He grabbed for the phone, then stopped. Was this the set-up? Did they let him loose in this store to monitor this very call, the very one that would send the Rangers to Diller's secret location. Was Tony Tetro sitting in the mansion with his own set of earphones on? Jack punched the counter in frustration, then dialed the DPS Ranger's office, sat on the floor and waited.

"Ranger Wisdom," said a serious voice.

"Weaver, it's Jack."

"Where the hell are you, boy?" the Ranger asked in a fury, standing in front of 12 solemn and anxious men. They crowded in anticipation.

"Weaver, they got me, listen, I may be on a recorded line. I've been kidnapped, then...I don't know...halfway released? Aaah, Weave, I'm gambling that when I tell you this, if they are listening, they won't know what it means. But you will, Weaver. M.J, M.J."

"I know what you mean, Jack. I know. Where the hell are you?" said Wisdom.

"You take all yer men and take care of business. And Doc Boone, the veterinarian set me up. Send some other people to find that son-of-a-bitch."

"Jack, where are you? I..."

"Weava." shouted Kellog. "YOU. Go and get Diller. I don't want YOU lookin' fer ME. Go. Do!" Jack hung up.

Weaver slowly hung up and looked at the grave faces on his fellow Rangers and Ranger Captain.

"Jack's in trouble," he mumbled, "but he doesn't want any help. Diller Bailey is at M.J.'s place, at the zoo. I've been there before. I know where it is. M.J. was Jack's old training officer in Houston PD. Doc Boone, the vet on the southside helped the gang kidnap Jack. We need him in custody."

As the Captain reached for the phone to request 10 more state troopers to search for Boone, Weaver and the Rangers grabbed up their gear and left for the Falthom City Zoo some 50 minutes away. Though delayed, the timetable commenced.

*****

Spying through the glass counter, then the front windows, Jack observed the front doors and parking lot from his spot next to the front cash registers. He sighed deeply, relieved that Weaver was on his way. He spotted some counter shelves and began a search for paper napkins or tissues, finding some along with half-used package of Extra-Strength Tylenol. He quickly gobbled four, dry, and shoved the toweling into a pocket.

He crawled through a space in the counter hauling his knapsack across the storefront and back to the stairway where he first engineered his escape. Hating to lose sight of the retail floor, Jack dashed across the store, slipped down the steps and ran to the storeroom where Francis Allen sat.

"What happened?" He asked Jack.

"Well, I don't really know. We're alone in the store," Kellog said while pulling out the napkins. He tore off some ends, licked them and jammed them into his ears. He tucked two wet pieces into the ears of Francis Allen. Jack pulled a gun from his waistband and aimed at the padlock of the chains on the chair leg.

"Lift yer legs up," Jack ordered, and Francis complied. He fired the .45, splintering the small lock and tearing up the chair leg. Jack unwound the rest of the chain, and Francis jumped from the seat. Both men removed their makeshift hearing protection.

"How did you...what did you do to get away from them? Where are they? I heard a gunshot," Allen babbled.

"I don't know what's goin' on," Jack said. "I got away from them, then they left me alone in this big store. I think that if we stroll outta heah somebody's gonna kill us."

Allen just stared at Jack with his mouth open.

"You ever been in the service?" Jack asked.

"No," said Allen.

"You hunt any?" Jack asked.

"Yeah, pheasant, some deer." From his expression, Jack could tell Francis thought it an unusual question.

"Good. Take this." Jack handed the man a loaded .45 from the knapsack.

"Let's get back upstairs where we can see outside."

But Allen stopped Jack. "Why haven't you called the cops?" He asked the detective.

"Don't know who I can trust. The only cop I do trust I just called, but he's got to do something much more important right now than rescue two heavily armed men inside a dark store. Anyway, this whole deal is a fucking death trap that I'm not sending anybody into until I figure out what the play is."

When both men got to the top of the stairs, they kneeled down and surveyed the store and what all they could see of the parking lot outside.

"If you will take a position in the back of the store near any service doors or back doors, I'll watch the front. I figure if we can wait this thing out about two...maybe three hours, I'll be able to call my friend and he'll help us get outta heah."

"Who is this friend?" Allen asked.

"He's a Texas Ranger, and he might come with a small army. Not that he needs one." Jack winked at Allen and squeezed his arm. "You'll see that family soon, Francis Allen. Now watch the back. If ya hear anything holler or come fer me."

As Allen left in the darkness, Jack crawled near the front windows and studied the parking lot and the occasional passing car on Loop 9. Just across the street, some state narcotics officers sat naively listening to electronic silence, not even aware that all their eavesdropping devices had been thwarted. What did Tetro mean when he said, "as a matter of fact, we got them under surveillance, ya might say." Would a call to those narcotic agents for help mean an ambush on them if they responded?

"Damn." Jack cursed. He had spotted yet another reason to curse, another reason not to call for help. The very front end of what looked like a Blazer protruded into view from the northwest corner of the store front. He inched up along the glass for a better angle. A gust of wind blew the smokey white trace of exhaust fumes around the edge of the building. There were men watching the store. Why? Confused, Jack crawled back away from the glass. Those cowboys made him an armed hostage. Why? He hoped for a few hours' peace at least. He wouldn't get it.

CHAPTER FIFTEEN:
SHIT FIRE, YANK.

Just 30 minutes later a stretch limo pulled up directly in front of the store. A stream of cars also appeared on the road, all leaving the mansion and filing out onto the Loop. The party was over. A very jovial Tony Tetro jumped out from the driver's side, and none other than Raymond Pontecorvo himself opened his own rear car door. Kellog watched them exchange smiling words. Taking absolutely no safety precautions, Tetro casually selected the front door key, opened the doors of Western World and both men stepped in, headed for the front stairway down to the basement.

"And to you two, I say a good evening," said a growling voice from the dark. Startled, both men stopped and squinted to discern the dark figure crouched nearby, half behind a wall in the shadows, holding a handgun. Recognizing Kellog's voice, Tetro slowly retreated away from his boss. He knew that crowd control was always tougher when targets stood at a distance from each other.

"What was it we blood brother cops say? Oh, yeah... that'll be far enough," Jack said menacingly, and Tetro froze.

"Guess ya'll got a funny operation here," Jack continued. "The northern hands don't know what the southern hands are doing."

"Hey, Jackie baby. We are here wit' a fabulous deal fa ya." Tetro proclaimed.

"Shut up." Jack barked. "The only deal I want from ya'll is surrender. I have warrants fer yer arrests. Get down on yer knees."

"Look you hick muthafucka', if you think you are gonna make me beg..." Pontecorvo threatened as Tetro dropped.

"I'll blow yer fuckin' feet right off," Jack barked.

Clad in his tux, Pontecorvo knelt in an uncoordinated, unathletic, stumbling motion.

"Now lay face down on the floor," Jack commanded.

"You book us you asshole, you're dead. We'll be out in an hour," said Pontecorvo.

"Oh, we're not going to the Police Station," Jack said. "Won't be any lawyers, any no Scooter Gleason's to get cha out."

Tony Tetro started to kneel down, knowing handcuffs would be next. His face showed disbelief, as if he couldn't comprehend what Jack had planned next for him, or for Ponty. He sprung to his right and reached for his beltline as Jack jerked his .45 over off Ponty and fired at Tetro instinctively. A round pounded into Tetro's tuxedo shirt, and his elbows flew up higher than his head. His pistol flipped through the air and a stylish black shoe slipped off a foot. The pistol struck the glass windows, and Tetro collapsed backward into a display of western boots. His quivering lip and the grimace on his face told Jack that Tetro saw himself dying.

"That's the sound of your last heartbeat," Jack growled.

Pontecorvo jaw dropped. He looked devastated. Tetro's chest gurgled and he coughed up blood as Ponty scampered over to him and cried out his name in a high-pitched almost feminine voice, "Tony. Tony. Tony. Jesus, Joseph and Mary."

Jack stared at the two and thought of all the pain, the suffering they had caused, and now Pontecorvo had tears in his eyes over this twisted, torturing, murdering henchman.

"You muthafucka." Ray screamed at Jack while he struggled to his feet. "You crazy muthafucka. You're friggen dead. DEAD." He shook clenched fists, spitting with almost every word. "I'll have 20 button men on the street hunting you by morning. They'll BREAK you. They'll CUT you to fucking pieces." He stopped for a sobbing, slobbering breath. Jack slowly raised his pistol and aimed it at Pontecorvo's chest.

"Why, shit fire, Yank," Jack said quietly with a sneer, "you'd do that to me?"

In that instant, Pontecorvo understood he was finished, as in his tale of the old racketeer and the Houston pawnbroker, the Texas parable. Jack's gun discharged, the bullet went straight to the heart, and the Yank mobster tottered over, spazzed and died in a pile of cowboy boots beside Tetro. Kellog stood before them, glowing in an elated rush of pleasure. He glanced outside. No one responded to the gunfire, sitting toasty warm in their Blazers, engines running, and stereos cranked.

Now, Francis Allen came running madly for the storefront, babbling as he charged. Jack turned and stepped out in the same aisle as Allen was some 50 feet away.

"It's okay." Kellog shouted.

Francis Allen fired his gun at Jack while at a dead run. The bullet ricocheted off the tile floor and whizzed past Jack's feet.

"What the....Shit." Jack cursed out. "It's me. Kellog." He shouted, waving a hand. "It's okay."

"You son-of-a-bitch." Allen cried out, still advancing, and he fired a second round right at Jack as the detective dove out of the aisle and out of Allen's eyesight.

"You son-of-a-bitch cop." Allen screamed.

Francis Allen, it seemed, was not Francis Allen. With a .45 in each hand, Jack popped up and opened fire four times. Two from each gun. Allen's dash ended in a bloody, rumbling, rolling crash and burn, spilling merchandise everywhere. Jack slowly approached the twitching body and saw yet another horrible death mask spreading over another face, etched with rabid shock and pain.

"You weren't supposed to escape." Allen howled between bloody gritted teeth while shaking spastically. "You weren't supposed to escape."

Jack just stared at him, then stepped over him to retrieve the .45 lying he gave him a half hour earlier, on the floor.

"You weren't supposed to escape." He bellowed over, over, and over again, spitting up blood in a haunting cadence.

"I get it, dipshit. I'm not supposed to escape."

Jack turned him over an dpulled his wallet out. He stepped back and opened it. The drivers license read "Louis Delmonte, Bronx, New York."

This Francis Allen was a plant. A plant in the closet for Jack to befriend. Maybe, just maybe, they planned for Jack to reveal details to Allen, like where he'd hidden Diller Bailey maybe in their escape plan. The cowboys let Jack escape, but the Yankees didn't know it? That's "Tanseed One, Pontecorvo zero," or rather - "Pontecorvo dead," as Jack kept score on the obvious game of deception. Jack looked down at the plant in his last throes. A plant for the weed eater. It was the weed eater scene that had instantly overcome all his doubts and suspicions about Francis Allen as a prisoner. Yes, that weed eater business, suckered him good.

"Get...get a doctor," Delmonte/Allen begged.

"Get dead," Jack answered.

Jack wondered just exactly what was supposed to happen next. He topped off the magazines in his guns. He pulled the car keys from Tetro's pocket and grabbed up the knapsack of guns and ammo. He could see the stretch limo across the front sidewalk, close to where the window display rooms began. Jack searched the front wall and found the first camouflaged wooden door to the window display room.

Once inside the display window, he found himself in a brown-felt covered room behind the famous stuffed trademark, the 17-hands tall, golden Palomino. The logo, brand of West World. Outside the front glass, across the brick sidewalk, he could see the passenger portion of the limo, and the very back car door that Pontecorvo emerged from just moments earlier.

Jack reared back, and then rushed the solid horse with his elbows up, hitting it like an angry linebacker. The horse's body pitched forward, toppling through the front glass and onto the sidewalk in a shower of jagged glass and splinters. Jack leapt through the opening, slipping on the pieces of glass on glass, but remained in motion. He ran for the limo and yanked the right-side rear door open and dove in. The two Blazers, one from each end of the store, bolted around the corners and bore down on the limousine.

With the ignition key gripped in his palm, Jack scrambled across the plush passenger interior over the seats and squeezed through the small opening into the driver's front half of the vehicle. He disliked seeing the rapidly approaching Blazer ahead. Arms appeared from its windows. Hands holding guns. Jack stuck in the key as he swung a leg under the steering wheel. Guns erupted - sitting duck - no time to move or - bullets pelted the limo. This, he thought, well, was it!

Nothing entered. Nothing. Jack looked around him. It was a bullet proof limousine. The kind made for business-men and diplomats, and for mafia people like Pontecorvo. Jack laughed. He laughed out loud! Then he calmly en-gaged the electric door lock, turned the key and started the vehicle while still under something of a barrage. Jack drove off toward the line of mansion party guest cars descending from the hill. The trailing gunfire therefore ceased. The Blazers remained behind him.

A fellow limo driver even stopped and let Jack maneuver into the line that led up to the Loop. The Blazers waited im-patiently to follow suit. Jack could see the men in the blazers wore cowboy hats. With about a 10-car lead, Jack turned west bound on the Loop. He had three-quarters of a tank of gas. Another laugh burst impulsively from his mouth.

"Even though I'm not supposed to, I think I might just be escapin'." He couldn't help but say to himself, savoring his temporary sanctuary. He knew, however, that soon the entire Tanseed and leftover Pontecorvo Confedera-tion would join in on the hunt, with Tanseed as the new, ruthless general.

"It's a new Civil War," Jack concluded out loud. "North versus the South. And I think...I think they just made me...somehow...kill Grant and Lincoln."

*****

With this head start, Jack floored the long auto out onto the beltway. He now was the cover, the distraction as Weaver's posse picked up Diller. His hands scoured the dash and console for the car phone. He found it and lifted the receiver, then slowly replaced it. He knew he had to act alone. Wanted to. He fled north on Highway 45, the limo full out. He pulled off at the exit of the Crossroads truck stop. He circled the place and looked for two tails. Tails from Tanseed and a "tail" named Clara. He saw her van on the lot, pulled beside her and beeped the horn.

"Youuu hoo, honey." Clara said, rolling down her window.

The dark limo window slipped down, and she saw Jack at the wheel.

"Oh, damnitt Jack. I thought I had me a rich one."

"Just a poor one."

"You don't look poor to me. Whatchu' doin' in a limo?"

"Leaving it here. Clara can you give me a lift?"

She nodded her head. "Yeah."

Jack pulled the limo behind the truck stop. Clara followed. He snatched up his knapsack and got in her van.

"I need to get near my house."

"Near it?"

"Yeah, around a block or two. It's being watched. Remember those guys I left with weeks ago?"

"Yeah."

"They're trying to kill me for sure now. On sight."

"What's in the bag?"

"Stuff to kill them back."

CHAPTER SIXTEEN:
KILL THEM BACK

Clara had some snacks and chocolate milk in her van and Kellog devoured them. She dropped him off behind a nearby medical complex. Jack walked a block then blended into the landscape of the neighborhood, ducking into the yard behind his house. He hung over the fence top, dropped the knapsack and vaulted his backyard privacy fence, falling into a heap on the dark lawn. He surveyed the manicured grounds. He noted his automatic light timer had tripped on several of his interior house lights, layin' down a collage of projected lights in rectangles and squares on the grass and driveway.

He low crawled to a row of thick bushes bordering his driveway and eased his way down until he attained a view of the street. Sure enough, the Lincoln that had terrorized him and tailed him before sat parked several houses away, loaded with occupants. He always felt they were from the Army of the South, not the North and now the South needed Jack more dead than followed.

He carefully inched back up the drive, typed in the alarm code and slipped through a side door in his garage. While he caught his breath, he put the Western World knapsack in the bed of his old truck, the War Wagon. Then he began to partially undress while getting a ring of keys from the truck's glove box. He unlocked the large heavy-duty toolbox welded to the bed-the box still specially packed from the Las Vegas trip, and pulled out a canvas bag. Other cities had SWAT teams, but West Forge didn't. The detectives were the SWAT team, and this was his war bag. He opened the black bag. Jack popped open and unzipped the front of his Wrangler jeans and inserted an athletic cup into his underwear. Then he removed his t-shirt to put on a Second Chance bulletproof, body armor, as the T-shirt came with the armor. Next, he put back on his soiled white dress shirt. Then came the heavy-duty lifesaver, a green combat vest with bulletproof panels and strategically placed lightweight armor plating. These levels of protection would stop almost all gunfire and greatly reduce blunt trauma.

Jack pulled his cordura black nylon police pistol belt from the bag, the one he wore in the East Texas drug raid and strapped it on his waist. From the Western World sack he produced a gun for the empty nylon holster. The belt contained nylon carriers for his magazines and cuffs, which were already stocked.

He tossed both the canvas bag and the nylon knapsack into the passenger side of the cab and slid in behind the wheel. He placed a loaded, cocked and locked .45 in each deep flack vest pocket and glanced at the automatic shotgun, always in the cab behind his calves. He pulled it up and rested it too, on the seat.

The garage door was the old fashioned, single piece, spring lifted, manual type. He opened the door slowly.

There in the quiet dark of his garage, he took a moment to reflect, for in the next moment he planned to lay down a blazing smoke screen to clear a serious path for Weaver to deliver Diller. But, no, he knew that wasn't the whole truth, the complete truth. Jack had grown tired of drugs, loan sharking, gunrunning, prostitution, contract bone breaking, contract killing. He had grown tired of playing a game, playing under strict rules against a monster that knew no rules. It constituted a no-win situation. They'd kidnapped, beaten, and shot at him. Some officers lay buried with their wives and kids crying for them. Another officer lay in the hospital near death. Their side - the wrong side - instantly bonded out with cash so they could get back to their illegal work, to maybe face charges - years later in court, where a whole new host of legal games, tricks, deceptions and rules began, sometimes involving payoffs to the judge and jury, or death threats to the lives of their families.

NO MORE. Tonight no constitution existed. No FUCKING MIRANDA. NO BOND. NO BAIL. Tonight the jury would ride the streets and no one could pay him off or threaten him again. It felt damn good when Tetro and Pontecorvo hit the floor of the damned. Damn good.

He took one long deep breath, his hands clenching the wheel, his expression wild. Layer by layer, he began to shut off all the decency in him, all the civilized notions and arm-chair theories. It was good versus evil. Equalized tonight.

He took a deep breath, turned on the ignition, hit the accelerator, blasted out the garage and barreled down the brick driveway. The men in the Lincoln may have even heard his scream over the engine's roar.

As soon as the truck appeared in view, the Continental's headlights came on and with its gas pedal floored, the dark sleek sedan's tires screeched as it sped down the street right behind Jack's turning truck. Jack purposely kicked on his brakes and the luxury car swerved away but not enough to clear the harsh impact into the suddenly stopped truck's tailgate, causing the back of the truck and the sedan's front to rock upward.

Cowboy hat brims hit the dashboard and the back of the front seat, then toppled into the laps of three of the four jostled occupants. On the impact, Jack instantly ejected from the truck both hands full of firing .45's, and as he let the truck slowly coast forward. The Lincoln froze deadly still as Jack pelted its windshield, hood and doors with 12 rapid rounds. A back door opened, and as its glass shattered to pieces, a large man with a revolver dove out on the street firing in wild abandon. A magnum round caught Jack's vest on his left shoulder and tossed him down on his front lawn. One of his .45's flew into the air. The man who shot him lay stone dead on the street. Flashes and explosions of gunfire from dead men twitching aimlessly erupted from inside the car. The roof itself ripped open from an automatic burst from what looked like Tec 9.

Now the Lincoln began to coast forward, and its back-left tire ran right over the man down on the street. Jack got up and pulled a pistol from his vest pocket. His left shoulder felt numb from the impact of the magnum. He noticed all four doors of the car now stood ajar. As the sedan rolled by, another passenger tumbled lifelessly out. The car came to rest against the incline of Jack's lawn. Carefully, Kellog approached the car, saw the grotesque red mashed insides, then reached in and cut the engine.

Lights. Shouts. Screams. Neighbors appeared in a flurry, and Jack ignored them all as he walked solemnly back to his truck. The truck coasted into a neighbor's parked Chevy. The back of the truck was buckled a bit. The rear tires looked fine. Jack got in his truck and roared off down the street. He heard distant sirens. The night of madness was just beginning.

*****

Jack drove down Corsicana Avenue toward downtown West Forge, knowing full well the Confederation men scrutinized the police station ahead for him and for any sign of Diller Bailey. They assumed Jack would escape to there, as well as house Diller for protection in the jail. Surely this assignment would call for their best. Surely, Ira Tenpenny waited ahead, the radical hand experienced in shooting federal and city police officers. Near the station, Jack saw the infamous dark custom van parked north, across from his headquarters.

A few dull, yellow streetlights burned across the wide empty streets and reflected off the front windows of closed businesses, guiding no one against the dark patches of downtown. A huge, round, white lamp on a metal pole by the front door of the station lit the stairs for no visitors to the police station. Sirens raced to Jack's neighborhood.

Jack accelerated toward the street-side of the van, passing it so aggravatingly close the War Wagon's rear view mirror smashed against the van's passenger side mirror, ripping both mirrors off and they fell in a clanging, tangled mess on the street.

"Shit." The van passenger proclaimed, as Tenpenny started the step side van and eased past the station front, then floored the gas pedal as he turned down the street where he last saw the truck turn.

"We donna know if dat was him, fa' Chrissakes." The heavy-set passenger shouted. "Maybe just a drunk in a truck. Kellog has a Cadillac."

Tenpenny ignored the remark from the New Yorker and continued a slow, searching pace.

"Should I call da' guys on dis C.B.?" he asked.

"No!" barked Tenpenny as he toured the streets of the

business district, his head leaning out of the windows to catch any vehicle sounds above the already frantic C.B. radio traffic. Handell sounded on the airwaves, frantically trying to raise Baker Tanseed on their personal channel.

"Dere's da truck," the Yank yelled, and Tenpenny tried to pursue the distant pick-up with the heavy, sluggish van, but it quickly disappeared again behind a bank.

"Do ya really tink dis Kellog would be playin' such games like dis?" The gangster asked in bewilderment.

"Without a doubt," the stoic Indian mumbled.

"Hey. Hey, dat it?" The thug questioned as they turned yet another corner to see a lonely truck parked by the West Forge Gardens Recreational Park entrance. The park looked as pitch-black as a jungle.

Tenpenny coasted to within 15 yards behind the truck, hit his high beams and studied the vehicle.

"Find your drunk."

"Hummph." The thug grunted, stepped out and adjusted his shoulders, a semi-automatic pistol with a silencer in his right hand. Tenpenny shoved open his door and half-stepped out. While the thug preoccupied himself with the dark park across the broad, stone sidewalk to his left, Tenpenny's eyes swept the whole scene. The thug still wasn't certain he'd find Kellog there, maybe just a sleeping drunk who…

BLAM. FLASH.

The thug's chest shredded from a shotgun blast as Jack sprang up from the truck's bed. The hood spun lifeless through the air, squeezing off his last silenced round.

Jack pivoted and pelted the Good Times van with automatic shotgun fire. The windshield exploded. Tenpenny caught some pellets in his face, neck, and arm while diving to the floorboards in a shower of fragmented glass. Since the van's engine still ran, he put the shift into drive and pushed down with his left hand on the gas pedal. He guessed where the truck was. The van flew off wildly and crashed into Jack's truck, knocking the detective off his knees onto his back inside the bed. The shotgun left his hands from the harsh impact and bounced first off the cab roof, then to the front hood and finally onto the street.

After the collision, Tenpenny tried to bail back out of the driver's door dragging a small machine gun in his right hand. Jack leapt from the bed, with a foot on the van front and scrambled over the open van door. They both hit the sidewalk, tumbling and rolling as the machine gun spun loose from the Indian's grip.

Jack stood. Tenpenny stood. Jack sprung angrily at Tenpenny and smashed him into the van until the metal dented. Jack threw a punch into the pellet wound area of Tenpenny's face, but he dropped his guard long enough for Tenpenny to counter with a sweep of his right arm and an elbow into Jack's head. Jack crumbled away and down to the ground, but he recovered to see Tenpenny wiping the streaming blood from his eyes and removing himself from the body mold they had crunched in the side of the van.

Jack mechanically got to his knees, but Tenpenny kicked him square in his padded chest, flipping him over. He managed to scramble so quickly to his feet that a surprised Tenpenny attacked him again, executing a perfect spin kick catching Jack on the bicep. Next, he snap-kicked Jack in the groin, all protected spots and Jack felt very little pain.

Tenpenny returned to his fighting stance expecting to finish off a suffering mass before him. Instead, he found a strong, solid Jumpin Jack Kellog. Jack turned as though to run for his truck and the vision impaired, dazed Tenpenny started to give chase. Then, Jack did something of his own spin, turning swiftly, parrying down the Indian's outstretched arms and rocketing a fist to Ira's eye. Jack tried to repeat this same blow, but Ira blocked it. Jack countered with a left uppercut to the bottom of Ira's jaw, with deep power generated from the pivot of Jack's hips. It could have stopped a Mack truck, and it did lift Tenpenny completely off his feet and whiplashed his head. He fell back in a loose heap, barely conscious. Jack flinched as though to jump on him but realized the move would prove too dangerous. The fighting was over. He pulled the .45 from his holster.

"Stay there."

The Indian just lay there, beaten, shot and bleeding, experiencing something he'd rarely, if ever felt. Losing.

"Let's get this straight up front," said Jack while gasping for breath. "I know you shot Roy Timmes, and I'd like nothing more that ta' shoot you dead with my .45. Now roll over on yer' chest."

"Fuck you."

Jack shot Tenpenny in the left ankle. It splintered red.

"AHHHHH."

"Roll over on yer' chest, or I'll shoot you again."

He rolled.

"Put yer arms out, palms up."

He did.

"Turn yer head away from me. Face the van."

He did.

"Spread yer' legs apart, toes out."

He did.

"You know what comes next? I am either going to shoot you dead or handcuff you, you skunk piece of shit. Makes no matter to me if I split yer' head open like a stinking melon. I've already killed about 7 of you monther fuckers tonight and I ain't done yet."

Jack cautiously approached Ira, cuffed one hand and brought it to the small of the Indian's back, then ordered him to put the free hand there, too. With the metallic clicks of the cuff's engagement, Jack allowed a small portion of relief.

"Now roll yer sorry body across the sidewalk. Look at me now and look to where I'm pointin'. Roll yer body right up there to that fence and lay beside it, chest down."

While Ira rolled over and over to the wrought iron fencing of the Garden Park entrance, Jack produced a second pair of cuffs from his belt. When the Indian lay face down beside the fence, Jack elevated the cuffed wrists uncomfortably upward, cuffed one end around the links between Ira's hands, then cuffed the other end to the fence, leaving his arms suspended in an awkward position six inches above the small of his back.

"You are under arrest," Jack growled, "for the attempted capital murder of Officer Roy Timmes and ME. I oughta just kill ya, but I'm gonna do worse to you. I'm gonna CAGE you fer life instead."

He searched Ira and found only a jeweled-handle knife.

"And yer' gonna limp out that life too because I've blown yer' ankle to shit."

Jack looked over at his truck. The back looked severely smashed from both the rear impacts of the night. A rear wheel hissed, going flat from the sharp point of a van fender. He gathered up his equipment and climbed into Ira's van.

"Hey." Ira shouted, "I'll bleed to death here. Hey."

Jack ignored him and drove off in the windshield-less van, the cold rushing air thrashing his hair wildly and invigorating his body and spirit.

The voice of Johnny Handell blared over the expensive C.B. radio.

"This is Everlast. Suspend the Kellog thing. I repeat, drop the Kellog search. All must meet at the West Forge Bus Terminal in 30 minutes. Our boy will be there fer payoff. We'll take care of that bidness, then get back to Kellog."

Silence, as he expected no confirmations? Then he said, "Red Indian. Red Indian."

Silence. Was he calling for Tenpenny?

"Red Indian come in," he implored again.

Jack swept the shattered glass from the radio, picked up the mike and, for the second time in a month, pretended to be Ira Tenpenny.

"Red Indian here, go ahead," he mumbled.

Silence.

"Boss man says you go there to the bus station but leave yer passenger at the... your lookout location, go ahead."

"Okay," said Jack into the mike, trying to guess how Tenpenny would acknowledge such radio traffic. He replaced the mike on the dash clip.

Payoff. Boy? Diller? The bus station?

CHAPTER SEVENTEEN:
THE BIG SET-UP

"It was all a big set up. We set Diller up for a deal to testify. Diller set us up for a money deal. The bad guys set each other up for a power deal. It was all one big set-up and none of it worked." - Weaver Wisdom, Retired Texas DPS Ranger, Round Rock , TX 2003

Archie Lennox Interview, tape 8

Jack whipped the van down Tom Ball Boulevard toward an all-night 7-11 store, screeched to a halt, vaulted out and dashed into the store.

"Jumpin' Jack." said Rod, the night manager, eyeing up all the gear and damage on the detective's body. "You... look like death warmed over ...what..."

"Need a phone, Rod."

Rod quickly obliged, waving Jack to the back office. Jack frantically dialed M.J.'s number on the office phone.

"M.J., are you alright?" Jack asked.

"Yeah. Diller's gone. He slipped out on me a few hours before Weaver got here. He took all his bags and boot-scooted. Weaver and half of his men are here now, the other half are at the DPS office hoping you'll call. I..."

"Jack." interrupted Weaver from an extension phone somewhere at M.J.'s house. "The police radio sounds like all hell is breakin' loose. What's going on?"

M.J. chimed in, "Jack, Diller took my revolver."

"You think that hippie son-of-a-bitch has double crossed us?" asked Weaver.

"I think," Jack said in a remarkably composed tone, "that at the last minute, Diller decided to gamble. He decided he wanted to be rich instead of being a plumber in Welder, Wisconsin."

Weaver unleashed a string of curses.

"Weaver, you know where the West Forge Bus Terminal is, right?" Jack asked.

"Yes."

"I've heard on the CB radio that Diller will be there in about 20 minutes to try and get rich from Baker Tanseed."

"He's a fool." said the Ranger.

"Pontecorvo and Tetro are dead," Kellog added.

"What happened?" Weaver asked.

"I killed 'em. They're lying in a pile of boots on the floor in Western World. They walked right in on me. They didn't know I got loose in the store and was armed. They walked right in on me like they were set up, an ambush. I think Tanseed set them up to let me do the dirty work. And we got a problem with the state surveillance team. The black hats know about them. They found our bugs and are watching the team back."

"I'll send some Rangers over."

"See ya at the bus station," Jack said.

"Cavalry in route." Weaver growled.

Kellog slowly hung up the phone and stared at the floor.

"Trouble Jack?" asked Rod, handing him a large cup of coffee, as was the routine.

"Big trouble in little West Forge," grunted Jack, shaking his head no first to the cup. Then he took it. He stood with a grunt and tapped Rod on the arm.

"Let me grab a sandwich and I'll pay you tomorrow."

"Okay."

Jack left for the van, and almost swallowed the sandwich whole with the coffee, which was luke-warm anyway. It was a 20-minute drive to the small bus station of West Forge, fully expecting to see Diller, Handell, Tanseed, Weaver, armed muscle, and Texas Rangers. It was all coming together in a horse opera nightmare.

*****

If Diller Bailey expected a crowd of witnesses at the West Forge Bus Terminal at 2:50 a.m. to ensure his safety, he calculated dead wrong. All alone, he stared at his reflection in the huge glass windows that secured the dark lobby from the garage/bay area. Even the janitors had gone. Parts of the station were locked at night. If you rode the bus lines after midnight the station locked you out of the lobby and you waited on benches outside. Green benches lined the bay where passengers could wait and purchase tickets from the midnight drivers. But Diller felt too nervous, too chilly to sit on any bench. Instead, he paced inside the huge, oily, dingy, garage area. With each step his cough echoed through the empty chamber, rippling off the few parked buses, storage bins and the heavy 1930's decorum. The open garage entrance and exit allowed a steady funnel of damp wind to dust through and slightly flap at the legs of his parachute pants.

Diller's head bobbed in anticipation, looking from the exit east to entrance west, waiting for the big rendezvous, his chance to go for the big hustle. He just could not go through with this informant thing, just couldn't do it, making up his mind at the last minute to slip away from the good, protective M.J. and dial Tanseed's number. Getting that damn Handell first, then Tanseed, Diller set up his deal. $100,000. But Tanseed had a job for him to do too, he said. Inside his sweatshirt pocket he fingered M.J.'s revolver, in case things went south. Take a chance, take a chance, take a chance, chance, chance.

Screeching tires and brakes. Diller snapped his head toward the station entrance to see a Special Edition stop and block the opening. Another car, this one a Lincoln, pulled across the exit way, its back windows slowly, electronically lowered. Diller took a deep breath through his tightening throat. He moved his feet in a nervous pantomime against the cold he no longer felt. This was it.

The back door of the Lincoln opened and Baker Tanseed himself emerged, dressed in an off-white Stetson, a full-length black wool coat, black tuxedo and ostrich boots. In a gloved left hand, he held a leather satchel. Diller caught a glimpse of the beautiful long legs of a woman clad in a short skirt pressed against the back seat just before the door shut. Those legs did not belong to Tanseed's skinny wife. Tanseed strutted across the station, glaring at Diller.

Johnny Handell, also in a tuxedo, stepped out of the other car and walked within 10 feet of Diller, bearing an exaggerated sneer. Diller gripped the concealed pistol with his good hand.

"Hi, butt-fuck." Handell said.

Diller refused to even acknowledge him, choosing instead to watch the satchel as it hit the asphalt, when Tanseed stopped. Diller slowly looked up at his former bar buddy's--now crime boss's--face. Diller had prepared quite a speech for this moment about the good old days.

The doping, dancing, carousing days. How Diller set him up with the pilot that later set him up with the Gallantis. The good old days surely earned Diller something? His freedom and some traveling money at least. He thought it a great speech, but suddenly Diller fell speechless.

"Ya thinkin' thar's booty in that?" Tanseed drawled dramatically about the satchel.

Handell laughed an evil chuckle.

Diller's mouth felt dirt dry.

"Ya thinkin' that I'd pay ya fer sumpthin? You know you already owe me coke money, and I'm a not buyin' shit from you. Hippie." Tanseed wandered in a circle around Diller.

"Guess who's dead, Diller? Raymond Pontecorvo's dead. Tony Tetro's dead. Ya man at PO-lice headquarters killed 'em fer me. Oh, he didn't know it was for me. I sorta'... arranged it all. Like a stage play. Shake-a-spear."

Tanseed grinned.

"Like a ...like a chess game. Let Kellog escape, knowing Tetro would go back to get 'em. Kellog bushwhacked them both. Like a hit that ain't a hit. I used the PO-lice like a hit man. Now that leaves little ol' me here without those Yankee interlopers."

"Carpetbaggers," Handell said.

"Yeah. Carpetbaggers. No revenge vendettas against me to worry about from New York. I'll be a takin' care of their revenge fer them myself. Kellog won't see daylight."

"You got it all figured out all right," Diller said.

"Neither will you see daylight, Diller. Neither will you. You are my last little problem, trying to fuck up my good thang, talking all about grand juries. Snitching on me and mine. You ain't nothin' but a weak little pussy, hippie boy. Now you wanna' come down here and spare me the embarrassment of being indicted? Fer a nice fee? Well, I'm not a gonna pay you shit, you stupid little hippie-bastard boy."

Tanseed turned for the Lincoln.

"Bake. Bake." Diller shouted. "You an' me, now... we go way back. I remember when you had to stick yer' fist up the rear end of tired horses tryin' to breed more tired foals. I...you...I use to buy you groceries, man." Diller kicked the empty satchel. "I set you up in all this." He'd spat out about one-tenth of his prepared speech, with all the wrong inflections.

Baker spun around in anger, pointing a finger at Diller like a dagger, "And you fucked my wife in the meantime."

"Oh, is that what this is? Huh? Is that why you had Pontecorvo killed too?" Diller shouted back at him.

Tanseed cooled down and his twisted expression unwrapped itself to a half-smile when he realized Diller would soon become a lifeless carcass.

"Sayonara, amigo," Tanseed said. He finger-flicked the brim of his Stetson and nodded to Handell.

"I'll show you a sayonara." Diller shouted. With his good hand, Diller drew out and emptied M.J.s revolver into Tanseed's chest and face.

BAM. BAM. BAM.

One hit his throat. Tanseed gasped and gurgled, grasped his throat and fell to his knees quivering.

BAM.

Then he tried to get to his feet, but instead slid sideways.

BAM. BAM.

He tried to speak but couldn't.

Click. Click. Click Diller clicked away at the empty pistol as the cylinder turned on empty shells.

Four of Diller's six shots rocketed airborne before Handell even reached for the 9mm under his jacket. Handell fired twice into Diller's left side and Diller, wounded, stumbled over the bench, hit the cement wall with his head and shoulder and then slid down the wall.

Handell would have gone to the aid of his fallen boss, but for the shocking noise and surprise of the crashing automobiles behind him. Ira Tenpenny's van roared into view and knocked aside the Special Edition. Handell spun around and looked confused.

"Ira?"

But instead, he saw Jack Kellog eject from the van, just as four Texas Rangers rounding the bay afoot like shock troops, each with shotguns.

Handell snatched up a metal garbage can and heaved it through the large bus station lobby window.

The chauffeurs and bodyguards piled out of the two Confederation cars with their guns blazing every which way.

The Rangers dropped to their knees and spread automatic shotgun fire throughout the garage. Everything was fair game. Screams ripped the air, and ear-piercing gunfire, and diving and ducking and weaving. Blood splattered walls, floors ceilings. Even once sleeping pigeons were cut down from the air as they tried to escape the nests in the rafters.

While Kellog and the Rangers advanced from their positions, then stopped under the counter-fire, Handell had leapt through his newly made opening in the window. Two of Tanseed's men darted from the other side of the Lincoln through the far exit and onto the street, but on the sidewalk outside, they ran right into the barrel of a growling Weaver Wisdom.

"Stop right there."

One of the two men dropped his pistol. The armed one instinctively raised his, and the Ranger cut him down immediately with .45 firepower.

Jack gripped his shotgun tight to his chest and vaulted through the broken window into the lobby right behind Handell. He slipped and crashed onto the broken glass scattered on the floor, and quickly discharged a wild blast at Handell who reacted by diving airborne some six feet into a row of plastic chairs. He and the chairs went sprawling. Jack struggled to his feet. Then a sudden explosive fury struck him in his back. It shoved him down on his face and stole his breath. He turned.

Aubrey, Jack's nemesis from the store, ran across the bus garage outside, firing. One of his rounds hitting Jack's protected back and floored him. Ranger pellets raked Aubrey's side, and the henchman lost his balance just before he could jump through the opening in the glass. Aubrey's face went from anger to shock to blank as he fell.

Jack saw Aubrey tumble into a huge piece of plate glass still stuck on the bottom frame, its position so steadfast that it didn't snap even after it stabbed through Aubrey just below the rib cage. The sharp, red glass peak exposed itself above his back and Aubrey just hung there. He babbled syllables making no sense with the last of his wind.

Jack and Handell exchanged gunfire while dodging through the lobby, oblivious to the new sound of machine gun fire out on the street.

Rangers frantically leapt and dived over the tops and sides of their cars in an effort to escape the automatic gunfire crackling from the windows of a Blazer as it approached the station. A maniac machine-gunner fired from the street. Two of the older, heavier Rangers didn't make it to the safe side. Rounds pelted into them as they crumpled then crawled trying to escape.

After the assault passed, Weaver stood and fired at the Blazer screaming, "Som-a-bitch."

In this confusion, one of the two surrendered suspects got up and fled south out of the station, another lay still. A Ranger took off in pursuit of the escapees but started out some 50 feet behind.

Weaver jumped into the first police car he came to and screeched off after the Blazer.

"Som-a-Bitch." he yelled again like a madman.

Weaver saw he would soon pass one of the fleeing suspects running down the sidewalk beside him. He released the steering wheel for a moment, stuck his short-barreled shotgun out of the window and almost nonchalantly blasted the lower legs of the runner, never once looking back as he past. The man's legs folded, and he ended up in a rolling ball of legs and arms. That chase was over.

"RUN from me." Weaver declared grabbed the wheel with one hand and radio mike in the other.

"Send that ambulance in. We've got Rangers down."

"Ranger, the scene is not secure. They won't go in," the dispatcher answered. "They are reporting gunfire from inside the station."

"Secure? You tell that first ambulance to grow a set of got-damn balls and get in there, or their gonna need a second ambulance to fix them up when I get my hands on em. We've got Rangers down."

"10-4."

The Blazer ahead suddenly U-turned for another sortie, this time the back-seat passenger half-climbed out of the window, with the machine gun out, up and ready, bracing himself for some serious accurate shooting.

"SON of a bitch." Weaver said, in shaky whispered this time.

The two vehicles bore down on each other like two jousting knights. Weaver grabbed the auto shotgun in his left hand, exposed it and his whole arm from the window, and the bullets and double-ought buck started flying. Weaver's target? The driver. The Blazer began to cut radically right and left, the driver's face a mask of panic. The machine gunner tried to throw some rounds at the police car but couldn't hold a bead with the erratic driving.

Double-ought, its scattered, heavy pattern won, and the

Blazer's shootist lost his concentration, then his balance, then his life. He fell from the window and rolled to a limp stop.

His shotgun now empty, Weaver dropped it to the street, yanked out his .45, and passed it to his left hand.

The Blazer zipped right past him; its two remaining occupants unprepared to return accurate fire after losing their main gunner. The Ranger steadily pelted the vehicle window-high until it swerved, left the road and bounded toward a used car lot.

The fallen machine gunner's body was right in front of Weaver on the street. The police car's left tires rolled right over him. Front and back, with bouncing thuds.

"Whew!" Weaver said, bouncing with every loose item in the car over each major bump.

Weaver cut the wheel hard to the left to give chase to the Blazer. But this chase was over too. First, the Blazer skidded into the low, metal rail piping fence that encircled the car lot, causing it to roll onto the right front quarter. The Blazer stood upright, on its right side, for a second as if the momentum wasn't enough to tip it over. Weaver coasted up to it. His jaw dropped as it seemed to hang there. He heard a man screaming inside. Then it toppled over, landing upside down on the top of the front ends of two, used cars.

Weaver pounded another magazine into his pistol, released the slide and stepped from his car. Gun up, he approached. He heard a man inside crying, whimpering. The driver looked dead. He'd been shot and all kinds of crushed. The crying passenger was laying on the inside of the roof.

"Hey now, don't you be crying now. It's too late," Wisdom said. "The milk's done been spilt. Gimme yer hand."

The man opened his hand and spread his arm Weaver's way. Weaver reached in and grabbed the man's wrist, all the while keeping his gun pointed at the man's face with his other hand. He pulled the thug from the wreckage.

"Ohhhhh, God. Oh MY God."

Weaver hauled him from the window.

"God? You say?" Weaver commented. "Oh, you is pleading to the wrong coach. Your coach is the devil, ain't he? That's the side you picked." Weaver handcuffed one wrist. "But, good news brother, I hear tell God is always recruitin' for some new teammates." Weaver pulled the man off the hood of the car toward a chain link fence. He snapped the other cuff around a solid post. "Think about that while your stewing here in the moonlight."

Weaver turned to leave.

"This car may catch fire. May explode."

Weaver stopped. "Now that would be the devil's work. Fire and all." He smiled. "Go team!" He turned and jogged toward his sedan saying over his shoulder, "If I knew me any prayers, if I were you, I'd be saying them right about now." He got in, kicked the gas pedal and raced off for the bus station back up the street.

Thinking Jack was down and out of bullets, Handell popped up to take aim as the detective rolled across the floor, only to have his own gun click on an empty chamber. Handell turned and ran.

Jack, however, was not out of ammo or, indeed, guns. But this situation had to end right, and ending right meant ending with a physical beating. Jack jumped to his feet, rushing after Handell's fleeing figure.

Handell darted wildly throughout the large terminal lobby, spotting each set of double doors were secured around their metal handles by chains. Jack tackled the big man from behind and the two slid across the floor, careening into old, seedy, lobby couches and then banging into the station's large, old three-tier fountain.

They struggled halfway to their feet, but Jack rammed

him again, and they splashed into the lower tier of the pink flamingo pond in the center of the terminal. Plastic birds with long metal legs toppled as Jack and Handell wrestled and sloshed to their feet. Toe-to-toe they traded vicious, rabid punches. Jack spit blood, anger, and curses in a growing rage. He had a momentum that turned his face and body numb against Handell's fists, as though his face too had a bulletproof hard shield. While Handell's sole purpose was to escape, Jack only sought to destroy. His right found its way through the wet, tuxedo-covered arms and smacked square into Handell's nose. Kellog felt the nose crush and break, and Jack managed to snap that same fist back again, fire away and knock the nose, mouth, and chin downward. Handell fell back against the second tier, completely stunned with his two clenched fists in the air. Motionless. Poised. Blood bubbled from his nose, his head wobbled, and knees quivered.

"Consider this my stunning rematch," Jack growled and gasped.

Then in a wild flurry of abandon Jack attacked, punching and kicking till the cocky, obnoxious, torturing, finger breaking, cop-shooting Johnny Handell bent way back over the tier, then slipped completely unconscious and limp into the shallow water at their feet.

Jack grabbed the curly, haired head out of the water. He was just a few seconds away from a well-deserved drowning. He shoved him back under. Handell's eye popped open. Bubbles burst from his lips. Jack saw all the shiny pennies tossed in the fountain surrounding his face in a shimmering backdrop. Each one tossed with a wish. Well, Jack has a wish too.

"Sarge." Came a voice from the garage. A West Forge patrolman stepped through the broken glass window

"Sooo much fer my wishes," Jack whispered, with a

sigh. Reluctantly, he yanked Handell's head back out. With both hands full of hair he hauled the torso to the fountain's edge and hung the head and shoulders over the brick border. Handell gagged and coughed. He flipped him over and handcuffed his hands behind his back. Water gushed from Handell's mouth, followed by some party hors d'oeuvres.

"Doncha get any of the horse-de-ervs on yer boots," Kellog warned the officer. They grabbed Handell by the arms and lifted him up.

"He'll be alright," Jack told him. "Just a ...little too much to drink.

What about you?"

"Me? I don't know about me. Ask me in the morning."

Jack left them and limped back to the broken bay window and stood near the suspended body of Aubrey in the glass frame.

The firefight in the garage had ended. All West Forge units had arrived. Officers searched the prisoners. Again approaching sirens, the sounds that seemed to serve as background music for Kellog all night long. City police. County police. State police. Fire department. Jack gingerly stepped through the open window past the impaled Aubrey. Jack saw he'd died with a gasp, his mouth open. He looked at Aubrey's tooled western belt with his name etched on in, all covered in blood.

"Looks like a mounted fish," he mumbled to himself.

The young rookie Officer Dale Cunningham, stutter-stepped toward the body, his eyes hypnotically affixed on Aubrey's form.

Jack stopped him and whispered, "Don't look too close, kid. You're too young fer this kind a nightmare."

The third ambulance arrived. A paramedic leaped from his van and raced toward one of Tanseed's wounded men.

"Whoa. Whoa," commanded Weaver. "You ferget about

him over there and you can start right here on this wound-ed Ranger," he said. The medic agreed.

Behind an overturned green bench, stuffed in the cor-ner beside some windblown trash and an overturned ash tray, Jack found Diller Bailey. One eye popped open at him, when Jack called his name.

"Diller. There you are."

Kellog shoved the bench away and straightened out Diller's body with care.

"You were straight with me Kellog. I shoulda known. Shoulda known you were the only one in town I could trust. Shoulda known."

Jack examined Diller's body. Two rounds to the left chest. Bad locations. Heart and lung locations. One out the back. One still in. Blood trickled for the corners of his mouth.

"Need an EMT here." Jack yelled out.

"Trouble breathing," Diller said with difficulty.

"Stands to reason Diller. You've been all shot up."

"Couldn't help but think- how boring my life would be. New name. Feds keepin' track of me. Some kinda steady fuckin' job. No dope. No hustle. Hey," he tried to grin. "I don't wanna work. I ain't never worked no kinda' job." He coughed again, only this time in a series. Jack saw more blood. He sat down on the asphalt beside Diller. Diller gasped as if from a drowning, suffocating pain. His lungs and heart beginning to shut down.

"Last hustle...Get some. From Baker...Then split. He... he wanted to set you up to kill the mafia dudes…"

"And I obliged."

"You did? They are dead? Water's comin' all up in my mouth...I shoulda known, huh, Sheriff?"

Jack nodded his head.

"I'm dying, Sheriff- I'm dying in a bus depot. Sheriff. I pissed in my pants," Diller gasped.

"Yeah."

"I don't even...I don't even own me a second...a second pair of pants to change into."

"In the very end, don't nobody own nothin', anyway," Kellog whispered.

Diller died. Jack remained there on the cold cement beside him. Sitting there he heard hysterical crying behind him. The tall, beautiful woman from the limo, not Tanseed's wife, hovered over Baker's body, wailing like a siren into the night air, competing with all those other damn sirens.

Jack blew out a gust of wind in a long sigh and shook his head. He took the small silver star from Diller's ear lobe. Bailey represented the most tragic informant Jack had ever seen, had ever heard of. Used by the good guys and the bad guys. He'd seen his girlfriend dismembered in Vegas. They beat him and now they'd murdered him. Jack rolled the star around in his hand and paramedics barreled toward Diller in a futile attempt at resuscitation. Diller was no ordinary dope dealing, pool-shooting, drug runner. Diller got them all. He made them all fall down and not like dominos, like an eruption.

Jack turned and stood, catching a glimpse of the yet unscuffed bottoms of Baker Tanseed's new boots pointing skyward.

"You alright?" Weaver Wisdom asked him.

"Yeah. You?"

"Yeah."

"Damndest, night though."

"Damndest," Jack agreed.

Weaver threw out a hip and rested a palm on the handle of his gun, looking over the scene. "Okay, he shot him. Then he shot him, and they shot...this is gonna take about 16 days of paperwork."

"The screaming banshee woman over there? Probably

saw it all play out from the limo."

"We'll have the governor...we'll have every agency here looking up our asses with flashlights for a week over this," Weaver said.

"Probably the U.N. too."

They walked over to Tanseed's corpse. Jack waved at Sgt. Willie Willaker and Willie came over.

"This damsel in distress?"

"Yeah?" Willaker said.

"Statement number one."

Willie gathered her arm at the elbow and walked her to his squad car.

"Ma'am are you hirt in any way?" Willie was asking as they walked off.

Jack lightly kicked at the clean soles of Tanseed's boots. "Looky' them boots. New boots each and every day until ya die," he muttered.

"That's the high rollin' life," Weaver said.

"And death. Maybe even the folks up east learned a little lesson from our Diller Bailey. Diller brought more justice in one night than most witnesses bring forth in two lifetimes."

All the aches and pains began to settle in, and Jack winced as he shoved Diller's tiny silver star into his vest pocket.

"My Caddy is...somewhere. Somewhere stashed by Tony Tetro."

"It'll turn up. You still have your pick up."

Gunther smiled and shook his head. "No, I don't." He limped off toward the Good Times van.

"See ya later, Weave."

"Jack. Where ya goin?"

"The night's not over yet," Jack said without looking back. He climbed back into Ira's van and backed away from the limo and out of Weaver's sight.

"Owww...I just hate it when he talks like that." Weaver

said with a deadpan face.

*****

The van turned down a still busy 16th Street. Despite the chill and the hour, plenty of people congregated on the porches, sidewalks, fire escapes, and in the streets. Radios blared. Drugs and liquor flowed. Jack's found his quarry, Rasp "The Trampus" Wilson, in such a crowd.

Rasp saw the van suddenly stop, and he snarled at it, until he saw the monster step from inside. The white-faced, bloody, black and blue, tattered and ripped, monster marched toward Rasp like a zombie, leaving the van door open, oblivious to the honking traffic behind it.

Taken aback, even stepping backward, Rasp said, "Watchoo' want?"

Jack marched on, cleaving through the crowd and shoved Rasp violently. Wilson bounced off a parked car and stumbled between two vehicles toward the sidewalk.

Jack reached out to grip Wilson by the shoulder and belt and spun him around quickly. Once, twice. Rasp's feet slightly left the ground.

"Unner' arrest." Jack declared. He cuffed Rasp.

"Hey, hey...leave my man..." a bystander objected.

"Back the fuck up." Jack ordered, in such a manner, in such a voice that the friend and all else nearby, just... backed the fuck up.

Jack hauled Rasp off his feet, his shins, and knees ricocheted off the cars. With a roar from the bewildered crowd, Jack heaved him airborne and sprawling into the passenger side of the van.

"That ain't no kinda' PO-lice car?"

"Any car I'm in is a police car," Jack replied.

Jack had his pistol in his left hand. Rasp was not handcuffed.

"Say, you can't..."

Jack floored the accelerator and the van roared off.

"What the fuck are you arresting me for now?"

"Beating up your nephew. Leaving him in a trash dumpster."

"Mother fucking bitch."

"You talking about Ida?" Jack slammed on the brakes and put the van into park. "You talkin' about Ida?" He back fisted the handcuffed Wilson three powerful times in his face. One of them landed really well.

"You can't...do this."

"Can't? Too late? Check yer' diary. It just happened."

Jack drove on.

"Where we going? This ain't the way to the jail."

"Trash dump. Cemetery. Crematorium. A bridge in Galveston. I haven't decided yet. But not the jail."

"Not the..."

"You and me, Rasp? You and me are beyond jail."

"You can't..."

"You have to understand. People cross lines. You crossed the line with your steak knife. And your aunt, and her little boy."

"What the fuck do you care? Huh? You don't even know that kid's name."

"Don't have to. But, I know your name. I know your name, and I know where the line is."

"Where's your line, huh? The Po-lice have a line..."

Jack hit the brakes and pointed out the window. "Right there."

It was a street of abandoned buildings and apartments. There were piles of rubble and the last dead orange glow from some working streetlights. It looked like a war zone. At one time, it was in a way.

Jack grabbed Wilson by his collar with both hands and hauled him across the driver's side seat and out onto the street. He shoved him across an alley, and belted Wilson across the face with his pistol. Wilson collapsed in a pile of trash. Jack rolled him over. Wilson was gasping for breath, tattered trash stuck to the bloody mess of his face and neck.

Jack looked down at him. He pointed the pistol at Wilson's face.

"You're a maniac." Wilson shouted.

"And you're a real bad man, Rasp. Well? Be bad now."

CHAPTER EIGHTEEN:
THE ZOO

Gangland Gunfight in Texas.

"Many questions remain unanswered today in West Forge, Texas, a suburb of Houston where something akin to a gangland war occurred yesterday and into the early hours of this morning. Unofficial reports suggest as many as 12 men were shot, five of whom appear directly related to the New York Gallanti crime family. The family is currently under investigation by New York State and Federal Authorities for organized crime activities.

The incidents reportedly center around a West Forge Detective, Sgt. Jack Kellog, and the Texas Rangers, and a witness bound for a State and Federal Grand Jury. This witness, now dead, was potentially murdered by the criminals. There was a major gang war, gunfight between authorities and suspects in a city bus station.

Authorities are still searching for one suspect, Ira Tenpenny, a former A.I.M. member, who apparently escaped custody after he was handcuffed to a fence by an unknown officer.

The Gallanti family lawyers have refused comment. The entire incident remains under investigation by both Local and Federal Authorities." - New York Times

At 6 a.m., the monster collapsed onto M.J.'s couch after unplugging the telephone. M.J. treated the bruises and stitched the wounds as best he could. Out from under the wet, bloodstained layers of bulletproofing, Jack was nothing but sweating, stinking, black and blue.

"I've cleaned up dead animals that smell better than you do," M.J. complained.

Jack drank tequila heavily for about an hour and barely spoke, refusing to call the station. Then he slept undisturbed for 18 hours, oblivious to Chief Shrewdy Collins' manhunt for him. Had Jack awakened in the fifth hour, he might have overheard the visit of Weaver Wisdom with M.J.. Weaver guessed where Jack was but didn't reveal his hunch to anyone.

Weaver felt content that his "podna" lived through the night, and damn to Shrewdy Collins for a while. And so, Jack slept there with the monkeys and the zebras. Shrewdy Collins, the reporters and the world could wait.

"When he wakes up?" Weaver advised, "Tell him to report in that he's passed out from his wounds. I am only starting on the paperwork. I'll keep the city, state and feds busy for a while. A day or two."

"Okay."

"Oh and tell him that Ira Tenpenny was not where he left him. He got away somehow. And Tenpenny may come after him. Keep a gun handy."

"Diller took mine."

"Well here, take mine."

"No, no it's okay. Jack came in with about five of em."

"And tell him that Pontecorvo and Tetro? They bodies are gone. M.I.A. He said they were shot dead in Western World? But, they are gone. Or their bodies are gone. He needs to know that before he makes any… ahh…statements."

"I'll have him call you when he comes around."

"Yeah. Good idea. Have him call my house first. My wife will call me. I'll catch him up."

CHAPTER NINETEEN:
THE LESSONS OF JACK KELLOG

One month later, Jack knocked on an apartment door.

"I'm Sgt. Kellog of the West Forge Police Department," said Jack to the man who opened the door. "This is Officer Kirkbride and Officer Moore. You must be William Corners, Jr."

"Yeah, I am."

"Then you must be under arrest," Jack said and aggressively stepped into the residence.

"For what?" the young man replied.

"Fer knockin' down an old lady and stealin' that plant sitting in your window right out of her arms. Ya know she lay in the hospital for two weeks? Now she has to... has to walk around in one of those metal walkers cause of her hip. I'd dearly, dearly love to put you in the hospital fer two weeks, but we're just gonna have to settle fer the jailhouse instead. Here's an arrest and search warrant and boys - here's yer man."

The officers searched and cuffed the man, and Jack

made a mental note to call the recovering Roy Timmes and tell him how good a case the patrolman had put together. He had some bad news for Timms, too. Jack would have to tell him that one of his shootists, Ira Tenpenny, had somehow completely escaped the double-handcuffed predicament Jack left him in at the park. He would have to explain that members of his own police department were duped and/or paid as spies and one had probably set Tenpenny free.

Jack leaned into his Caddy with the plant. Weaver had found the car behind the Tanseed mansion a few days after the bus station gang war. He was careful to place the frail potted pine on the rubber floor mat, careful to squeeze its branches inside the passenger door opening before closing the door. The squad car and its prisoner roared past him headed for downtown. Jack rounded the front of his car and, sliding off his Stetson, climbed behind the tilt wheel and sank into the plush interior.

The police scanner caught a dispatcher mid-sentence with a turn of the ignition. Jack pushed an 8-track Sinatra tape into his Alpine stereo and the Don Costa orchestra filled the air. His hat floated onto the backseat.

Anyone else might have enjoyed returning Mrs. Fredrick's pine tree to her at her home, like a special gift, reporting to her the details of the arrest, bringing justice to an elderly woman. But not Jack. Jack planned to carry an evidence-tagged pine to the property officer, who, in turn would notify the Fredrick family to come get it. An assistant DA would then contact her about prosecution. He swung the Caddy out into the rush hour traffic, thinking about some of the next steps in his pending cases.

"West Forge 101." said the dispatcher. Jack turned Frank's voice down.

"Go ahead."

"Call a complainant Carolyn Marks, 392-1114," the radio crackled.

"10-4," said Jack.

"Stand by for CB traffic."

Within a few seconds, the dispatcher called him on the unrecorded, CB radio.

"Jack, this is Betty. Come in."

"I'm here Betty."

"Mrs. Caroline Marks is very mad and impatient."

"Ain't they all? I just got handed that case this morning."

"Just a heads up. She's fixin' to chew you a new one."

"Welcommmmme to my worrrrld. Won't yooouuu come on in." Jack sang a few lines from the old Ray Price song.

"You can serenade me all day Jacky, but it won't work with her."

"Thaaanks Betty."

"Over."

Caroline Marks was a complainant on a crime from the previous night, wondering where the hell the police were, what they were doing, and just why in the hell hadn't she been called yet?

EPILOGUE BY ARCHIE LENNOX

"I thought...that if I could only work cases, that I would be happy. No distractions. So, I cleared the deck. That was my life. Cases. I was happy for a while. A few years. Then, it didn't work for me anymore." - Jack Kellog, West Forge, Texas 2002

Archie Lennow interview tape 2

The whole nasty affair of the "Crime Confederation" - as the newspapers and Time Magazine came to call it - was over. Over, that is, except for the public critique. Some armchair philosophers, politicians, lawyers like Scooter Gleason, media people and the West Forge City Council declared the police operation against the Confederation a failure, a flop, a mess. They said Detective Jumpin' Jack Kellog dropped the ball, flubbed the play, and lost his informant, causing a torrential, violent bloodbath instead of clean, civilized justice through the courts. Chief Shrewdy Collins took a lot of heat. Other folks applauded the police effort, even if in secret.

Some ten years later while working a child murder

case, Jack suffered a nervous breakdown. This breakdown involved beating the killer within an inch of his life. This beating by the way, occurred just after Kellog rescued the next potential victim -- a young girl -- from the trunk of the killer's car. Chief Shrewdy Collins was forced to fire him this time, under the pressure of the new West Forge Mayor (and Boston immigrant). The mayor should have been a little more grateful that Jack was employed just long enough to pop the trunk of the car open.

Jack returned to the badge after one of his lifelong, old archenemies escaped the Texas Penitentiary and began a statewide crime spree of mayhem, murder and robbery with a new gang. Ranger Weaver Wisdom convinced a reluctant governor that Jack was needed on a special task force. But that my friends, is another story

In over 20 years, the bodies of Raymond Pontecorvo and Anthony Tetro were never found. In his police reports Jack clearly stated that he shot them while "in a fight" inside Western World. He stated that he thought they were dead, but since no bodies were found, no authorities cared to pursue the matter (this was, after all Texas in the '80s). Probably they wound up in the alligator lake, the pig farm or the mink ranch, shoved there by Tanseed's henchman in a massive cover-up.

No one reported any contact with Ira Tenpenny. He mysteriously disappeared while double-cuffed to a strong wrought iron fence in a downtown West Forge Park. I'll let you, the reader, guess what really happened to the radical Indian and cop shooter. I have my ideas. Maybe Ira disappeared in the same place the Good Times van did? Jack's a little vague about all that.

Nor has anyone ever seen or heard from the Steak-Knife Rapist, Mr. Rasp Wilson again after that crazy night. Police reports show Wilson was never officially arrested.

Decades later, Jack claims he only pointed his gun at Wilson and warned him to simply "behave" and "leave Dodge," as it put it. He'll say nothing else about it. I'll let you to decide on that one too. I have.

And, needless to say, if my wife or daughter were in trouble or in danger, I'd want Jumpin' Jack Kellog on the case.

IF YOU LIKE THIS, TAKE A LOOK AT
THE LEVON CADE OMNIBUS BY CHUCK DIXON

FROM BEST-SELLING AUTHOR, CHUCK DIXON,
COMES THE LEVON CADE SERIES – A CAN'T-PUT-
IT-DOWN VIGILANTE JUSTICE SERIES.

Levon Cade left his profession behind to work construction. He just wants to live an anonymous life and be a good
dad to his daughter. But when a local girl vanishes, he's
asked to return to the skills that made him a mythic figure
in the shadowy world of counterterrorism.

Follow Levon and his daughter while they go on the run
from the feds and a growing army of enemies that Levon
makes along the way.

"Levon is bad ass. Makes Jack Reacher seem like
crossing guard."

AVAILABLE NOW

ABOUT THE AUTHOR

Hock Hochheim is a former U.S. Army investigator and 22 year veteran Texas police investigator, patrol officer, former private investigator and award winning author.

He currently owns and operates Force Necessary, an international combatives training company and teaches combat techniques and strategies in 11 allied countries around the world annually. He is the author of 10 non-fiction books and four fiction, and countless articles on policing, the military, street survival, close quarter combat and conflict psychology. He lives in Texas.

In 2013 Hock's book My Gun is My Passport won the Beverly Hills Book Award for Best Military Fiction. You may read more about him at http://www.forcenecessary. com or email him at hock@hockscqc.com